# ❧ *Dedication* ☙

*This book is dedicated to my Jake ... you're my heart and my absolute reason for being. Everything I do is for you ... thank you for being such a wonderful son. I love you.*

# ᴔ *Acknowledgements* ᴒ

*Gaylan ... this never would have happened without you ... thank you so much for doing everything you do. You'll never know how much you mean to me. Thank you for your patience ... I know you have had to have a lot to deal with me. Thank you for making this dream a reality.*

*Jason ... you've always believed in me even when I wanted to give up. Thank you for everything ... I love you and your words of wisdom ... 'if it was easy, anyone could do it.' That kept me going. And thank you for all the help you've given me ... and for all the endless reading you've had to do.*

*My sister Holly who shares the same kind of humor I do. Thanks for reading endless pages over and over again, even though this is not the type of book you'd normally read. And for actually liking what I wrote even when it was so unfinished.*

*The kids that have inspired me more than they'll know ... Jeremy Mosley, Max Scherff, Lindsay Sims, Tori McCormick, Brock Brett, and Charles Knight. Thanks for reminding me what it's like to be a kid again!!*

# ❧ About the Author ❧

Zoey's life long passion for writing surfaced in her first book *Everything Changes*. Even as a young girl, she had a love for reading and active imagination that sparked an interest in writing. She has always dreamed of writing books ... now that that dream has come true for all of us to enjoy.

Her love and understanding for teenagers is apparent in her books. For many years she has worked in the Alabama schools, teaching, working with students, and sponsoring youth clubs and events. Being around teenagers is a joy for her and spurred her to write about teen issues.

Zoey currently resides in Athens, Alabama, with her son Jake and is currently working on her next novel.

Zoey would love to hear from you. She can be contacted through the Eudon Publishing website *www.EudonPublishing.com*

# ❧ Chapter One ☙

"Are you and Jane going to the pool this afternoon?" I heard my mother ask me from the hallway.

I was lying in my bedroom with the door shut, trying to escape into privacy, but she was talking to me anyway. I hate it when she does that. I went to the door and opened it just a crack, enough to satisfy her that I was listening but not enough so that she could actually get in. She was standing right in front of my door and yet she hadn't even bothered to knock. In fact, she talked to me like the door didn't even exist.

I stood there with a towel wrapped around me for better coverage and peeked around the corner. "Yes, we're going to the pool." I said to her, sarcasm lacing my words. In an attempt to end the conversation, I quickly shut the door before she could say anything else to me. I was a little irritated that she had even asked. We live in Atlanta, Georgia, where the afternoons are hot and muggy, especially in July. Of course we were going swimming! Duh! Sometimes my mother can be so dense. I slipped a big T-shirt on over my swimsuit then ran out of my room, down the stairs, through the kitchen and outside.

I was sprawled out on the grass in my yard waiting for Jane Hunter, my best friend, to come over so we could ride our bikes to the pool. The pool is actually in our neighborhood, but it's closer to my house than it is to Jane's. So we usually meet up at my house before heading over to the pool together. The community swimming pool is surrounded by trees and a privacy fence and it's only supposed to be used by the people who live in the neighborhood. As a result, it's very private. Jane only lives two blocks over from me and we go swimming almost every afternoon that we don't have anything else going on. That particular Thursday was one of those lazy, no-activity days, perfect for swimming. As I saw Jane approaching the driveway on her bicycle, I realized I had left my swimming bag in my bedroom.

"I'll be right back, Jane!" I yelled to her as I sprang to my feet. I hurried into the house, raced through the kitchen and ran up the stairway. I was halfway up the stairs when I heard my mother talking on the phone. She was in her bedroom, which is situated at the top of the stairs, so I couldn't help but overhear. My curiosity roused, I slowed my pace so I could hear what she was saying. I'm normally not *that* nosy, but I could just tell by her tone that whatever she was saying was something serious. My curiosity piqued, I had to know what she was talking about. I would have just asked, but I know my mom, and she wouldn't have told me anyway. That's why I always have to snoop around to find out what's going on around here. My ears perked to attention, I heard her say something about a realtor and then her voice faltered so I didn't catch the rest. I crept up another stair so I could better hear what was saying.

"Yes, I think tonight we should sit down and talk to her." "Her," I assumed, was me. "She's going to have to know sooner or later and tonight is as good a time as any." There was a pause and then, "No, William." William is my father, so I now knew who she was talking to. "I'm not looking forward to telling her, but she has to understand this isn't under our control. And since we have to be in Sarasota before school starts, we'd better just get it over with."

Reeling from that statement, I felt my head start to spin. I sat down on the stair so I wouldn't lose my balance. Sarasota ... wasn't that in Florida? Why did we have to be in Florida? That was miles and miles from Atlanta. Florida was where we went on vacations. Maybe that was it, I reasoned, trying to calm myself. Maybe this just had something to do with vacations and I was getting worked up over nothing. But even as I rationalized, I knew in my heart that it couldn't be right. I wanted to confront my mother, but I knew that Jane was waiting. I didn't know what to say anyway, so I figured it best to just avoid the situation altogether. Forgetting all about my swimming bag, I ran back downstairs.

"What took you so long?" Jane was sitting at the kitchen table, eating an apple and making herself right at home. She looked at me for a moment and then, seeing the look of worry on my face, asked, "What's wrong?"

That's Jane. She can always tell when something is bothering me. She and I have been friends since we started kindergarten and she knows me better than anyone else in the world.

"I heard my mother on the phone just now," I tried to explain.

"Yeah?" She took another bite of her apple and threw the rest of it away. As she crossed the room, she paused and said, "So, what's so important that you had to listen in on her conversation?"

That's also Jane. She isn't a nosy person and she doesn't like it when people do things like listen in on private conversations.

Deciding it best to change the subject, I grabbed a handful of cookies and said, "Let's go to the pool."

I walked to the back door and Jane obediently followed behind me. I had on my bathing suit and T-shirt, but I didn't have a towel or my sunscreen or anything else, for that matter. It was all in my bag and I didn't want to go back upstairs to get it. I just wanted to get out of the house as quickly as possible. We decided to walk instead of ride our bikes since Jane could see I needed to talk, though once I started I wasn't sure what I could even tell her. I just told her what I'd heard.

"Do you really think you're moving?" she asked, her eyes widening.

I nodded. "What else could it be?"

She nodded too, and the rest of the walk was silent.

80   03

That night at dinner, I knew I was finally going to be officially informed about everything that was going on. I knew because my mother was a wreck. My dad had gotten home at his regular time, but my mother fussed so much that she had everything finished a half hour early. By the time we actually sat down to eat it, our dinner was cold. I didn't mind though. I couldn't taste anything anyway. I knew that a bomb was about to go off, yet I was helpless to do anything to stop it.

I kept thinking about that afternoon at the pool, how Jane and I had had so much fun. We'd stayed too long though, and my skin now looked a little shriveled from the water logging it had endured. I kept thinking about other things too—in particular, our neighborhood and how I didn't want to leave it. I thought about school and how I was supposed to be starting high school with my friends, the same ones I'd known since I had started elementary school. This was the only place I'd ever lived. Would I now have to leave all those memories behind? I didn't want to move, but I knew that we were going to have to. I just didn't know why yet. That was what I wanted to find out, but my mom and dad were playing a game and, in the process, were dragging out the torture. Neither wanting to be the bearer of bad news, they were waiting each other out. They wanted to see who would make the first move. Thinking I was unaware, they kept stealing glances at each other, but neither of them would talk. Finally, my mother flashed Dad a really hard look and put her wineglass down with a clink.

My parents always drink wine with their dinner. They also play what they call dinner music. I don't like it—it's Celtic music. I think it would be better if we could listen to what I want to sometimes, though I can't imagine my parents consenting to listening to Eminem, or The Strokes, or even something tamer like Britney. So every night it's the same old thing. We listen to Celtic and I just endure it. To make matters worse, I don't even get to taste the wine. I have to drink milk or juice—because it's good for me. What's fair in this world?

"Kathryn, your dad and I really need to discuss something with you."

Mom looked at my father across the table and that was supposed to be his cue to say something. But he completely ignored her hint and kept right on eating. He took another bite of cold mashed potatoes while I looked to him for confirmation of Mom's statement. I waited for him to say something, but he just looked from me to her.

Finally, Mom took a deep breath and said, "As I was saying, your dad and I need to talk to you."

I looked back at her, feeling like a tennis ball they were serving back and forth to see who was going to finally say it to me first. I wanted to make it easy on them but I couldn't. I wanted to yell, "I already know, we're moving!" But the words wouldn't come and I felt a lump building up in my throat. I took a sip of milk to wash it down, but it only grew worse.

"It's actually good news, depending on how you look at it," my mother finally said, trying to ease the crushing blow she was about to deal. I doubted that. "Dad got a job promotion, and we're moving to Sarasota. You'll be starting a new school in the fall."

So there it was—the bomb. My dad's job was the reason behind it. I should have known. He works in advertising, although I didn't think that fact would ever be the cause of us having to move.

"Sarasota?" I barely choked out the word. Even though I knew we were moving, it was still quite a shock to hear the words actually uttered.

"It's in Florida," Dad told me, as if I didn't already know. Out of the corner of my eye, I saw Mom flash him a dirty look, I guess for stating the obvious.

"Your dad will be making more money and we can live in a really nice house and send you to a really nice school. It's going to be great, Kathryn, I know it will." Mom was talking too fast in an attempt to glorify the less than glorious and I just looked at her, not knowing what to say. What I did know was that whenever a parent has to sell you that hard on something, it's never a good thing. To make matters worse, my mother's fake, overblown voice was really grating on my nerves.

"We already live in a nice house and I already go to a nice school," I said sullenly, playing with the peas and carrots that were sitting uneaten on my plate.

The game again. Mom looked at my dad and this time he spoke up. "Kathryn, we're sending you to a *private* school."

I snapped my head around to him and dropped my fork with a loud clunk. "What!" This wasn't happening. It couldn't be. Send me to a private school? My mind was spinning out of control. "Why would you do that?" I practically yelled.

Dad sighed. "With everything going on in schools today, we just don't feel it's safe. I never liked the idea of you going to a public school. Now we can afford to have you attend a private one and that's where you're going. We want to keep you safe." He picked his fork up again and began eating. I guess that was his way of ending the discussion.

I was so angry. So that was it, I thought. I don't even get an opinion. Well, no way! I wasn't going to just sit back and take being walked on like a rug. I jumped up and shouted, "I'm not going anywhere. I'll stay here with Nana or I'll stay with Jane, but I'm *not* going to Sarasota!"

To emphasize my point, I pushed my chair in so hard that it tipped over. The hardwood floor in the dining room echoed from the impact of my chair falling onto it. Always one to hide from drama, Mom put her head down in her hands. Dad said something, but the anger pounding in my ears was so deafening that I didn't hear him. I ran up to my room and slammed the door for added effect. Something about being mad makes me love making loud noises. I always get a thrill out of being loud when I'm angry—mainly because it upsets my mom. I know it's wrong and I can't explain it, but I love making her angry.

I can remember that when I was younger my mother and I had a great relationship. She's never worked outside the home so we were always very close. But lately, we haven't been getting along so well and I don't really know why. It isn't anything specific. It's just that in the past few months I've felt closer to Dad and I've been pushing my mom away as a result.

When I got to my room, I dramatically fell across the bed and sulked. Being an only child is really hard work. People don't always understand that. All my friends who have brothers and sisters think that being the only one is wonderful. The reality of it is, though, that all the attention is placed on you. Everything I do, my parents know about right away. Nothing—and I do mean nothing—goes unnoticed. I can't even so much as sneeze without someone uttering a "God bless you" in response. Also, being an only child means that parents expect more out of you and are very protective of you. Like this private school stuff. No matter how much they buttered it up, there was no way I was going to a private school.

I got up from my bed and strode over to my CD player. I turned my music up really loud to match the level of my anger—I picked Ludacris's "Roll Out" on purpose. My parents hate that kind of music, so it seemed somehow sweet revenge. I kept it really loud like that, allowing the song to play through twice for double effect. I knew by that time that my mom and dad were probably going crazy so I turned it down and called Jane, figuring a sympathetic ear might lessen my anger a bit. She answered on the first ring and I started right in on my tirade. "We *are* moving, Jane. And they want me to go to private school."

"Private school?" Jane mumbled. She was chewing on something that sounded like ice cubes.

"Yes, can you believe this?" I went on to talk about how angry I was about it and about how unfair the situation was, but Jane was silent. "What's wrong, Jane?"

"You mean besides the fact that you're moving?" I waited for her to go on. Then she spoke the theatrical words I had expected from her all along: "Oh, Kathryn, what will I do without you? This is our first year of high school. I can't start the ninth grade without you. We've talked about high school since the fifth grade and it just won't be the same."

Then to top it all off, she started crying. It was just like her to do that! This was *my* moment, my personal pain and she had to make it hers. I tried to be sympathetic, but it was annoying. Finally I said, " *You?* At least *you* still have the same friends. You know people. Who will I know?"

Put off by my bluntness, she stopped wailing. "Yes, I know, but it's not the same without you. We've always been best friends. I don't want a new best friend. I just don't want things to change."

Didn't she see that I didn't want them to change either? Given the circumstances, however, I couldn't bring myself to join her pity party so I just said, "Change is a part of life, Jane. Deal with it." Then I hung up.

# ဆ Chapter Two ßെ

The next day, Friday, I had a tennis lesson scheduled for eight a.m. I didn't go. In fact, I didn't even get up to cancel. I guess my mother handled it for me. After my phone call with Jane, I had taken a bath and fallen right into bed. I hadn't wanted to talk to my parents. For that matter, I hadn't wanted to talk to anyone. Sleeping straight through the morning, I woke up around noon and soon realized that the house was quiet. That's what I loved about this neighborhood. It was set in a kind of wooded area, which was why it was named Woodland Acres, and the houses weren't lined up like cookie-cutter homes. Each home in the development had its own original twist to it. Better still, they were all spaced out nicely so you didn't have neighbors right in your face every time you walked out your front door. But it was even more than that. I loved our house and I really loved my room. It was special because I'd stamped so many personal touches on it. What's more, it was the room I'd grown up in, the only bedroom I'd ever known, and it held memories that could never be replaced.

In one corner of my bedroom, I had a little open space that was just big enough for my desk. It overlooked the backyard, which was really nice because I could see the seasons changing before my eyes as I gazed out the overhanging window. This room was where I spent so much of my time—writing in my journal, doing my homework, listening to music, doodling pictures ... just everything. I didn't want to give all that up just for the sake of a job promotion. I loved everything about my room. The hardwood floors were strewn with throw rugs that made it look cozy. The full-size sleigh bed was a gift from my parents after I begged them for almost a year for it. Of course the bed would go with me, but I'm sure it wouldn't match my new room the way it does this one. Nothing would be as good as it is here. Nothing.

I looked at the clock again and decided that, given that afternoon had already arrived, I should probably get up. I slipped on a T-shirt and old shorts and went downstairs, my stomach grumbling on the way. I found my mother in the living room talking to someone I didn't know. The woman my mother was talking with was young and she had on one of those suits that made her look as though she were trying too hard to come across as professional. She even wore high heels.

As I walked in, my mother gave me an exaggerated smile. "Kathryn, this is Monica Reeves. She's going to be helping us sell the house."

Oh, the realtor. Realizing she was not to blame, I didn't smile or say anything to her. I just looked at my mother disgustedly then went to the kitchen and got some juice. I drank it right out of the carton, another thing that really annoys my mother, just to spite her. I just wish she'd been there to see it.

The day already off to a horrible start, I decided to go back to bed since there wasn't anything to do anyway. I didn't want to call Jane and I wasn't in the mood to swim either. So I jumped back into bed, buried myself beneath the sheets and stayed there the rest of the afternoon. Despite the huge amount of sleep I'd gotten the night before, I dozed on and off. I remember my mother coming in and checking my head for fever, but I didn't move when she touched me. I didn't want her to know that I was half-awake because then she would have talked me to death. I guess I must have really fallen into a deep sleep at some point because I don't remember my dad coming into my room.

"Katybug, you need to wake up." Katybug is my nickname, one that only Dad uses. It's kind of embarrassing now that I'm older, but I don't want to say anything to him about it. It might hurt his feelings and I don't want to do that. "Mom says you've been sleeping all day."

I rolled over on my side and looked at the clock. It was after seven o'clock. I didn't know it had gotten so late. "I don't want to get up," I mumbled.

Dad sat down on the edge of my bed and tried to coax me out of my doldrums. "So, you're going to just stay up here until the moving men take you away?" It was a poor attempt at humor and I let him know that's exactly what I thought of it.

"I don't want to move to Sarasota, Dad."

"I know, but sometimes change is a good thing."

"Not this one. And I don't want to go to a private school. All the kids will have known each other forever." I started twisting the sheet with my hands, trying really hard to concentrate on not crying. "I won't belong and I don't want to go. Why do we have to move anyway?" I almost started crying then, but I didn't want to give him the satisfaction of seeing tears. I was angry more than I was sad and I wanted him to know that.

Dad didn't say anything for a minute. He just stared at me as if he were trying to find the right words. "I know this is hard on you, but you're too young to see the big picture. It's a huge opportunity for me. Well, for all of us really. It's going to be a better job for me and more money and a better place for you to grow up."

"I'm already grown up," I asserted, sitting up in bed to emphasize the point. He smiled and his eyes crinkled in the corners.

"No, Katybug, you're not. That's exactly what I'm talking about. You're too young to realize that this is a good move for the entire family."

"But why do I have to go to private school?" I knew I was whining but I couldn't help it.

He sighed. I hated to hear him sigh. It meant that he was losing patience and that wasn't what I wanted him to do. I just wanted to understand why he was forcing me into doing something I so didn't want to do. "Because, Kathryn, I don't want you to go into a dangerous situation. The school your mother and I have decided on isn't far from the house we're considering buying and it's so nice. It has wonderful teachers and a great curriculum and I think you'll like it if you'll just give it a chance."

"So, you've met these wonderful teachers?" I challenged him.

"Well, no, but they come highly recommended and the school has a reputation for being one of the best private institutions in the entire state of Florida."

Institution: Good word, Dad. "Well, I don't want to go to a private school and I don't want to change houses. I don't want to do any of this."

He nodded as if he understood, but deep inside I knew he didn't. No one could understand. I was all alone in my misery.

ಬಿ   ೞ

I didn't get out of bed the entire weekend. On Saturday, Jane called but I told Mom to tell her I would call her back, only I didn't.

By Sunday, I guess my parents had had about enough of my sulking because my dad called me downstairs to look at the house he wanted to buy. I didn't even bother getting dressed. I dragged myself downstairs in my Atlanta Braves T-shirt, the one that I use as a nightshirt because it's three times too big on me. I found him in the den, smiling stupidly at the computer. "This is it," he said proudly as I approached.

I looked but I wasn't as impressed as he was. It was a white two-story house, colonial style, with a swimming pool right in the backyard. It even had a few palm trees in the front yard, for architectural landscape purposes, I supposed. How typical. The inside was big. Really, it was *too* big for just the three of us, and I told Dad exactly that. As he shook his head in response, he had a glazed look on his face, the kind that children have on Christmas morning when their excitement has prevented them from getting enough sleep.

"This is the house of our dreams, Katybug, and I know you'll love it once we get there. You're going to be within walking distance of the beach. How lucky is that?" he enthused.

Lucky? Who will I go to the beach with? I didn't have any friends there. And did he suddenly become blind? Couldn't he see that I was not the beach type? It was one thing to go to the swimming pool in my own neighborhood, but it was another thing altogether to hang out at the beach! Those Florida girls had lived on the beach all their lives. They were probably born in bikinis and I would never fit in. I was just simply not pretty enough and certainly not thin enough. He still wasn't getting it, though.

With a few simple mouse clicks, Dad zoomed in to where my bedroom would be. Instantly I knew the only thing I could even possibly like about it was that I would have my own bathroom. While the bedroom was big, it wasn't as big as the one I'm in now. Worse, it had some kind of ugly carpet blanketing it, although I couldn't see what awful color it was.

"I don't like the carpet," I told him point blank.

"We can change that," he assured me.

Then he zoomed in on his and Mom's room. It was so big that it was almost twice as big as the room they had now. It also had a sliding glass door that opened onto a wonderful view of the backyard and the pool. It figured that I didn't have a view. My bedroom was situated in the front of the house, where the only thing I'd be able to see was the street. I wouldn't have the view I have now. In fact, I wouldn't have anything I have now.

The anger inside me grew to a boiling point. Seething, I just picked up a book that my dad had on his desk and I threw it against the wall. It was a big hardback and it bounced off the drywall before hitting a lamp. In response, the lamp toppled over and broke. I didn't wait to get yelled at. I ran upstairs and slammed the door shut behind me. I was getting good at slamming doors, I realized. Then I turned on the music again, only this time I blasted AC/DC. Let them think I was becoming a retro metal head—I really didn't care.

# ප Chapter Three ඥ

Monday morning arrived and my mom came in to wake me up. "You've pouted long enough and you're paying for the lamp out of your allowance and baby-sitting money."

Don't bet on that, Mom, I thought. But I didn't say anything. I just rolled over and looked at the clock. Had she gone mental? It was only eight o'clock.

"You are not going to lie around in bed all day like you did this weekend," she warned. Then, as if to affirm her point, she walked over to the window and pulled the curtains back, letting the sunlight stream in. I pulled the blanket over my eyes to drown out the blinding illumination.

Satisfied with her work, she breezed out of the room and I hated her more in that instance than I had in a long time.

I thought about Mom for a minute before I got out of bed. When did I start hating her so much? I could remember when I was younger, I was so proud of her. She always looked younger than the other moms, not just because she was—since she and my dad had married young and had given birth to me the very next year—but also because she took care of herself. She took exercise classes and she always wore nice clothes. She played tennis and even though it was just a hobby for her, she was really good at it.

My mother is also very attractive, and not just in my eyes. I hear it all the time. People say, "She's your *mother?*" Like it's completely unbelievable that we could even be related. I guess it's because we're so different. She's around five foot seven; so far, I'm only five foot one. Of course, I'm still growing, but I just don't think I'll ever reach five seven.  Mom also has naturally blonde hair and her eyes are a mesmerizing green, like cats' eyes. When she's angry they turn a wild green and that's when you know you're in trouble. When I was little, I always wanted to look just like her, especially her eyes. Mine are blue like my dad's. Unlike my mother's, his hair is brownish blond while mine is just plain brown. It's not even a light or a dark shade; it's just medium brown. It's what most people would call mousy. In the height and weight department, my dad was also blessed, standing about six feet tall and still sporting a slim physique. I guess I got my height from my Nana. She stands barely five feet tall, while my grandfather stood over six feet tall. Funny how opposites attract that way.

Given that I was now wide awake, I decided that I should just get out of bed and take a shower. After all, it had been days since I'd done so and maybe that would make me feel better, though I doubted it. Following through with the plan, I went down the hall and got in the steamy shower, allowing the hot water to cascade down my tense body. Afterwards, I stood in front of the full-length mirror and examined myself from every angle.

I rued the fact that I would never fit in. Florida was not the kind of state where people like me fit in. Not only was I short, I realized that I'd also gained some weight as of late. I had noticeable problem areas around my thighs and stomach. Given all that, I didn't want to even think about wearing a bathing suit on the beach. Florida's the kind of place where girls wear bikinis everywhere they go. And running around half-naked is something I could never get by with. I knew I'd feel out of place the instant I arrived, but how could I get out of going? I knew that Nana would let me stay with her, but my parents would never go for that. I was completely doomed, I realized. And since I knew there was nothing I could do to prevent the inevitable move, I knew then and there that I had to do something about my excess weight. I hadn't realized how big I was until now. My flesh appeared as if I was looking in a three-way fun house mirror. I gave myself a disgusted look and turned away from my reflection. That was it, I decided. I was officially on a diet from there on out. No more sugar or junk food, I warned myself. If I was going to fit in, I had to at least look the part.

I knew that Mom wasn't going to let me get by with going back to bed, so I put on my oldest pair of shorts and a ratty T-shirt. Sure, it had holes in it, but I didn't care about what I looked like. Dressed, but not raring to go, I then I snuck into my dad's den. I wanted to get on his computer for a while. My plan formulated, I decided to look up diets that were supposed to work fast. I didn't have a lot of time, I reasoned, so time was of the essence. I decided to Google 'fast diets' and found several that matched that criterion, but nothing that seemed like it would work for me. I also found several diet pills that were supposed to work but you had to be eighteen with a credit card to order them. So I couldn't go that route either.

After about an hour of unproductive surfing, I finally hit upon something that might work. I was right in the middle of reading about it when Mom burst into the room yelling at me.

"Kathryn, get off the computer and go clean your room. When you're finished with that, straighten up the living room."

"Why?" I mumbled, so absorbed in my discovery that I didn't even look up from the computer.

"Because Monica Reeves is coming by to show the house, that's why." She stormed past me, picked up a stack of books and then put them back on the bookshelf. I didn't want her to see what I was doing online, so I minimized the Window and pulled up Kazaa instead. I began downloading music as Mom walked toward the door.

"Kathryn! Your dad and I have told you over and over to stop downloading music. You're causing the computer to have viruses with that nonsense. Now, get off there and do what I told you to do," she ordered. As she walked out of the room, I typed in four more songs to download, just for spite. Then I went up to my room, made my bed as instructed then sat down at my desk. I didn't want to clean the living room. Let her do it, since she was the one who wanted to sell the house so badly. I decided to write in my journal instead. Two pages into it, I heard the doorbell ring. I wanted to go downstairs and see what kind of people were looking at the house, but I didn't want to look obvious. I decided to be patient and wait until they came up to see my room. I figured it would only be a matter of minutes before they intruded and I was right.

"Knock, knock!" Miss Reeves sang as she peeped into my room. She stepped back and let three strangers—presumably a father, mother and daughter—enter my bedroom as if she owned it. The man was tall and he wore a suit. The woman was short with medium blonde hair and she looked a little dumpy. In fact, they didn't look like they fit together. Their daughter was probably my age, but I couldn't be sure. I didn't ask them in; they just walked in and started looking around without permission. "Kathryn, I want you to meet the Petersons. They want to look around your room. Is that okay?" Miss Reeves asked a little too late and didn't even wait for a response. They all just barged in like they'd been there forever.

"Oh Bianca!" the dumpy mother exclaimed. "Just look how big this room is! It's much bigger than your old one. And the view!" Mrs. Dumpy walked over to my window and went on and on about how she would have loved to have a view like that when she was a young girl. I just rolled my eyes, but Bianca looked excited.

Then Bianca walked over to my closet. Oblivious to my privacy, she actually opened it and started rooting around inside it. It was then that I began to feel anger welling up inside me again. The man in the suit, obviously not interested in the contents of my closet, told the dumpy mother that he would be in the master bedroom. He left the room, leaving Bianca alone with her mother to explore my closet.

"What do you think you're doing?" I hissed, voicing my discontent. I stood up and walked over to the closet.

Bianca looked at her mother and Mrs. Dumpy walked over to us.

"Oh, I'm sorry," she told me and looked at Bianca. "Apologize for opening the closet without permission," she instructed her daughter, but Bianca just looked at me and said nothing.

"This is still my room," I yelled and pulled her out by the arm. I slammed the closet door shut behind her. "You have no right to snoop in here," I continued with my scolding.

Miss Reeves looked embarrassed and the three of them filed out of the room without another word. I wondered if she would tell Mom about my outburst, but at that point I really didn't care if she did.

That night at dinner, I found out. Dad noticed that I wasn't eating the way I normally did. "You've hardly touched your food, Kathryn. Are you feeling okay?"

"I'm fine," was all I said in response. I was still mad at him and my mother and I didn't feel like having a conversation. Because of Miss Reeves and her big mouth, however, we were about to have one, like it or not.

My curt response set it off. Mom put her wineglass down and glared at me. "You just had to be rude to the Petersons, didn't you, Kathryn?"

"I don't know what you're talking about." I picked up a lima bean and moved it to the other side of my plate, feigning disinterest.

Based on the requirements of the diet I'd chosen to follow, I decided the only thing I could eat from the plate of chicken and starches was my lima beans and they weren't something I even liked.

"Don't play that game with me, young lady. You *do* know what I'm talking about." Her eyes bulged with rage and I knew she was getting angrier by the second.

"Well, I don't know what's going on," Dad said, taking a big bite out of his chicken.

"Well, William," Mom started in, really dramatic-like, "it seems that your daughter threw a fit when the Petersons came in to look at her room." I'm always *his* daughter when I do something she doesn't like.

Dad looked at me, shocked by my mother's accusation. "What kind of fit, Katybug?" He seemed like he didn't care anyway, so I told him.

"Dad, that girl just went into my closet and started looking around. I didn't want her going through my closet and clothes."

Mom glared at me. "She wasn't going through your clothes, Kathryn Ann. She was only seeing the size of your closet. It's what people do when they look at houses."

"Did they go through our closets too, Abby?" Dad asked my mom, giving me the benefit of the doubt.

"They look, William. They don't go through anything."

Dad went back to his plate, mumbling about how he didn't want people going through his things either. I almost laughed but I knew better. Mom found nothing funny about this.

"Why do I even bother talking to you about anything? You just end up on her side." Mom's voice had that shrill tone to it as she accused us of secretive teamwork.

"I'm not taking sides. I just understand where she's coming from."

Mom just glared at him and then turned back to me. "From now on, the house will be shown when we're not home. It's the way it should have been anyway, but I thought that you were mature enough to handle someone coming into your room."

"That's not it—" I started to explain, but she interrupted me.

"I don't want to hear another word about it. Eat your food and let's not talk about the Petersons anymore."

"I'm not hungry." I told them and put my fork down. I got up from my seat and glared at my mother. "I'll be in my room."

I heard Mom complain to my dad about me not eating. I didn't hear what he said because I went straight up to my room and called Jane. I was feeling bad about not calling her back but it had been a hard weekend.

"You missed a great party Saturday night, Kathryn," she informed me right away.

Saturday night? Oh yeah, I was having a sleep-a-thon. "What did I miss?"

She went on to detail to me how Kevin Stanley's parents had gone out of town and how he had thrown a huge party on the spur of the moment. "I tried to call you, but you never called me back," she explained by way of apology.

I didn't care. Missing a party wasn't really important since I wasn't going to see these people much longer anyway.

After a minute of awkward silence, she said, "Jeremy asked about you."

I sat up on my bed when I heard Jeremy's name. "What did he say?" I'd been crushing on Jeremy Matthews for two years now; only I didn't know he knew I was alive.

"He asked why you weren't at the party."

Oh no. "What did you say?" I held my breath in anticipation of her response. I wasn't sure I wanted to know yet I had to.

"I told him you were busy and couldn't cancel your plans."

I smiled. "Thanks, Jane. That sounds *so* like I'm cool."

She started laughing. "Though we both know you're not."

That threw us into wild fits of laughter and I felt better for the first time in days. Then everything got quiet and she said, "So, are you still moving?"

I told her about the house Dad had shown me online and about the awful school he wanted me to attend. After we got off the phone, I wanted to cry. Jane had gone to a party without me. In my heart, I knew that was her way of separating herself from me slowly. I didn't know why it bothered me, but it did. But just thinking about Jeremy asking about me made me smile. Maybe I'd run into him before I moved. After all, I still had some time left before the eventual became the unavoidable.

# ജ Chapter Four യ

July went by too quickly and although I tried several times, I didn't run into Jeremy at all. I even boldly walked by his house in an attempt to get a glimpse of him. It was lucky I didn't since I really wasn't sure what I'd say anyway. His house wasn't exactly on the way to anywhere, but fortunately (or unfortunately, depending on how you look at things) I didn't have to worry about making up a story because I didn't see him once.

During the second week of July my parents informed me that the Petersons loved the house (even though they thought *I* was a brat), and were putting in an offer to buy our home. If the offer was accepted, it wouldn't be long until we moved out. Mom was right; we would be in the new house by the time school started. The mere thought of it completely depressed me.

On the plus side, I was doing really well on my diet. I was eating only fruit on Mondays, Wednesdays, and Fridays; on Tuesdays and Thursdays I ate only vegetables. Saturdays and Sundays, to shake up the routine, I ate a little of both. I had lost a few pounds but not enough, so I was trying to figure out what else I could do to improve my results. I didn't have long until we moved and I didn't want to go to Florida looking like an overweight sow.

Realizing our time together was limited Jane and I stayed at the pool almost every day. It was then that I realized how much bigger I was. She had always been thin, but because she was a few inches taller, I figured it all evened out. Now I realized I was just a beach ball on legs while she was a willowy twig. I wasn't happy about the obvious difference in our body shapes, so I started keeping a T-shirt on when I swam.

"What is with you and that shirt?" Jane finally asked.

"I don't want to get a sunburn." I tried to sound nonchalant about it, but Jane always saw through me.

"Like you ever do! You always have a tan and besides, you're moving to Florida! You want to be brown. People expect it." They also expect people to be thin, I thought, but I didn't say it. Jane dove under the water and when she did she splashed me so hard that I had to go under to grab her ankles in retaliation. We were playing and splashing and having so much fun that I almost forgot about the T-shirt and my overweight body.

At night, we hung out with our other friends. Sometimes we went to the movies and other times we had sleepovers. It was at one of our sleepovers where it was just the six of us that I told the other girls I was moving. Besides Jane and me, our inseparable sextet included Tori Holt, Kammy Phillips, Shelly Donaldson and Ashley Campbell. That particular night, our sleepover happened to be at Tori's house.

Upon breaking the news to them, they were so upset to hear I was moving that I thought I might burst into tears. After we discussed it for like an hour, Kammy said that in honor of my moving we should color my hair.

"Color it? Why?" I was skeptical.

Kammy informed me that since I was moving to Florida, I should have blonde hair.

"I don't know." I hesitated. "I've never put a color on my hair."

Kammy was one of those overzealous people, who just can't take no for an answer. She was also very intimidating. Taller than all of us, we always joked that she was looking down on us.

"Oh!" Tori shrieked. "It'll be so much fun! It's like a makeover."

"Yeah, come on," the other girls encouraged me. And then Kammy said, "Let's have another sleepover next Friday night, and we'll do it then."

I saw the look on their faces. They were so eager to help me and how could I refuse? I mean, after all, wasn't I the one who'd said I wouldn't fit in? Maybe with blonde hair I would feel like I could fit in better. We decided that next week we would have the sleepover at Ashley's. I didn't want to do it at my house. In fact, I didn't want to tell my mother I was coloring my hair until it was done and too late to change things. That way she couldn't say, 'no'.

ᛒ    ᚷ

When the next Friday finally arrived, my dad dropped me off at Ashley's. She doesn't live in our neighborhood, so I couldn't just walk over the way I do when I go to Jane's house. We didn't talk much on the drive over because lately I didn't know what to say to him. Every time we talked, it seemed like I got angry and I didn't want to always be angry with him. So we conversed very little. The air conditioner was blowing full blast in my face and it felt so good. August was really hot and I couldn't help wondering what the weather in Florida would be like. I knew that I would miss the seasons once we moved, especially autumn. It was my favorite time of the year. I didn't like to think about it. Besides, tonight was going to be fun. We were going to color my hair, even though I was still a little apprehensive about it. When we arrived, I just jumped out of the car and barely said 'bye. My dad drove away with a dejected look on his face. And for a minute, just a very short minute, I felt very lonely.

Mrs. Campbell answered the door and told me that the girls were already upstairs. I was the last to arrive so I ran up to meet them. As I prepared to enter Ashley's room, I discovered that they were listening to the Backstreet Boys and I felt like we were back in grade school. All the girls were laughing and having fun in my absence and I instinctively thought about how much I would miss them once I was gone. Would I ever find friends like this again? Not likely, considering that I'd known them all my life.

I reluctantly entered and threw my bag in the corner. As soon as she saw me, Jane rushed over to me and told me that she'd seen Jeremy at the mall that afternoon. She and her mother had been shopping for back-to-school clothes and she said that Jeremy had asked for my phone number.

I shrieked, "No way!"

"Yes, way," she countered then laughed. "So, I gave it to him and he said he was going to call you tomorrow."

Kammy wanted to know what was going on, so Jane told her and before I knew it all the girls were shrieking.

"You're *sooo* lucky," Shelly said. "I've always thought he was so cute."

I nodded. "Yeah, but I thought you were kind of talking to Robert." All of a sudden, it occurred to me that even if Jeremy did call me, it didn't really matter. We could see each other only a couple more weeks and then I was moving. I didn't know if Jeremy knew that or not. I would hate for us to start seeing each other and then have to leave him. This was *so* not fair! After crushing on him forever, he finally notices me the same minute I have to move. At that thought I got angry with my parents all over again.

I guess Jane sensed my mood was getting dark because she yelled out, "Let's do Kathryn's hair!"

Everyone got really excited then, and we went into Ashley's bathroom and started reading the instructions on the back of the box. Mulling over my choices, I decided on the honey blonde color because I thought that wouldn't be so dramatic. I wanted change, but nothing drastic.

How could someone go *so* wrong?

Kammy was in charge of mixing the solution while Ashley read her the instructions. Tori and Jane watched while Shelly called Graham Greiss, a boy in our class. I was trying to concentrate on something else because I was getting more and more nervous by the second. Kammy spilled part of the solution, and although I glared at her, she assured me it didn't matter. "They always put more in there because they know people will spill some."

That logic didn't make sense, but I didn't say that to her. I just eavesdropped on Shelly's conversation so as to keep my mind off the fiasco that was unfolding before me. The bathroom door was open so I could hear most of what she was saying. Shelly was giggling at something Graham had said and then I heard, "Well, I guess we could try to come by." She laughed again, but it wasn't her usual laugh. It was a high-pitched giggle that sounded fake. I rolled my eyes. Then I heard, "Well, of *course* I want to. Why don't all of us meet at Woodland Park tomorrow afternoon?" Who was she talking about?

I soon found out because about nine seconds later she was jumping up and down and saying, "We're all meeting tomorrow afternoon at Woodland Park." She went on to explain that Graham had told her how Bobby Moore wanted to meet up with Tori. She told him (apparently when I wasn't listening) that Jeremy had said he would call me. She informed us that Graham was going to round up Jeremy, David, Kevin and Brent to meet us at the park the next afternoon.

I felt the trickle of solution running down my back and it was cold. I shivered. "Be careful, Kammy."

She wasn't listening, though. She said to Shelly, "I really, *really* like Brent. But you didn't tell Graham that, did you?"

Shelly shook her head. "No, of course not. You know how they all run around together. They're meeting us tomorrow afternoon at five."

My mind was racing. What if Jeremy didn't want to come? What if that whole thing about a phone call was just his way of being nice? I thought about that for a minute, then I realized that Kammy was finished putting the stuff on my hair and was setting the timer. She then twisted mousy brown locks in a towel so the solution wouldn't drip out on the floor.

We filed out of the bathroom and everyone decided they
were hungry. "Let's order pizza," Jane suggested. I realized that I
hadn't brought any fruit with me and this was my fruit day. I was
sure that Mrs. Campbell would have fruit, but I was embarrassed
to ask. Oh well, I really wasn't hungry anyway, although the
other girls acted starved. After deciding what they *didn't* want on
our pizza, Ashley called and placed our order. Then we went
downstairs to get something to drink. While most of the girls
opted for soda, I just got bottled water.

Ashley's mother was sitting at the kitchen table, drinking tea
and writing what looked like a list. "Girls, do you want to order
pizza tonight? I really haven't been to the store, so I don't know
what we have to eat."

"We took care of that, Mom," Ashley told her. "And we
have plenty of junk food since you and Dad don't eat that stuff
anymore."

It was true. At the beginning of the summer, Mr. and Mrs.
Campbell had decided that they were going to eat only foods
that were good for them. They even started shopping at a
grocery store that specialized in organic foods. They were
sticking to their promise so well that even my mother had said,
"I admire Joan. I wish I had her willpower." I'm glad that she
doesn't because my mother would be the type to make *me* join
her in the quest for being healthy. I wanted to diet my own way,
not the organic way.

Everyone grabbed drinks and, as we headed back upstairs,
we heard the doorbell ring. All of us started for the door in one
mad dash, but Ashley's dad must have been trained to hear the
doorbell and instinctively know that he was needed, because out
of nowhere, he appeared with his wallet in his hand. He paid the
pizza guy and we all started back upstairs. On the way up, we
heard the hair-coloring timer ringing.

"Oh no, how long has it been going off like that?" I asked.

My anxiety growing, we ran to Ashley's room, almost spilling
the pizza in our rush. Kammy and I went straight to the
bathroom while the others started eating. Jane turned on MTV2.

I was really worried about my hair, but Kammy told me she had everything under control.

Fifteen minutes later, I was ready to kill her. I looked in the mirror and let out a scream that made the other girls come running. Kammy had used the blow dryer before I could see, and then there it was, the finished product: my hair, only you'd never know that by the looks of it. The ends were completely fried, and it had two colors to it: vibrant blonde on the top and burned blonde on the bottom.

My hair is long and falls way past my shoulders. As the girls kept running their hands through it, I realized it was falling out. Tori and Shelly had handfuls of my hair in their hands. I was so furious that I was just shaking by then. "Stop! Don't put your hands in my hair like that. Just look at what you're doing!"

Tori's eyes grew wide with amazement with the fistful of strands she held. She tried to drop the hair, but I'd already seen it.

Then Kammy started to cry. "I'm so sorry, Kathryn. Please don't be mad at me."

Why was *she* crying? I kept looking in the mirror, trying to decide how to salvage this predicament, but there was no way. My hair was ruined, utterly destroyed. I picked up the box of hair coloring, seeking out answers to my burning questions.

"It was that towel!" I yelled at Kammy. "You twisted my hair in a towel and it didn't say anywhere on this box to put my hair in a towel! Not to mention, there's no telling how long that stupid timer was going off."

"Ashley was supposed to read the instructions," Kammy cried, throwing blame somewhere else.

I was just too upset to say anything else. Then it hit me ... I was meeting Jeremy at Woodland Park the next day and I had to go looking like sideshow freak.

I guess Jane was thinking the same thing because she said, "Don't worry, Kathryn, we'll go shopping tomorrow and buy lots of hats."

Hats? Like that would solve this. But Kammy stopped crying and said, "Yes, that's it. We'll start a hat fad." Left with no other alternatives, we decided that early tomorrow morning we would go over to the mall, but my heart wasn't in it. I didn't really look right in a hat since I was so short. Despite the many times I'd despised it in the past, at that moment I just wanted my old hair back.

ᏉᏃ    ᏉᏆ

Going home the next day was a dreaded event. Although we had been shopping that morning and had bought lots of hats, I didn't think my parents would let me get away with wearing one every minute of every day. And since they didn't know about my hair color party in the first place, I'm sure they wouldn't be happy when they found out how poorly my sneaky action had gone.

After Mr. Campbell dropped me off at my house, I ran up to my room before my parents could see and locked my door. It was already two thirty, and I had to get ready for my encounter with Jeremy soon. I looked at my hats. I had to admit some of them were cute. I had one that looked like a sailor's hat and one that looked like a beach hat. It had a wide brim and was very elegant. I also had some that reminded me of the sun hats I used to wear as a child. I hadn't realized how pricey hats were, so I was glad that I had had my mother's credit card with me. She had said it was only for emergencies, but I would imagine this was as 911 as it gets.

I decided to try out the floral sun hat on my mother. I put it on and tucked the bottom of my hair behind my ears. That way, you couldn't tell so much that it was fried. I ran downstairs, hoping for a positive reaction. When I arrived, Mom was sitting on the deck, reading a magazine. I had to step over boxes to get to her because some stuff was already packed. I hadn't helped with the packing, of course, since I didn't want this move to happen, but at least my parents were taking everything slowly. At the pace they were going, we wouldn't be finished until after I graduated high school. Which was fine with me, but it was getting to be a pain stepping over boxes every day.

I opened the sliding door and saw that my mother was reading *House Beautiful*. Oh pa-lease, I thought, is she going to try to make our house like something out of this magazine? I just ignored it, however, because I had enough to worry about as it was.

"Mom, Jane and I are meeting the girls at Woodland Park at five, okay?"

She hadn't looked up yet, so my heart was beating fast at the thought of her noticing my hair. But all she said was, "Okay, just be careful and be home at a reasonable time."

She hadn't even taken her eyes off the magazine. She just turned the page, practically oblivious to my presence. I really needed to see if this hat thing would work, so I cleared my throat to make her look at me. She tilted her head and peered at me over her sunglasses. My mother has very sensitive eyes, and she always wears her sunglasses when she's outside. "Did you need anything else, Kathryn?"

I shook my head. "Not really. I just wondered what time I had to be back, specifically?"

She looked at me quizzically. I normally don't ask questions like that. "I think you know what time is reasonable." That was all she said before turning her attention back to her magazine. Well, she'd looked and said nothing, so I guess my experiment had worked. I was heading back inside when she said, as an afterthought, "Nice hat."

# ❧ Chapter Five ❧

Jane walked over at four forty-five and we went to the park together. Woodland Park was just right outside our neighborhood and it was only a five-minute walk for Jane and me. I loved going there, even as a child. It was just another thing on my ever-growing list that I would miss once I was gone. Trees and picnic tables surrounded Woodland Park and they were spread out everywhere so families could come and enjoy their afternoons by eating and playing baseball, soccer, or even football.  But the thing I liked most about it was that at night, everyone knew that it was a place for the teenagers to hang out. As a result, grown-ups didn't bother to come around so much.

I had decided to wear something casual since we were only going to the park. I had chosen white drawstring shorts. The strings were on the side and the shorts were really cute, though I thought they might be a little too short considering my problem areas. But Jane assured me that I looked good. To top them off, I wore a pink scoopneck T-shirt with Gap written across it. And of course, I wore my white sun hat to finish off my wardrobe masterpiece. To match my shirt, I sported pink sandals that I'd gotten at Old Navy months ago but still hadn't worn. I even had the matching bag to go with them. I felt pretty good, considering what my hair looked like underneath it all. Jane looked even better. She wore her hair in a French braid that coiled all the way down her back. On top, she sported an Atlanta Braves baseball cap, even though she'd never watched baseball a day in her life. I think she wore the cap so I wouldn't feel so bad, but it actually made me feel worse. I'd never find such a good friend as Jane.

Once we got to the park, the rest of girls were already there but the boys hadn't yet arrived. Since Ashley's dad was going to rent movies anyway, he had picked up the other girls and brought them to the park. With nothing else to do to idle away the time, we sat there and waited for the boys, all of us nervous but not wanting to admit it. I glanced at my watch. It was already ten after five and none of them had shown up yet. I looked at Kammy for reassurance. Wrinkles of anxiety creasing her face, she looked almost scared. She looked nice, but it was almost as though she were trying too hard. She had on too much makeup and her hair had been rolled so she had all these really big curls all over her head. It would have been cute if we'd been going somewhere other than just the park.

I hoped that she and Brent hit it off. He was the only guy in our class who was taller than she was. I wondered if that was one of the reasons why she liked him. She had talked about him nonstop for about a month now, only she wouldn't talk *to* him. She was hopeless in her romanticism, but then again, who was I to talk? I was the same way. I'd liked Jeremy for so long that I didn't remember *not* liking him and I never really talked to him either. I guess that's what made all of us such good friends. We were all kind of pathetic in our own ways.

To our great relief, the first of the males to arrive were Graham and Bobby. Graham's dad had dropped them off and I wondered why, since it wasn't that far for either of them to walk. Then I noticed that they were both loaded down with blankets, a CD player, CD's, and a cooler. Why hadn't we thought of that? I wouldn't have ever figured the boys to be that thoughtful.

"Where is everyone else?" Graham yelled from the curb after his dad drove away.

"They're being fashionably late," Jane yelled back and laughed. We walked over and helped Graham and Bobby bring the stuff to the middle of the park. Settling down under a huge tree, we unfolded the blanket. We were all standing there uncomfortably, none of us certain what to do next, when Jeremy, David, and Kevin finally walked up. The guys started doing that stupid high-five thing they do and we girls just walked over to a picnic table and sat down. I sat in the middle of the table with my legs folded underneath me. Kammy came over and sat on the bench part.

"I wonder where Brent is?" she whispered.

"Oh, you know how he is. Always late, always laid back. He isn't going to rush for anyone. It might look like he's not cool or something." I didn't know what I was talking about but it must have sounded good because the next thing I know, Kammy is smiling and the boys are turning on a CD. They chose Linkin Park and were so absorbed in the beat that they didn't seem to even notice that we weren't sitting with them.

It was around five forty-five before Brent finally arrived.

"Where have you been, dude?" Graham asked as he sauntered over to his friends.

"Sorry. I had a phone call and I couldn't get away any sooner." I looked at Kammy for her reaction and she just shrugged.

Since everyone was finally there, Kevin suggested we all walk to the middle of the park, where it was more secluded from the adjacent road's traffic. Besides that, where we were currently sitting, we were facing some of the houses from Woodland Acres and we didn't want any of the neighbors spying on us. All of us in agreement, we took the stuff Graham and Bobby had brought with them and moved it to a better location. It was still light outside but the trees hid the sun so it seemed later than it was.

At that point, Jeremy approached me. "You look great, Kathryn. I like your hat." He started to play with the ends of my hair that were sticking out, but I couldn't risk him finding out about my fiasco. I instinctively pulled away, and I think he took it to mean that I didn't want him touching me. He looked at me kind of funny and I felt bad. I didn't want him to get the idea I didn't like him, but more important, I didn't want him to see my freakish hair.

Jeremy sat down, so I sat down beside him. As I did so, he smiled at me and my knees went so weak that I was glad I was no longer standing. Everyone else followed our lead and sat down on the blanket too. Graham then changed CDs, this time putting in Nickelback. It was a good choice, and everything seemed so perfect at that moment. The weather was nice and I was with my best friends. And for the first time ever, Jeremy Matthews had noticed I was alive. It was so blissful that I wanted that moment to last forever.

Without him noticing, I tried to look at Jeremy. He really was the cutest guy at school, I decided. He was tall, but not as tall as Brent, and he had that Ashton Kutcher hair that always made me want reach out and touch it, but I'd never had the nerve. He had really pretty blue eyes but the thing I really liked most about Jeremy was his smile. When he smiled, my knees went completely weak, just like they felt at that moment. I was just glad I didn't have to stand up because I think I would have fallen right back down.

"Hey, I have an idea." David broke the silence. "Let's play dare."

Kevin groaned. "What are we, third-graders?" But David kicked him and gave him a knowing look. I guess it was supposed to mean something between them because right away Kevin said, "Oh, sure, okay. Let's play dare."

I had never really liked that game because you had to do foolish things in front of everyone. I knew that it would just get embarrassing, but everyone else agreed so I had to go along.

Graham jumped in and said, "I'll go first." He looked around the circle. "Kammy, I dare you to kiss Brent."

Everyone giggled and Kammy instantly turned red. I felt sorry for her. How could Graham be so mean to start out with a dare like that? Then Kammy gave Shelly an accusing look as if Shelly were the one who'd told Graham that she liked Brent. But Shelly just shrugged and looked back at her innocently. Contemplating whether to take the dare, Kammy got up slowly and walked toward Brent. He stood up and they just looked at

each other for a minute before Brent dropped his gaze to his
feet. I felt embarrassed for both them, the way everyone was
staring. Kammy gathered up the courage to make her move,
leaned over and kissed his check, then ran back and sat down.

The boys started laughing, and then Graham said, "Okay,
Kammy, it's your turn."

She gave him a really dirty look. "Okay, Graham, I dare you
to sing 'My Country, Tis of Thee.'"

I laughed out loud. "Good one, Kammy," I said. The thing
you had to know about Graham is that he can't sing one note in
tune. He's always the one who, at the teacher's request, just
stands around and moves his lips when we have to sing in school
plays. To sing in front of us would be completely humiliating.

"And," Kammy added, "you have to stand up and face us
while you sing."

Graham looked like he wished the ground would swallow
him up. He stood up and cleared his throat twice. Then he
began, "My country, tis of thee, sweet land of liberty, of thee I
sing. Land where my fathers died, land of the ..."

At that point, everyone was laughing so hard that he had to
stop. No one could hear him anyway. Well, except maybe dogs.
His face turned as red as Kammy's had and I thought it was
sweet justice. Graham couldn't take another turn so Kammy got
to pick someone. "Okay, Shelly, it's your turn."

You could tell Shelly was scared to do something mean
because it might come back to haunt her as it had to Graham.
Taking the easy way out, she chose Ashley. "You have to do
three cartwheels in a row."

Ashley got up and immediately did three cartwheels. It was
easy for her because she'd been taking gymnastics for the past
two years, but she got dizzy doing three in a row and fell over on
top of David. He didn't look like he minded and we all laughed.
The rest of the game was fun. Before it was over, people had
been dared to stand on their heads, hop on one foot, or chant
some stupid cheer that we'd heard at football games. Bobby had
even been dared to kiss Tori, but neither of them seemed to

mind. In fact, I think they liked it so much that Kevin finally yelled out, "Get a room!"

When it came my turn to be dared, I had to give Jeremy a head massage. At first, I panicked at the thought of touching him, but then again, I'd always wanted to touch his hair. This was my chance. Initially, I was nervous, but after a minute, he relaxed and so did I. I liked the way his hair felt in my fingers and it smelled good too. I didn't know how long to keep going, so I just kept on rubbing until Kevin said, "Okay, Kathryn, you're enjoying it too much." I wanted to hit him. Since when did he become the game commentary?

In sum, we played for almost an hour, time slipping by without us being aware. After my turn, Jeremy took my hand and held it the rest of the game. I was having so much fun I almost forgot about all the bad stuff that was going on in my life.

Before I knew it, it was getting dark. I didn't want the night to end. After the game ended, Graham put an Usher CD in, and everyone got sodas out of the cooler the guys had brought along. I was glad they'd also brought bottled water because my mouth was really dry. I think it was because I was suddenly very nervous.

I watched Brent walk over to Kammy. They started talking, and then they started dancing—if you could call it that. They were so close to each other that they were barely moving, but you could tell it was their attempt at performing, even though neither one of them knew how to properly dance. I watched Jane as she talked to Kevin and the idea dawned upon me that she was starting to like him. From there, everyone started pairing off. It was then that I realized this would be the last time all of us would be like this together.

As a really sad feeling grew in my heart, Jeremy whispered, "Let's go for a walk."

I got up, straightened my shorts, and put down my water. Obeying his command, we started walking deeper into the woods. I wasn't scared because I knew these woods like I knew my own house. I'd been in and out of them since I was little.

When I was younger though, my parents always made me carry a flashlight, even in the daytime, if I was coming into the woods. Now, though, I didn't need one.

We got to a stopping place, away from the others and Jeremy turned to me. "Where have you been all summer, Kathryn?" He kind of whispered it and the way he said my name sent tingles all over my body.

"I've been around." I shivered a little, not because I was cold, but because I was so nervous. He pulled me closer and then he kissed me. It was my first real kiss, not counting stupid junior high kissing at the skating rink. My heart was beating so loudly that I was sure he could hear it.

"You know—" He pulled away for a minute then started looking me up and down. "You look good. Not that you *ever* looked bad, but you look like you've been working out."

I hadn't been working out, but maybe my fruit and vegetable diet was actually working. If Jeremy thought I looked good, then maybe I was on my way to being able to fit in when we had to move. Maybe if I could lose more weight, I would be able to wear bikinis like the other girls and I wouldn't feel like the beached whale I was sure I looked like. And maybe Jeremy was onto something, maybe I *should* work out. That would only help the weight loss go faster!

While I was thinking about all this, Jeremy kissed me again. Overwhelmed by a mix of emotions, after a few minutes, I had to pull away.

"I'm moving, Jeremy." I just blurted it out.

He looked at me, confused for a minute, and then said, "Moving where?"

I looked down at the ground and started kicking a rock back and forth with my foot. "Sarasota."

He looked at me funny and asked, "Florida?" I reluctantly nodded. "Why are you moving to Florida?"

After I explained to him about my dad's job, he was quiet for a minute. The reality of it all sinking in, he kind of pulled away from me. "When do you have to go?" When I told him how we were moving before school started back, he just said, "Man, that sucks."

I nodded and agreed that it did indeed suck, but what could I do about it?

"It's too bad you have to move. I thought it would be cool for us to hang out more. You know, like start dating."

I thought about that. How wonderful it would have been to start the ninth grade as Jeremy's girlfriend. At that moment, I hated my parents more than ever. I hated them for taking me away from all of this ... and now especially from Jeremy Matthews.

That night, as I lay in bed, I thought about the evening. I thought about Jeremy and how he'd kissed me good-bye before we left the park. But, knowing it was soon all going to come to a crushing end, it just wasn't the same. When I came home, I went straight to my room. I didn't want to talk to my parents. I just wanted to be left alone. Finally, after tossing and turning for what seemed like hours, I fell into a dreamless sleep. I woke up the next morning feeling more drained than rested. Why did life have to suddenly become so hard?

# ❧ Chapter Six ☙

It wasn't until Sunday night that my parents finally found out about my hair. Except for the long run I decided to take in the early morning hours, I stayed in my room for most of the day. I got up early, even before my parents woke up and I ran around the block three times. I was still in pretty good shape from my tennis lessons so I barely broke a sweat and running felt freeing somehow. It was like I could block everything out—my parents, the move, leaving my friends, even Jeremy. I just ran and concentrated only on my feet hitting the pavement. But after I got back, I felt exhausted and went straight back to bed. When I woke up the second time, it was almost one o'clock in the afternoon. I could hear my parents downstairs, but I didn't feel like facing them. My throat dry, I went to the bathroom and drank like ten cups of water out of those little Dixie cups. I was so thirsty! Then I went back to bed again. I guess I slept on and off the rest of the day until finally, my mother knocked on my door and demanded I join her and my father for dinner. I wasn't hungry, but I thought this would be the perfect time to shock her. Going for broke, I left my hat in my room and went downstairs as though nothing was wrong. I took my place at the dining room table as usual.

"Well, Kathryn, it's so good of you to—" My mother stopped mid-sentence. As she noticed my hair, she actually gasped. I thought she might have a heart attack the way she reached for her heart. My dad was less dramatic.

"So, Katybug, what's this? A new hair trend?"

"Well, more like a hair trend gone bad, I guess," I told him as I reached for the broccoli. It was a fruit and vegetable day so I decided on just broccoli.

My mother was shaking her head. "How long has it been like this?"

"Since the sleepover Friday night." I was so calm that I think it made her even angrier. I just played with my broccoli, deciding that I didn't really want it after all.

I went to the kitchen to get some water. When I got back to the table, my mother just started ranting about my hair. "How could you do this to yourself, Kathryn Ann?"

Whenever she used my full name, I knew I was getting to her. After I drank my water, I said, "It was an accident, *Mother.* Do you think I would do this to myself *on purpose*?"

She sighed heavily, as though the weight of the world rested on her shoulders. "Well, we'll just go to the hairdresser's first thing in the morning and have it fixed." She said Preston, her miracle hairstylist, could fix anything. I doubted that he could fix this disaster, but I didn't want to even talk to her. I just excused myself.

"But you didn't eat anything, Kathryn." Mother was in one of her feisty moods, and her eyes were turning that wild color. I didn't get up right away. "And don't think your dad and I haven't noticed this little food trend you have going on." She was getting all worked up. "Fruits and vegetables are fine, but you're not eating enough of anything to even matter. So you'd just better stop this insanity before you make yourself sick." She took a breath and then added, "And you need protein and calcium, and you're not even taking a vitamin." By this point, she was raging. All the while, my dad was sitting back, eating, looking at her like she'd lost her mind.

"Fruits and vegetables are good for her, Abby. What's the problem?"

"The problem, *William,* is that our daughter isn't getting a balanced diet and you are just too oblivious to realize what's going on."

"Well, we'll get her a multivitamin." He kept on eating as if that solved the problem.

"You're going to sit there until you eat something, Kathryn Ann," my mother threatened, completely ignoring what my dad had said.

"Whatever, Mother." I stomped out of the room before they could say anything more. As I drifted away, I heard my mother say something to Dad about how I was getting out of hand. I didn't care what she thought. I just went to my room and called Jane. Once I had her on the line, we talked for over an hour, and then I went back to bed. Even though I couldn't sleep, I felt comforted just being in my bed.

ক্ষ   ল্প

The next week turned out to be a crazed time in all our lives. Every morning I continued to run, although my mother didn't know about this obsessive activity. I always went before she and Dad woke up so as not to arouse their suspicion. It was so peaceful that early in the morning and I could completely block everything out of my mind. My running ritual seemed to be the only time that was completely mine.

On Monday, true to her word, Mom took me to Preston to have my hair fixed. His face showed a little shock when he saw me, but he recovered quickly. First, he shampooed my hair, and then he cut off all the split ends. My hair, which used to fall past my shoulders, was now sitting *on* my shoulders. It was a big change, but I knew I couldn't go through life with burned hair. Then he colored it a chestnut brown, and even I had to admit it looked good. As we left, I overheard him tell my mother that I shouldn't play with my hair like that. His miracle touch ended up costing her almost three hundred dollars. She just looked at me hard at the salon, but on the way home she told me that I was paying for it out of my allowance.

Yeah, right, I thought. Just like I paid for the lamp. And besides, how much allowance did she think I got anyway? If you ask me, I think she was spending too much time watching TV

Land reruns. If she thought she was a June Cleaver mother, she was seriously off balance.

ಐ ೞ

The rest of the week we spent packing everything up and it was just a very confusing time for me all around. Since I'd never moved before, I didn't know where to begin. Jane, who was very organized, came over to help me. She even made lists to ease the flurry of activity and although I rolled my eyes at her, I have to admit the lists proved very helpful. We worked almost all week just packing up my room. Every time we would start accomplishing something, we would come across a note or a picture or even a childhood toy that would bring back memories. So, we ended up talking more than we packed. It was just a hard time for me from every perspective. Jane was very moody throughout most of the packing and I knew it was hard on her too. Sure, she had the other girls as friends, but it wasn't the same.

Mom said that we would be leaving on Sunday, so Friday night I spent the night at Jane's for the last time. That same night, my parents had been invited to the Jessup's house for a going away party. Everyone was going to be there, including Jane's parents. It never occurred to me that it would be hard on Mom and Dad to say good-bye to their friends too. At the same time, it was hard to feel bad for them when it was their own fault for moving.

Jane and I tried to have fun, but when you know it's your last time to do something, it's hard to enjoy it. It's like you're trying so hard to hang on to the moment that you can't really savor it. Most of the night, we just talked quietly about how strange high school would be without each other. We also talked about Jeremy and how he'd called me only once since the night at the park. While it pained me to think about, I told her I completely understood. "It seems so unfair that I could have started out high school with a boyfriend as cool as Jeremy and now I have to move to a place so far away that it might as well be the moon."

Jane nodded as though she understood but I doubted she did. Lately, I felt like no one really understood me, not even my best friend.

&#10086;  &#10087;

When the dreaded Sunday arrived, Nana came over around eight o'clock in the morning to help out. Mom said everything was under control but I think Nana just wanted to see us one last time before we left. For as long as I'd been alive, we'd only lived thirty minutes away from my grandmother and it was going to be hard to adjust to living so far away from her. I knew she felt the pangs of distance already too and I wish that dad would see how he was hurting his mom. To be away from us would hurt her. Didn't he even care? Didn't anyone care about anything besides more money and bigger houses?

Jane also came over to see me before we left, even though I told her she didn't have to. We'd said goodbye so many times that it was getting harder instead of easier. The movers were already there and had everything in their truck and were ready to leave. The control freak, my mother, was flittering around, making sure every last-minute detail was taken care of and my dad was whistling like this was the best day of his life. Jane pedaled up the driveway on her bicycle. I knew I would miss seeing that. There was so much I would miss that for some reason I was reminded of the play we had put on in the seventh grade, *Our Town*. All of a sudden I felt like Emily, one of the characters, even though I wasn't dead. In her speech, she was saying how everything moved too quickly and how she missed the little things—like clocks ticking and the smell of coffee. I knew my list of things to miss was different from hers, but the point was the same. I would miss everything that I had taken for granted before. And again, anger built up inside me for my parents that I couldn't control.

"I brought you something." Jane handed me a gift bag. I opened it and inside was a journal with an angel on the front. It was pretty. She also gave me an address book with everyone's e-mail address in it. "Even Jeremy's!" She nudged me and we started giggling.

"Thank you so much." I hugged her and she told me to e-mail her as soon as I could.

"I will," I promised her.

She nodded and looked like she was going to cry.

Finally, after a few minutes, my dad called me to hurry. He said 'bye to Nana and she hugged him extra hard.

"Take care of our Katy, William." He winked at her. Nana just gave Mom a stiff hug and then Dad turned to me and told me it was time to go.

Regretfully, we had to leave. Jane and I hugged one last time and I got in the car, thinking of it as my final ride before my execution. In the front seat, my parents were talking nonstop, making all kinds of plans. I felt completely left out, like I had no choices. I also felt like I had no control over anything that was happening to me. For the first time in my life, I felt small. I just wanted to crawl in a hole and stay there. The saddest part was that my parents wouldn't even notice. For once, I wasn't the object of their attention. This move was the center of their universe. Dad's new job was all they could think about. Everything was more important than I was and I didn't know how to handle it. I felt like I was losing control, with no idea of how to regain it.

# ౪ Chapter Seven ౫

The first week in our new house was a nightmare for me. I was living out of boxes and my room wasn't as big as the one I had had before. It was on the right side of the hall at the very top of the stairs, while my parents' room was at the end of the hall on the left. My new room had light yellow walls, and the carpet was a dark, putrid brown that I hated, even though I knew in advance that I would. On the wall closest to the door stood a built-in bookshelf and a big closet, not a walk-in one like the one I had in my old room, took up most of the left side of the wall. I had my own bathroom, though, and that was nice because I'd never had my own bathroom before. The first thing you could see when you walked in was a huge picture window facing the street. It also had a window seat, though I couldn't imagine why. There wasn't anything to see except the neighbors' houses. To make matters worse, we lived in the kind of neighborhood I didn't even like. All the houses looked the same and they all stood side by side in cookie-cutter rows. I was glad that we had a privacy fence in the backyard because I could already tell I wasn't going to like the neighbors. It turned out, I couldn't have been more right in that assumption.

The first night we were there, the neighbors from across the street came over to introduce themselves. They were David and Sally Morgan and they had a daughter who was my age. She had come with them, so my parents made me come downstairs to meet her. I was right in the middle of trying to get my room in order when their request interrupted me. All the clutter was upsetting me and I couldn't imagine why anyone would come over the first day someone moved in.

Mr. and Mrs. Morgan's daughter's name was Tiffany and I knew I'd hate her right away. She was tall, thin and blonde. In pretty pertness, she looked like a model. Even though she had on a casual tank top and shorts, she looked pretty. She had perfect features and I instinctively felt embarrassed standing next to her. My features were just the opposite of hers and I felt inferior, even though Dad always insisted that people couldn't *make* you feel anything.

"No one makes you feel bad about yourself, Katybug, except you. You're the only one in control of how you feel." He told me that all the time. But standing next to Tiffany, I couldn't help but feel embarrassed. She was so tall and thin, standing beside her I feel like a big round beach ball with legs.

"Let's all go into the kitchen and I'll make some coffee," my mother suggested to everyone. We had been standing in the living room surrounded by boxes and you would think they would have known that we had lots of unpacking to do. But the Morgans followed my mother into the kitchen where she busied herself making coffee and setting out a cake that another neighbor had dropped off when we had first arrived. At least Mrs. Sumter knew to just drop something off and not stay. These people, on the other hand, were downright rude!

Uninterested in domesticity, Mr. Morgan and my dad went outside to look at the yard. I think they were talking about Dad's plans for fixing it up. Although it was a big backyard, the previous owners hadn't taken care of it and it did need work. I wished I could have gone with them. Mrs. Morgan, Tiffany, my mom and I sat down at the table, even though Mom had to move several boxes off it just to make room.

Mrs. Morgan spoke first. "Well, Kathryn, I hear you'll be attending school with Tiffany."

She said that like I should be happy or something. I just nodded.

My mother chimed in. "Won't that be great? You'll already know someone." She had that stupid fake smile going on that made me want to vomit. Why did everyone have to be so bogus?

When I didn't say anything, my mother went on. "Ever since Kathryn found out we were moving, that's been her biggest complaint, not knowing anyone at school."

I looked at my mother hard and wished I could crawl into a hole. I couldn't believe she'd just told them that. I was just mortified, but Mrs. Morgan said, "Oh, before the first week is over you'll know absolutely everyone, won't she, Tiffany?"

"Oh, yes." And then Tiffany looked at me and smiled brightly. "The classes at Vanguard Academy are really small, and you'll find that everyone is very friendly."

I'll bet they are, I thought. But instead I just said, "Yeah." I think my mother was embarrassed by my sudden lack of verbal skills, but I didn't care. I had a lot of unpacking to do and there I was stuck talking to the Brady Bunch. Tiffany was someone I had nothing in common with and she was so unlike Jane that it made me miss my best friend even more.

"Kathryn, why don't you go up and show Tiffany your room?" my mother suggested.

What were we—kindergartners? "My room isn't really ready, Mother," I reminded her. "I still have boxes everywhere, considering this *is* our first night here." I knew my voice sounded hateful but I couldn't help it. I was angry that I was stuck talking to these people.

I thought I would throw that hint toward Mrs. Morgan, but she just ignored it and said, "Oh, if you need any help, Tiffany is a wonder at decorating." She smiled at her daughter as if she were most proud of her for being able to put a bed in the right spot and scatter a few pictures around. "When Chad— that's our son ..." Mrs. Morgan turned to my mother as if to explain, "... went back to college last year, Tiffany helped him and his roommate with every room in their apartment. They were very pleased with the results."

Well, of course they were. They were probably just glad they didn't have to do the work. "I'll keep that in mind," I told her sullenly and my mother glared at me.

"Kathryn, will you go out back and tell your dad and Mr. Morgan that the cake and coffee are ready?"

I got up and walked toward the back door but not before I heard my mother whisper, "She's just having a hard time adjusting." I didn't hear the response because I was just so angry that after I called my dad inside, I went straight up to my new room and stayed there until everyone left.

🙰    🙰

Finally, by the middle of the week, my room started looking more like *I* lived there as opposed to some stranger. I wanted to pull up the carpet, but Dad said I should wait until we got someone who knew what they were doing. I still put my throw rugs out, even though they didn't match, and I put all my books on the bookshelf. I didn't have enough to fill it so I scattered in some pictures of my friends and me to fill in the gaps. When I was done, it didn't look that bad. I didn't like the color of my room but I decided to talk to my mother about that another day.

I was glad that I'd chosen a white comforter because it didn't clash so much with the yellow, but I just didn't like the yellow walls. They were definitely not me. I thought about hanging up pictures or posters, but since I was going to try to get the room painted, I didn't see the point.

School was starting the next week, so that weekend—the first weekend in the new house—my mother asked me if I wanted to go shopping with her. It was a Saturday morning and she was so cheerful that she was making me sick. "Oh, it'll be so much fun!" She was actually gushing.

We were in the kitchen. Ignoring her excitement over the proposed shop-a-thon, I got some water and sat down at the table. She was making pancakes and my dad was reading the newspaper. He peered over the top of the paper and said, "Oh, go have fun with your mother, Katybug."

Fun, coupled with Mother, was an oxymoron. That was a word I learned last year in English. It meant two words that were totally opposite, like the big little car. You can't have a big *and* a little car; it was one or the other. Just like my mother and fun. I could be with my mother or I could have fun, but not at the same time. "No thanks. I don't want to go shopping," I politely declined.

She put pancakes on all of our plates, but I just stared at mine. "But, Kathryn, you have to have school clothes and this is the last time to go shopping. You know, school starts on Monday."

"I'll go myself, Mother. I don't need anyone there with me. I can make better time alone." She looked hurt and started to say something else, but Dad put his hand over hers as if to stop her. Then he put his newspaper down and started eating. I looked at the pancakes as if they were poison, knowing full well I wasn't going to eat them. "Don't we have an apple or anything in this house?" I sounded so hateful that I almost didn't recognize my own voice.

"We have fruit, but I wish you would eat something else, Kathryn." Mother was calm this time but she was making herself clear. She wanted me to eat.

I was making myself clear too. "I'm not hungry." I drank a glass of water and went to my room. All of a sudden, I felt drained. I don't know if it was the week I'd had, the changes we'd made or if I was coming down with the flu, but I just felt tired. I looked at the clock and it was only nine o'clock in the morning. I hadn't even been up long. I couldn't figure out why I was so tired. I decided to call Jane to see what she was doing. I had talked to her only once since we'd moved and that was the day after we arrived. I had told her all about Tiffany and how I knew I was going to hate school. That time, we had talked for over an hour.

I dialed the phone and her mother picked up. "Is Jane there? This is Kathryn."

"Oh, Kathryn! How are you? How are your parents?"

"Everyone is fine. We're just getting settled in."

"Well, tell them I said hello," she said and then added, "I'll let Jane know you called. She stayed at Tori's house last night and she isn't home yet."

I thanked her and hung up. I felt so bad that I was missing out on a sleepover, but I decided that maybe I would feel better if I went outside and ran to the beach. It wasn't very far, so I just threw on a pair of old shorts and a shirt that I wouldn't let anyone see me in and I went outside. The breezy air felt good against my skin. I took a few deep breaths and started running. Running here felt different than it did back home, but it wasn't bad. I had to admit that the salty air from the ocean felt amazingly refreshing. I ran so far and so hard that when I got home, I was exhausted. I put my Atlanta Braves T-shirt back on and crawled into bed. Dead tired, I stayed there until the afternoon.

Finally, around four o'clock, I got up and decided to go to the mall. My mother was right—I did need clothes but I just couldn't imagine going shopping with her. I found my dad hanging out in his new den. It's a really nice room. He bought a leather couch to go in there and he had filled the built-in bookshelves with actual books, not pictures, like mine. The computer was set up in there too, and his desk was really great. I like to sit at it when he's not home, pretending that I'm working on something important and can't be disturbed. Most of the time though, I'm just doodling my name with Jeremy's inside hearts.

Dad also had a really nice TV installed in the den. It's a flat screen, and it's better than the one we have in the family room. I think it's his favorite part of the new house because it's where he spends most of his time.

"Hey, Dad."

The door was open so I went inside. He was sitting at his other desk, the one that is slanted perfectly for his work. As I entered, I discovered that he was working on layouts for a project that was due. That's the way my dad is—he's always working on layouts.

"Well, sleepyhead, glad to see you're up." He smiled at me. I loved to see him smile in which his eyes crinkled up like he was really smiling with his eyes.

"Can you drive me to the mall and drop me off?"

"Sure, sweetie, but why didn't you go with Mom? She and Mrs. Morgan left a few hours ago."

Mrs. Morgan went? Hearing that, I was so glad that I hadn't gone with them. I couldn't imagine hours of shopping with those two. And maybe Tiffany had gone too. Just the thought of that made me cringe.

"I didn't want to go with Mom. So, can you please just drop me off?" He looked at the way I was dressed, skeptically raising his eyebrows.

"Well, let me know when you're ready and I'll take you." I ran upstairs, threw on a white T-shirt and blue denim shorts, and ran back downstairs. I barely brushed my hair. I didn't know anyone here, so why should I care what I looked like? I was ready to go in five minutes flat. "Really?" Dad said in a flat tone. "You're going to the mall like that?"

"Yes, Dad, I really am."

Giving up, he just shook his head at me and told me to get in the car. He put his work down and we drove to the mall in silence. On the way, he tried to make conversation, but it didn't work out too well. I didn't feel like talking. Instead, I turned up the radio so he would take the hint and stop chatting. It didn't take long to get there, but it felt like hours.

As Dad was dropping me off, he handed me money and his credit card. "Get what you need, Katybug, and call me when you're finished. I'll come and get you." Then he added, "Or maybe you'll run into Mom and you two can ride back together."

I said I'd call him, then I took the money and went into the mall.

It felt good to get inside, away from the heat and away from my dad. Malls are always so cold and this one wasn't any different. I wasn't sure where to start since I usually did my school shopping with Jane. I felt bad, thinking that this year she was probably shopping with Tori instead. I had to block that vision out of my mind because it hurt too much. Everything felt so lonely now.

Random shopping, I went into several stores, but I couldn't find anything I liked. I usually shopped at the Gap, but nothing looked like what I wanted there. I walked the first floor of the mall without actually going into any stores. Then I saw Hot Topic. Although I'd seen the store before in Atlanta, I'd never actually gone in. It wasn't a store that Jane and my other friends would imagine we would ever shop in. But as I walked inside, I was completely intrigued. I found myself in the middle of everything from Marilyn Manson T-shirts to Care Bear stuff. It was bizarre. Most of the clothes were black and there was one shirt that said, "Pink is the new black." If that was true, why was everything mostly black?

I looked around for a few minutes and actually found a couple of cute shirts that I liked. They were black but they fit my mood, so I ended up buying everything I needed in that one store. I found jeans, shirts, and even a light jacket that I liked. I also bought a pair of sneakers in, you guessed it, a matching black. Later, after I surveyed everything I had bought, I realized that nothing had color to it. When piled together, everything was an endless sea black or gray and I suddenly felt better. I was finally in control of something, even if it was just school clothes.

৵     ৎ

That night at dinner, my mother said she wanted to see what I'd bought. Wanting to avoid the criticism she'd no doubt express, I told her I'd show her later. We were having a roast that night, but I wasn't hungry. I pushed my food around so that it would appear as if I'd eaten.

"What did you eat at the mall?" Dad asked me.

I should have known. Mother was getting him on her side. Now he was going to start with what I ate and didn't eat.

"I had French fries at the food court," I lied. I didn't want to get into this with them. "I also had a cookie at the Cookie Company, so I'm really not hungry."

"Well, I wish you had come shopping with Mrs. Morgan and me. We had so much fun. She's a really nice lady and she belongs to the country club." My mother turned to my dad. "That reminds me, William. You and I are invited to dinner there next weekend. They want to see if we want to join."

My dad nodded but didn't say anything. He continued to eat. I pushed my food around some more and then asked if I could go up to my room.

"You need to eat something," Mother interjected. "You haven't even touched your roast."

"I'm thinking of becoming a vegetarian," I told them, as though I'd been thinking about this for a long time, when in reality it had just occurred to me.

"Oh, I don't think so." Mother looked at my dad and he just shrugged. "You're not becoming one of *those* people, Kathryn. I won't allow it." She looked at my dad again. "Would you please say something?"

"What kind of people, Mother?" I asked her, pushing her to the limit. She ignored me.

"What do you want me to say, Abby? She's just expressing herself right now. She'll get over it. It's just a phase."

They were talking about me like I wasn't even there.

"She's losing weight, William." Not getting the response she wanted from my dad, my mother looked at me. "You're losing too much weight, Kathryn, and I'm going to make sure that this stops. If you don't stop it, I will."

"I'm going up to my room," I defiantly told them then I ran upstairs and slammed the door behind me for good measure. She wasn't going to stop anything.

I looked at myself in the mirror. I didn't see that I was losing that much weight. Given the excess bulges that stared back at me, I still wasn't going to fit in here. Everyone here looked like Tiffany, and I certainly didn't look like that. I had a lot more weight to lose and nothing, not my mother or anyone else, was going to stop me.

❦ ❦

Monday morning, I got up and dressed for school. My heart wasn't in it, but I knew it was something I couldn't avoid. I put on my black jeans and a black oversize T-shirt. It didn't look too bad, but I wished that I didn't look so big in my hips. As the final touch, I then put on my black sneakers. I didn't even want to see what I looked like so I avoided the mirror. I should have felt smaller because black always makes you look thin, but instead, I felt like a big black bear. I really needed to start running every day, I thought. Maybe I would even start taking tennis lessons again. I might be able to talk my mom into that. She might see it as a sign that I was trying to fit in.

By the time I arrived downstairs, my parents were already in the kitchen. When I walked in, my mother eyed me distastefully and said, "So, this is what you bought at the mall?" She was standing at the stove stirring eggs, but when she saw me, she stopped and glared at me after eyeballing me up and down.

I had never gotten around to showing her my clothes. I just nodded.

"Young lady, you don't seriously think that you're going to wear black on your first day?" She put her hand on her hip for emphasis.

"Well, yeah, it's exactly what I *know* I'm wearing."

My dad looked up from his paper and facetiously asked, "Who died?" I rolled my eyes.

My mother shook her head. "I just don't understand you anymore." She put my breakfast on a plate and handed it to me. She'd made eggs and I couldn't even look at them. I was so nervous about starting school and didn't she know how many calories were in eggs?

Then suddenly my mother's mood changed and she said in a smiling voice, "Mrs. Morgan wanted to know if you wanted to ride with her and Tiffany this morning. She has to take Tiffany anyway." She sounded so hopeful.

I felt a terror in my heart. "No thank you. If you or Dad can't take me, I'll walk." School was only a couple of blocks from our neighborhood and I'd have walked a hundred miles as long as I didn't have to ride with that Stepford Daughter.

"I can take you, Katybug," Dad said in between bites. "I can drop you off on the way to the office."

"William, it would be so good for her to ride with Tiffany."

"Get off her back, Abby. Please don't make the first day any harder for her."

"Harder for her? I was only trying to make it better. Tiffany is very popular and she could really help her fit in." Mother was getting that tone in her voice I can't stand. It was a high-pitched, whiney tone and I hated it. What's more, I hated *her* when she used it.

"Kathryn fit in fine before we moved and I'm sure she'll do fine here."

"Well, I was only trying to help her." My mother sighed then, and all of a sudden I felt very tired. I got up from the table without eating anything. My stomach felt as though it had lead in it. If the morning were any indication of how the rest of the day would go, I didn't know how I could live through it.

# ಏ Chapter Eight ೮೪

True to his word, Dad dropped me off in front of the red brick building. As I emerged from the passenger's seat, I looked up at the sign that was written in huge letters: "*Vanguard Academy.*" Under it, in smaller letters it read "*Home of the Wildcats.*" I looked around and saw kids standing on the steps that led to the front door. They were all talking and laughing together like old friends and I felt envious. I wondered if I would ever laugh and talk with any of these kids.

I saw some other kids sitting under trees, talking like they didn't have any worries about anything. I couldn't help but wonder if I would fit in with any of these groups. I sighed deeply, rounded up every last ounce of courage and made my way to the front door. Some of the kids looked at me curiously as I approached, but no one said anything. Not even a smile or a hello greeted me. Trudging forward, I walked through the front door and found that it looked like any other school, although I don't know exactly what I was expecting. I found the office right away and explained that I was a new student. The secretary looked up from her pile of papers and smiled at me. I smiled back and she asked me my name.

"Kathryn Bailey."

"Of course! You're already registered," she told me. "Your parents had your school records faxed over to us and we've been expecting you." She gave me a locker number, a combination and my schedule. "If you have any problems, Kathryn, always remember the door is open to you." I smiled and nodded. I obediently took my things and looked at my schedule. I had to find Mr. Holden's room because that was my homeroom. This schedule also said he was going to be my math teacher. His room number was one hundred eight, which meant he was downstairs. I also had some classes whose room numbers started with two, so I assumed that those would be upstairs, but I couldn't be certain. The bell rang then and the hallway seemed to jam up with kids. Everyone was scurrying to lockers or classrooms and I didn't even know which I should do first. After a split second of indecision, I settled on finding my homeroom. I didn't have any books with me so I could wait on my locker.

I found Mr. Holden's class without a problem and gingerly walked in. Everyone seemed to already know one another and everyone was talking at once. The first person I noticed was Tiffany. She looked as if she were a queen holding court, sitting cross-legged like she was on top of a table at the back of the room. Several kids surrounded her and they were all laughing and talking like they were having the time of their lives. I saw her glance over at me, but she completely ignored me. She uttered something to two of the guys who were sitting with her, although I didn't know exactly what it was she said. It must have been something witty though because they started laughing and looking my way. I knew right away that it had to be something about me. I just glared at her but she looked right through me. Then she tossed her long blonde hair so that it fell across her shoulders and went back to talking with her groupies.

I didn't know where to go, so I just went to the desk where a man close to my dad's age was sitting. He was looking at a textbook, so I cleared my throat so he would look up.

"I'm new," I told him. I didn't know what else to say.

"Yes, you're Kathryn, right?" I just nodded and he went on. "It's nice to meet you. I'm Mr. Holden. I also teach algebra. I think you're in that class as well."

I confirmed that I was and he told me that I could sit anywhere. I didn't know where to sit since no one was in desks. Weighing my options, I finally decided on a desk closest to the window. I just sat there thinking about how strange it was that

Mr. Holden already knew my name. That just proved how small this school really was. All these kids had been together since Kindergarten, I reasoned. The grade school building, the K-8, was actually attached to this one by a breezeway. I was amazed at how a single school could hold all its grade levels in just two buildings. But looking around, I realized why. This class, the ninth-grade homeroom, only had twenty-seven students in the entire freshman class. At my old school, that would have been only one of several ninth-grade classes. I didn't know if I could get used to so few students. Everyone obviously knew everyone else's business and it was going to be much harder to fit in when the leader of the group was someone I already knew I didn't like, Tiffany. My mind was reeling with all these thoughts when the bell rang and brought my attention back to class.

As everyone scrambled to his seat, a guy who had been talking to Tiffany approached me and told me I was in his seat.

"I didn't know that these seats were assigned," I replied, since that's what Mr. Holden had told me.

"They're not, but I was sitting here first."

"If you were, you'd be here instead of me," I quipped. I couldn't believe I'd just said that, but it just came tumbling out.

Not used to being shot down, he was angry. "I always sit in the seat by the window and I want this desk." He was standing over me, glaring, and he threw his notebook on the desk to mark his territory. I looked away, embarrassed, but I didn't budge. Looking back, I realized that moving would have been the smart thing to do, but I felt like it was the principle of the matter. Why should I have to move when Mr. Holden had said I could sit anywhere? But that one brief lapse in judgment wound up causing me a lot of problems down the road.

"Children, find your seats, please," Mr. Holden instructed us. Everyone started toward a place to sit except for my tormenter. "Max, find a desk." Mr. Holden looked over our way. Apparently, Max was this guy's name.

"I found a desk, but this freak girl is in it."

Freak girl? He was calling me a freak?

"Maxwell Sutton, apologize to Kathryn right now and find somewhere else to sit." Mr. Holden was growing impatient.

Max grabbed his notebook and stalked off without apologizing and Mr. Holden began to call roll. Max took a desk on the other side of the room and slammed his things down so hard that Mr. Holden had to tell him to wait out in the hall. "I'll talk to you about this outburst shortly," he said.

I felt embarrassed, like I'd gotten him in trouble for not moving, but wasn't it my right to sit there? I guess the other kids felt it was my fault too, because some of them looked my way with disgust. I acted like I didn't notice, but I felt their eyes burning into my head. Out of the corner of my eye, I saw Tiffany lean over and say something to one of the other girls. They both gave me dirty looks and I turned my head away, ignoring them.

It was only eight fifteen and my morning was already ruined. At that moment, I wished I were anywhere but there. If only I could go to public school. At least there I wouldn't stand out so much. Here, I felt like I was sticking out like the freak Max said I was and I wished I could just completely disappear.

૪૦  ૦૪

The rest of the day proved just as bad, if not worse, than the way it had started. I went into the wrong room during second period and ended up in a senior Spanish class. It wasn't until the teacher called roll that I realized I was in the wrong place. I then had to go up and embarrass myself by telling the teacher that I was actually looking for ninth-grade history. The entire class roared with laughter over my stupidity. For seniors, they were very immature.

I dreaded lunch most because I had realized early on that I would have no one to sit with. The lunchroom was set up with round tables that were scattered throughout the room and by the time I had gotten my tray, I saw that all the tables were taken. Since the classes were small, so was the lunchroom. Of course there were plenty of seats left at the tables, but I didn't know anyone well enough to just take my tray and sit with them. Scanning the crowd, I spied Tiffany, who was sitting with her friends, and of course *her* table was full. Not that I would have sat with her anyway, but besides her, I didn't know anyone else's name. I felt foolish just standing there so I threw my tray of food away and went into the bathroom to wait until lunch was over. I wasn't hungry anyway, but I just wished I had somewhere better to wait. I couldn't go to the library, since everyone in my grade was supposed to be in the lunchroom and I couldn't go outside, since that would have been even more obvious. Everything was just getting to me, so I barricaded myself in one of the little stalls and tried to figure out how to convince my parents to take me out of this school. Maybe the afternoon would be better, I tried to tell myself, but in my heart, I knew it wouldn't be.

ɞ  ʚ

After lunch, things went from bad to worse. My locker got jammed and I was late for my English class. The teacher's name was Mrs. Jamison and I could only hope that she was nice and understanding about me being late.

It was completely mortifying to have the entire class watch me walk in five minutes late. And wouldn't you know it, the entire ninth-grade class took English together. It was the only one that we all shared besides homeroom. I tried to sneak in unnoticed, but that tactic didn't work.

"Are you Kathryn Bailey?" Mrs. Jamison was standing at the white board, but turned her attention to me when I walked in.

"Yes." My voice was small.

"Do you have an excuse for being late?" I froze and didn't know if I could even answer her. She didn't look friendly at all and I was scared to move. I just stood frozen at the door, embarrassed that I couldn't speak. Finally, I just shook my head no. I didn't feel like explaining about my locker and anyway, it would have come out sounding lame.

"Let's not make a habit of being late." To emphasize that warning, she looked at me over her glasses. They were sitting on her nose and she peered over them at me like she was the old maid in that classic game of cards. I nodded my head again but she continued, "Being late indicates that you think your time is more important than the other person's time. I'm not sure how it was at your old school, but here, we respect one another."

She paused and I didn't know if she was waiting for me to say something or not. I chose to say nothing. I guess that was the wrong choice because she looked even more frustrated, but finally gave up her scolding and told me to find a seat.

I scanned the room with my eyes. I had to walk to the back of the room because there were only two empty seats. One was beside Tiffany and the other one was beside a huge bookshelf. A no-brainer in my book, I went straight to the one beside the bookshelf and hoped beyond hope that it would fall down on me.

On the way there, I had to pass Max's desk. Still seeking revenge on my earlier actions, he put his feet out in a nonchalant way, like he was just stretching, as I passed. Only I didn't see them until it was too late. Falling into his trap, I tripped over his feet. My books and notebooks went flying all over the room and I fell flat on my face. It was the most humiliating thing that had ever happened to me. The entire class roared so loudly with laughter that Mrs. Jamison had to yell in order to get everyone quiet. I fumbled around, trying to get up and find all my things. All of my papers were scattered across the floor and no one even made a move to help me gather them. The task left entirely in my hands, it took several minutes to get my stuff back together. My ankle hurt from the fall, but no one was interested in that. All Mrs. Jamison said was "Since we've wasted enough time this afternoon, we have to get straight to work." She then passed out our assignments.

   &#8242;&#8242; &#8540;

I'd never been so glad for a day to be over in my life. I decided to walk home because I didn't want my mother to come and get me. She had told me to call her if I wanted a ride home, but I thought the walk would help me clear my head. Unfortunately, I ended up feeling worse. The entire day just swept over me in a massive tidal wave and I felt exhausted and drained. Worse, I dreaded the next day so much that I got a tightening in my stomach.

When I got home, my mother was actually standing at the door waiting for me. She was smiling with excitement. "How was your first day, Kathryn? Did you get a ride home with Tiffany?"

I just looked at her. Was she serious?

"Why would you think I got a ride home with Tiffany?" Not wanting to hash out the details, I tried to push past her and start up the stairs. The only problem was, she held on to my arm to prevent me from sidestepping her.

"Well, how did you get home?"

"I walked."

"I thought for sure, since you didn't call me, you must have ridden home with the Morgan's." She looked so disappointed. For a moment I wanted to tell her everything. I wanted her to really listen and tell me that she understood. I wanted her to admit that she was sorry she and Dad had sent me to such a horrible place. I wanted her to tell me that I could go back and stay with Nana so I could attend my old school. But I knew that she wouldn't say any of that and I knew that she wouldn't understand or believe anything I said. So, I just said, "My day was fine." Then I just brushed my way past her and started upstairs to my room.

"But don't you want to tell me about it? I made cookies," she bribed. She was calling after me in a singsong voice that I hated. I just yelled, "*No!*" and I slammed my door once I got inside my room. Slamming doors was something I was getting good at. Still filled with pent-up rage, I threw all my books down on my desk and proceeded to take off my shoes. For added effect, I threw them at the wall. It felt good to throw something and I looked at my history book. It was big so I threw it too. It made an even louder noise, which made me feel even better.

My energy spent, I lay down on my bed and started crying. I couldn't believe my mother had just told me that she had baked cookies. What was getting into her? Why was she acting like this? Why was she trying to make us into something we weren't? My mother and dad were losing it. They were joining the country club, my mother was baking, I was attending a private school and all of it was just so phony. I just wanted real things in our lives like they were before and I couldn't get my parents to understand that. I felt like nothing was the same. And changes weren't always good, like my dad had indicated.

I guess I fell asleep because the next thing I knew, my dad was waking me up, saying it was time for dinner. "I'm not hungry," I told him in a sluggish voice. I looked at the clock; it was already six o'clock.

"Katybug, I'm worried about you." Dad sat down on the edge of my bed. "You haven't been eating lately."

Good, I thought. You should worry. But instead I said, "I *have* been eating. It's just that you and Mom are too busy to notice."

He sighed. "That's not true. We're never too busy for you. Please come downstairs and have dinner. Mom and I want to hear about your day."

My day? That was something I never wanted to think about again. And I certainly didn't want to *talk* about it. Feeling an obligation toward his sympathy, however, I got out of bed and walked downstairs with Dad. That decision proved to be a poor one. The minute we sat down, my mother started talking nonstop.

"Oh, I met the nicest lady at my tennis lesson this morning. Sally introduced me, and we all had lunch together."

She started rambling about lessons at the country club and I just blocked it all out. As had become my dinner ritual, I started moving my food from one side of my plate to the other. It was a game I had begun playing and I had the technique down pat. Each night, I liked to rearrange all my food on my plate in a different way. For instance, I would put my peas where my corn was or my asparagus where my rice was. By this point, I had stopped putting meat on my plate altogether. All I had to do was make it appear as if I was eating so my parents wouldn't say anything to me. This tactic was even fooling Dad, something I was sure I'd never be able to do. I've always known it was hard to get anything past him, but this was working and I felt so good about myself. I didn't want to let that feeling go and eating all that food would do just that. I'd noticed that my clothes were fitting better, although not as well as I wanted them to. Even my rings were fitting looser. If I could just keep this ruse up a little while longer, maybe I would be considered thin. Maybe being thin would help me fit in better because so far everyone in the entire ninth grade hated me.

I was thinking about this when I heard my mother say something about Janet Sutton and my head snapped up. "Sutton? As in *Max* Sutton?"

My mother put her fork down and took a sip of wine. "Yes, I think she mentioned she had a son named Max. Why? Is he in your class, Kathryn?"

Her voice was just so sweet and happy that I felt anger swell up inside me. "Yes and he's the biggest butt munch in school," I yelled at her.

My dad said, "Kathryn, we don't use language like that in this house. What has gotten into you?" He looked over at my mother, who was just sitting there with a shocked expression on her face. She looked as though I had slapped her and at that moment, I wish I had. "Apologize to your mother," he demanded. Like 'butt munch' was the worst word in the world. Considering we were talking about Max, I thought I was being kind.

"I will not apologize," I yelled at him then I picked up my plate and slammed it back down on the table. Some of my food fell off my plate and although the plate didn't break like I had wanted it to, it did hit my glass and my milk went spilling all over the table. Pushing myself away from the table and leaving them to contend with the mess, I didn't even run out of the room. I stomped loudly, only this time my dad followed me.

"Don't go to your room, Kathryn Ann. I want you in my den. *Now!*"

Dad never raised his voice. He's usually very calm, but if you ever make him mad, you have to watch out. The way he emphasized the word *now*, I knew I was in trouble. I strode to the den, following him like a scolded puppy with my tail between my legs and he shut the door behind us. He was so angry that he couldn't even speak for a minute. Finally, after what seemed like forever, he broke the silence.

"What is going on with you? Lately, your attitude is out of hand and I've really grown tired of these outbursts. I've never seen you get so angry. You've ruined dinner more than once and you're sullen and rude. And now I find that your language is less than tolerable. I want to know what is wrong because this really isn't like you." His voice didn't even sound like his own – that's how angry he was with me.

Refusing to humor him, I didn't say anything. I just folded my arms in front of me, walked over to his bookshelf and looked at all his books. He had everything in alphabetical order by the author's last name, just like in a library. My dad was very organized. Although things were still in boxes all over the house, my dad's den looked like he'd lived in it forever. This was the first room he had started working on when we arrived.

I concentrated on the book titles so I wouldn't have to talk. Refusing to give up, Dad walked over to where I was standing and put his hands on my shoulders. My arms were still crossed in defiance.

"Look at me, Kathryn." I looked at him for a minute but I couldn't look into his eyes. Instead, I gazed down at my feet. "I know that you're going through a great deal of changes, but this behavior isn't going to be accepted anymore, do you understand?"

I nodded and he told me that if I wasn't going to finish dinner to just sit in his den and think about how I'd ruined the meal for all of us. As punishment, he left me in there, but I didn't think things through like he'd ordered. Instead, I walked over to his computer and turned it on.

I decided to excuse my own behavior and e-mail Jane instead. While I was logging on, I wondered what she was doing. I wondered how her first day at high school had gone. At that moment, I missed her so much that I wanted to cry. Instead, I wrote her a really long e-mail. I told her all about school, all about Tiffany and all about Max. I told her everything that had happened to me that day and after I was finished, I felt much better. If anyone could understand it would be Jane. I just wished that I could talk to her. But I knew that my parents wouldn't like it if I got on the phone long distance, especially after the way I had been acting. Not that I cared what they thought, but I didn't want my dad to get really angry with me again. It was one thing for my mother, but now she was getting Dad on her side and I didn't want that.

# ❧ Chapter Nine ❧

The next morning as soon as I awoke, I ran downstairs to the den to see if I had e-mail from Jane. I logged on, but my mailbox was empty. I was disappointed to say the least. I had wanted to hear from her so badly. I knew she was busy, but I kind of expected she would e-mail me back since she knew I was having a really hard time. I checked the status of the e-mail. She'd read my message at nine forty-three the night before. Well, she'd probably just read it and gone to bed. Maybe I would hear from her after school, I reasoned.

Just thinking about school and how much I didn't want to go made my stomach really hurt. I could hear my mother in the kitchen, and I could smell cinnamon rolls. My stomach started churning at the scent. I returned to my room and brushed my hair and teeth. I flipped through my closet and decided on a skirt and blouse. The skirt was black and came to the top of my knee. The top was gray, and it crisscrossed in the back. I thought it looked cute, although on someone else's body it would have looked better. Not wanting to dwell on my appearance, I put on a pair of black Birkenstocks that matched perfectly then ran downstairs. As I entered the kitchen, I found my mother standing at the coffeemaker and my dad reading the paper.

"Kathryn, are you going to wear black again today?" my mother asked in that voice of hers I'd grown to hate. "Don't you even *want* to try to fit in a little better?" She took a sip of coffee and waited for me to answer.

I just ignored her and got a glass of water. As I drank some, my dad said, "Katybug, do you want a ride to school?"

I shook my head. "No thanks, I'll just walk." I had decided that walking to school every day would be an even better way to exercise and shed some excess pounds.

"I really wish you would ride with Mrs. Morgan," my mother said. "You and Tiffany could get to be such good friends." Dad gave her a look of warning and for the moment she stopped.

What planet did my mother think we were on? Didn't she see that Tiffany and I were completely different?

"I'm going to school now, mother," I stated, putting an end to the charade.

"Please eat something before you go," she intoned.

I completely ignored her and walked out the door. The air felt good across my skin and I wished that I wasn't going to school. That's one thing I had to say about Sarasota. The weather was wonderful. I only wished that I could go to the beach and just hang, even if it was all by myself. I knew it was impossible, though and I went to school with a heavy heart.

&#10078;   &#10079;

The next couple of weeks proved just as harsh as the first day had. Every day I hated school more and more. While I had first stuck out like a sore thumb, I now felt completely invisible. Everyone was already divided up into groups and no one was willing to get to know me. The only thing that kept me sane was my running. I walked to school every day and after school I ran to the beach and back two times.

Things were bad, but it was about the third week in September when they started spiraling downhill.

On Tuesday, during English, I couldn't find my pencil. I'd had it with me when I came to class, because every day we had to write a short composition to get us ready for the big one at the end of the semester. Mrs. Jamison wanted us to write in pencil so we could erase any mistakes. But when it came time to compose my composition that day, I couldn't find anything to write with. So I had to ask Mrs. Jamison for a writing utensil. It was an agonizing proposition for me because as much as Mrs.

Jamison hated tardiness, she hated not being prepared even more. Every day before she began class, for the first five minutes she lectured on how we need to always have our things ready. She particularly liked to stress how we need to always have our pens, pencils, papers, notebooks, and textbooks with us. She said that we couldn't make it in college if we weren't prepared and I guess she took it upon herself to instill us with that preparation. So, on the day I couldn't find my pencil, I completely panicked. Unfortunately, I didn't have anyone else to ask, so I was forced to approach Mrs. Jamison.

She looked down at me again through her glasses. "Miss Bailey, when we don't come to school prepared, we are showing lack of respect for everyone." I hated how she called everyone by their last names. And I hated how every situation became the focus point of a lack of respect. "Now, does anyone have a pencil for Miss Bailey to write with?" I was so embarrassed.

Tiffany raised her hand. "Oh, I have an extra one, Mrs. Jamison." She reached over and handed me a pencil, smiling so sweetly I wanted to throw up.

As I grasped it in my palm, I realized that it was same pencil I'd lost! I knew it was the same one because it had a bright yellow eraser on the end and bite marks in the middle of the wood. I have always chewed my pencil, but not like everyone else. I just munch in the center.

"Well, thank you, Miss Morgan," Mrs. Jamison said. "It's wonderful that you're so prepared." Then she looked back at me. "You should thank Miss Morgan and don't forget to return her pencil at the end of the day." Enjoying watching me squirm, Tiffany looked over at the girls she was sitting beside and they all started giggling.

Thank her? What I really wanted to do was push her down a flight of stairs.

ᛞ   ᚷ

Every day I spent my lunch period in the bathroom. I started bringing a book with me so I wouldn't get so bored, but it was also very lonely. No one really noticed anything I was doing anyway. I felt completely invisible except when I was the object of ridicule. On Wednesday after lunch, I was about to walk out of the stall when I heard Tiffany and her friends walk in. Taking a deep breath, I just stood very still so they wouldn't know I was there.

"So, how did you do on your English test, Tiff?" one of the girls asked. I think her name was Allison.

"Not too well, actually. I've got to bring my grade up or my parental units are going to be a major downer for the rest of the semester."

The third girl, the one whose name I didn't know, piped in, "You know, that new girl is really good at English. I saw her last composition, and she got a ninety-eight."

"Yeah, what's with that freak girl anyway, Tiffany?" I heard Allison ask.

"How should I know?" I could see through the cracks that she was brushing her hair while the other girls touched up their makeup. "Well, your parents are friends with her parents. I just thought you two were *friends*." She had a mocking tone to her voice, and Tiffany just let out a hoot. "Yeah, right. Do you *know* what it's like living across from Wednesday Addams?" They all laughed. "And the weird part is that the parents are really nice, very normal. It's just too bad they had such a freak for a daughter." By that point, they were laughing so hard that when they finally left the bathroom, I could still hear their echoes.

By Friday, I realized that Tiffany and Max were dating. I think it was something that had just happened between them because it was buzzing all around school. Max's locker was next to mine (how perfect was that?), so he and Tiffany always blocked the door so I couldn't get to it. I tried politely asking them to move, but they ignored me. As a result, I was late to class so many times that I got a note to take home to my parents about my excessive tardiness.

I gave the note to my dad because he was usually more understanding about things than my mother is. I also knew he wouldn't lecture me like my mother would have.

"I didn't realize the school was so big that you couldn't make it to class, Katybug." His humor was very dry sometimes, but he signed my note nonetheless and didn't say anything else about it. I would have tried to explain, but I didn't feel like even going into it. And besides, he wouldn't have believed me anyway. How could anyone believe that someone would just not let you get to your locker? Even I wouldn't have believed it, except for the fact that it was happening to me.

ဆ   ෆ

Finally, I got sick of it. The next week, on Monday, I decided I wasn't going to be late again. I had grown tired of being nice and asking them to move. The last straw was when I went to my locker and Tiffany was leaning against it. "Move," I hissed at her.

She looked at me hard and said, "Make me move, Freak Girl."

By that time, I had so much anger built up that I was actually boiling over with rage. "Move or I *will* make you move," I threatened.

She just looked at Max and they laughed. I was sick of being laughed at and I guess I just kind of lost it because I shoved her as hard as I could. It was as if I were no longer myself. Every twinge of anger I'd had in me since I moved to Vanguard bubbled to the surface and I completely lost control.

Reeling from the impact, Tiffany fell to the floor. As Max was about to help her up, I kicked him hard in the privates. I guess I kicked him too hard because he too fell to the floor, doubled over in pain. He was groaning so loudly that people noticed the commotion and soon everyone in the hallway was surrounding us.

I wasn't through with Tiffany though. I knelt down on the ground and pulled that precious hair of hers. I then slapped her so many times that she started screaming and crying and flailing, but she didn't fight back. It was like I had her exactly where I wanted and I couldn't stop. It felt so good hitting her that I even made a fist and hit her right in the eye. I'd never even slapped another person and here I was completely brutalizing someone. The best part was, it felt freeing.

My soaring euphoria was interrupted. A strong hand lifted me way off the ground. It was Mr. Griffin, the principal. Tiffany was lying on the ground rolled up in a ball, crying her eyes out. Meanwhile, I was still trying to get to her. Max was finally able to get up, but he was still kind of bent over in obvious pain.

Before letting me go Mr. Griffin informed me that he wanted to see me in his office. I was gasping for air because of all the energy it had taken for me to tackle Tiffany like that, but I stalked off toward his office as if I did things like this every day. On the way, kids were giving me questioning looks. Some of them glared at me in a hateful way. But of course they did—they all loved Tiffany. I was the new girl, the freak ... the one who didn't belong. But for the first time, they also had a different look about them. They kind of looked scared—as if they did something wrong I might hit them too. And the best part about that was that I probably would have.

# ❧ Chapter Ten ❧

When I arrived home that day, I walked through the front door exhausted and full of anxiety. Mr. Griffin had tried to call my mother, but she wasn't home. He had tried to call Dad too, but he wasn't in the office. Unable to reach either parent, Mr. Griffin just sent me home with seven days' suspension. I now had seven complete days away from that prison. As if that were punishment! It wasn't all fun and games though. I also had to give my parents a note explaining to them what had happened. That was the part I dreaded. Normally, I loved giving my mother trouble, but this was going to affect Dad too. He had told me he didn't want any more trouble and here it was – the worst kind. I'd never gotten in trouble at school in my entire life. I just hoped that my parents would realize that this wasn't entirely my fault.

Then an idea came to me! Maybe they would finally understand now. I mean, I'd never ever gotten in trouble before, so maybe they would know that this had to do with the other kids and not just me.

I went upstairs to put all my things away and I checked the clock. It was only one. Since the "incident," as the principal had called it, had happened in the middle of the day, he wanted me to go home and start my suspension early. I didn't know where my mother could be in the middle of the day, but I figured that it had something to do with the country club. With the house all to myself, I decided to check e-mail. I'd gotten only one message from Jane in the entire month we'd been here. It wasn't very long either. She didn't say much about school or the other girls or anything. I guess she was having fun and didn't want to rub it in, but I really wanted to hear from her. I went to the den and logged on. I didn't have any messages, but I decided to write one.

Jane,

What's going on with you? I've only heard from you once and I miss you. I know that things are probably great there, but don't feel bad about telling me how much fun you're having. At least one of us can enjoy the entire high school experience. I'd like to know everything, so e-mail me soon! I have had a few really bad weeks. Mom told me I couldn't change the paint in my room. I don't like the yellow color, but she said it was sunny and it was staying. Sometimes I think she's becoming such a control freak that I don't see how Dad can stand her. I know I can't. But that's not even the worst news.

I just got suspended from school for an entire week. Well, 7 days actually, but whatever. It's a long story, but it ends with me beating up Tiffany and kicking her new boyfriend—who ironically is Max—in a very sensitive spot. I hope he's still hurting over that one. HA! But he deserves it, so I don't feel bad about it. Only my parents don't know yet. If I'm ever allowed out of my room again, I'll let you know what happens when they find out. Maybe it'll make my mother so crazy that her head will spin around like Linda Blair's did in that old horror movie we watched once. Maybe she'll go insane and my dad will forget everything I've done and he'll have to send her away. Keep your fingers crossed! And please write me back. I want to know how you are and how school is going on! ~Kathryn~

P.S. Do you ever see Jeremy? Has he asked about me?

I didn't have to confront my parents until dinner. Mother didn't get home until after three o'clock and she just assumed that I'd beaten her home. Putting off the news for as long as I could, I stayed in my room until I was called down to eat. In the meantime, I had rearranged things in my room just to keep busy. I cleaned out my closet and took out everything I didn't like. Everything that I'd brought from Georgia went into a big

box that I labeled "Katy's Junk," and then I surveyed what was
left. Everything remaining in my closet was the stuff I'd gotten
from Hot Topic. I'd gone back a few more times since the
weekend before school and gotten several more outfits, despite
my mother's pleas for me to shop elsewhere. I liked them
because they expressed my mood, which was dark and angry,
and because the clothes drove my mother insane. I cleaned out
my desk drawer and wished for the millionth time that I had a
computer in my room. My parents wouldn't let me have one.
They said there was too much I shouldn't see on the Internet. I
tried to tell them that all I wanted to do with it was homework
research and e-mail, but they said I could do that in the den.
They always seem to have the last word.

I was just in the middle of throwing away some old papers
when I heard my dad coming up the stairs.  He knocked lightly
on my door and told me that it was time for dinner. His voice
sounded strained but he'd been like that for a while now. His
easygoing manner wasn't so easygoing anymore.

"I'll be right down," I told him, like it was just any other day,
but I knew that it wasn't.

I put everything back into the closet in an organized way
then ran downstairs to confront my parents. I took my note
because I figured that would be the best way to tell them.
Besides, they had to be at the school the next morning to meet
with the principal.

"Well, Kathryn." Dad looked at me, as I walked into the
dinning room. I could tell right away that he already knew. I
walked over to my chair and sat down. "I got a very interesting
call from David Morgan today. Do you want to tell me what's
going on?"

My mother walked in from the kitchen, holding a casserole
dish of lasagna. The rolls were already on the table. The smell
kept wafting up to my nose and I felt really sick.

"What's going on, William? What call did you get?" The
lines on her forehead were visible and she looked worried. She
set the lasagna down and stood over him, waiting for an answer.

Obviously, he hadn't shared the news with her yet. I didn't say anything; I just handed him the note. After he read it, he handed it to my mother. "You need to read this, Abby."

She took the note from him and looked at me skeptically. Then the look went from being skeptical to horrified. She went crazy all at once. "Fighting?" she yelled. Though Dad rarely yells, my mother makes up for it. "You were FIGHTING? With Tiffany? Our neighbor? My friend's CHILD?" She sat down then, looking as though she didn't even know me.

She went on ranting and raving until finally Dad said, "Abby, that's enough! We haven't heard the entire story. Every situation has two sides. We need to hear Kathryn's side now."

My mother had become so irate that her face was actually red. She wasn't finished yelling though. "What do you mean, William? Is it okay to fight with someone under certain circumstances? Is that what you're saying to me? Is that how we have raised our daughter?"

Dad was very calm. "I'm just saying that we need to know what happened before we get so angry that all the neighbors hear us."

"Okay, I'm listening, Kathryn Ann." Mother turned to me, heeding Dad's advice. "What was so bad that you had to beat her up?"

They were both looking at me, waiting for my response. My mother was also nervously tapping her foot on the floor so that you could hear it echoing. Caught in their web, all of a sudden I didn't know what to say. I just stared at them, thinking about everything but realizing I could say nothing.

Could I really say, "Well, she laughs at me, makes fun of me with her friends, stole my pencil, won't let me in my locker and she and her boyfriend mock me daily"? They would think I was insane and then I would have even more problems. They would also think that it wasn't a good enough reason to hit someone. "I don't know," I just said.

"You don't know?" My mother was turning red again. "You are sitting there telling me that you simply don't know why you beat up another child."

I started feeling sick and I needed air. I ran out of the room and dashed outside. I was gasping for air because I couldn't breathe. Why did I think they would understand? Why did I think they would know that this wasn't really my fault?

Then I felt sick, really sick. I started throwing up, right there on the front porch because I couldn't make it to the bathroom. I realized that I hadn't had anything to eat or drink all day and I didn't have anything to throw up. I was dry heaving and it hurt, then everything started going black. I felt like I was falling, but I didn't care. The pain stopped, but I was scared that I was going to hit my head. I don't remember anything after that.

# ❧ Chapter Eleven ❦

When I woke up, I didn't know where I was. I just knew that I was very thirsty. I looked around and saw that I was in the hospital. I had an IV tube sticking out of my arm. It didn't hurt, but I felt that if I moved it would come out.

My dad was the first to come to me. "Katybug! You're awake." He was smiling down at me.

My mother ran over to the other side of the bed. "Oh, baby, are you okay?"

I nodded and started to sit up, slowly so my IV wouldn't move, but Dad told me to just lie back and rest.

"How long have I been here?"

"About eight hours," Dad told me.

"What time is it now?" I asked.

"About two-thirty in the morning."

"What's wrong with me?" I asked. I felt so confused. I was trying to think back to what had happened, but everything was a blur. The last thing I remember was throwing up on the front porch.

"You're going to be fine, sweetie," my mother told me.

Dad left the room for a minute and came back with a nurse. "Well, well, you're awake!" She was smiling and it wasn't the fake kind of smile my mother used most of the time. The nurse was a large woman with brown hair that she had pinned up. When she smiled, she had dimples in her checks. She came over and took my blood pressure and my temperature then checked my pulse. "The doctor wants to see you out in the hall," she told my parents.

While they were gone, I asked the nurse what was wrong with me. "The doctor will talk to you in a few minutes, Kathryn, but you gave your parents quite a scare."

I tried to remember, but I couldn't imagine what was wrong. All I had done was thrown up. That wasn't a reason to be in the hospital. Then I remembered thinking I was going to hit my head. Maybe I had and the bump was turning into a tumor.

I asked the nurse that and she just laughed. "No, you don't have a tumor, and you didn't hit your head that hard."

She was laughing all the way out of the room, but she wasn't laughing at me; she was laughing in a good way. Her laugh was contagious and she almost made me chuckle. Right after she left, however, a doctor came in the room and things turned serious once again. "Where are my parents?" I asked him.

"They'll be back in a few minutes. They went to get some coffee so we could chat."

I realized I didn't know this man. All my life I'd had the same doctor and now this man was standing in front of me and I wasn't sure I liked him. He was a young for a doctor, and he introduced himself as Dr. Brandt.

"How do you feel, Kathryn?"

"I feel fine, just thirsty," I told him. He nodded and said he would make sure I got plenty of fluids.

"So am I going to be okay?" I asked him. "What's wrong with me?"

"Well, you were severely dehydrated, young lady, and your electrolytes are low."

I didn't know what that meant and he didn't tell me. He just started asking me questions.

"When was the last time you had your menstrual cycle?"

My mind was spinning. I couldn't think. I had no idea. It had been a while and I hadn't even noticed it. "I guess I've missed a couple of months," I told him. He started jotting things down on his chart and I asked him if I moved whether the IV would come out.

"No, it's in there until we take it out." Then he continued his line of questioning. "Is that usual for you to skip like that?"

I shook my head no.

"Is there any reason to believe you might be pregnant?"

I couldn't believe he'd asked me that. "No, of course not," I told him firmly.

"What have you had to eat in the last twenty-four hours?"

I hesitated. I didn't really know how to answer. When my parents ask that same question, I always tell them I ate at school. But I figured a doctor would know better. "I wasn't hungry today. I don't feel well, which is why I'm in this place, don't you think?"

He ignored that and went on. "On a typical day, what do you eat, Kathryn?"

I shrugged. "The usual things."

"Your parents say that you haven't been eating breakfast in the mornings and at night you barely touch your dinner. They mentioned that you were on some fruit and vegetable diet."

I was scared to answer because I didn't know where these questions were going. I tried to explain how I alternated days on my diet—fruits on some days and vegetables on the others. He didn't seem to hear me.

"Do you eat lunch at school?"

I pictured myself in the bathroom during lunch class. I didn't want to tell him that though, so I didn't say anything. I started playing with my fingernails instead, peeling off the old nail polish. I guess my silence was all he needed to know.

"Do you know what an eating disorder is, Kathryn?"

"Yes, it's when people have problems with food."

"Yes, it's kind of like that. Do you have a problem with food?"

I shook my head.

"By the looks of things, Kathryn, I think you do have a problem with food and I want to understand the reasons why." He looked at his chart.

"You've been through a great deal of changes, haven't you?"

"Yes," I told him quietly.

"Why don't you step out into the hall and get on the scale. I want to chart your weight."

I didn't want to. When I didn't move, he informed me that it was something I had to do. He helped me get out of bed and roll the IV contraption out into the hall. A scale stood close to the nurse's station and when I stepped on it, I was surprised. It showed one hundred five. That wasn't bad for my height and I was pleased that I'd lost so much weight. The funny part was that I didn't feel that small.

"I had your chart faxed over from your last doctor's visit, Kathryn. In the past two and a half months, you've lost thirty-five pounds. Did you realize that?" I shook my head. "Your last recorded weight was the beginning of July and you were at one hundred forty pounds."

"I'm still very big in my thighs," I told him.

He shook his head. "You can't even see yourself as you really are because you have a distorted image of yourself. That's what I mean about an eating disorder."

He continued talking, but my mind started wandering. I didn't really understand anything he was saying anyway. I'd never weighed so little, but I still didn't understand how it had happened. I still felt bigger than Tiffany, bigger than the other kids in my class. Then I thought about the kids back home and I realized that I was smaller than all of them, including Ashley, who was always the petite one. Funny thing was, I didn't feel thin. Suddenly I wondered if Dr. Brandt was lying. I didn't feel like I weighed one hundred five pounds.

Then Dr. Brandt said, "Your ideal weight is between ninety-eight and one hundred thirty-five pounds, so right now you're about ten pounds away from being in danger of being underweight. What I'm worried about, however, is how much weight you've lost in such a short period of time. If you keep losing weight, you're going to have to come back to the hospital and then you might have a much longer stay ahead of you."

The nurse came back in then and helped me get back into bed just as my parents walked into the room.

"We're so sorry, Kathryn," my mother said. She sounded as though she'd been crying. "I don't see how we missed this right under our noses."

I was too tired to ask what they'd missed because before I knew it, I'd fallen asleep and when I opened my eyes, it was morning.

# ❧ Chapter Twelve ☙

I had to stay in the hospital for two days so they could monitor me. During that stretch of time, my parents were so nice that I almost forgot everything that had happened before I got sick. But then Mother had to go and ruin things by calling Mrs. Morgan. She explained to her that I was in the hospital and apologized for the fight. I wouldn't have known at all that she'd done this except that Mrs. Morgan came to see me that same morning. She brought a huge bouquet of flowers, daisies actually, which I thought was very generous, considering I'd taken down her daughter.

I was alone when she came by and I felt embarrassed. Given the recent circumstances, I didn't know what to say.

"How are you feeling, Kathryn?" She breezed into the room and put the flowers on the table, squeezing them in amongst the others I'd gotten since I had arrived. My Nana had also sent me flowers with a cute teddy bear perched in the middle. I don't think Mother had told her the real reason I was in the hospital. I just heard her use the words "intense malaise." Although I didn't know what that meant, I'm sure it had nothing to do with food.

"I'm better, thank you, Mrs. Morgan." Then I paused struggling for more words. "The flowers are beautiful, thank you."

She smiled. "You're welcome. They're from all of us. Tiffany said she was sorry you were sick and she felt bad about the fight you had. She told me to tell you hello."

I sat up, but not fast because the IV was still in my arm and I wasn't sure I believed anything Dr. Brandt had said, including his reassurance that the IV would not fall out on its own.

I looked at Mrs. Morgan in a funny way because I couldn't imagine Tiffany telling me hello let alone saying she felt bad about our fight.

She continued. "Tiffany is a very forgiving girl, although I have to say, she looks really beaten up. She has scratches on her face and her eye is swollen shut. She's even having to use a wrist brace for a couple of weeks from where she fell on the floor."

Mrs. Morgan paused for a moment. I guess she was waiting for me to apologize but I couldn't. I knew I should have, but I just couldn't. Picking up on my discomfort, she then said, "Kathryn, I know it's hard when you're in a new school. I know it's hard to fit in, but Tiffany really tried to make you feel welcome. She told me how you rejected her time after time."

Rejected her? What was she talking about? I must have looked confused because Mrs. Morgan just patted my arm and said, "But we completely understand now, Kathryn. We know now what was going on, so there aren't any grudges to be held."

"What do you mean you know what was going on?" I asked her.

"Oh, well, we just that know why you lashed out so. Tiffany told me how at the beginning of the year she begged you to eat lunch with her and her friends but you refused. And now we know that's because you didn't want the other kids to know that you have" —she paused then whispered— "an eating disorder."

I could not believe what I was hearing. That was just such a lie, only I had no way to prove it.

"She also told me about the crush you have on Max, which is ultimately what made the fight break out."

IV or not, I sat straight up and said, "Excuse me? What are you saying, Mrs. Morgan?"

She started busying herself, straightening the covers and fluffing my pillows. Then she sat on the edge of my bed and said, "Nothing, dear, just that Tiffany explained everything. She told me about how your locker is next to Max's and that you became jealous after he and Tiffany started dating because you had to see them together every day at his locker."

"Mrs. Morgan, that's not true. I—"

She interrupted me before I could give a full explanation. "It's okay, really, Kathryn, you don't have to explain. Tiffany forgives you, and so do Mr. Morgan and I. We just want you to get better."

I couldn't believe what was happening. So, this was what Tiffany was telling everyone. I fell into a stunned silence. Mrs. Morgan took my sudden quietness to mean that I was exhausted, so she stood up to leave. "If you need anything, please let us know and have your mother call me when you get home. I've made a casserole."

Then she walked out of my room, and I was left feeling drained again. I couldn't believe how so many things could go wrong at once.

⋙ ⋘

Dad came by to see me after work. He brought me some magazines so I wouldn't get bored. I thanked him, but my mind just wasn't there. It was still with Mrs. Morgan's words and everything she'd told me. Dad hugged me and said that I could get out the next morning if I continued to eat. I told him I was trying, but the food was gross. And I was telling him the truth; I really was trying. The only time I hadn't eaten was lunch after Mrs. Morgan left. I got a visit from Dr. Brandt because of it, but I told him I was nauseous. He instructed the nurses to give me some phenergan in my IV, but all it did was make me sleepy. I'd slept soundly until Dad came by after work. While I slept, apparently my mother had been by, Dad told me.

"Where is she now?" I asked him.

"She ran home to get some clothes. She's staying the night with you in case you wake up and need something."

I didn't want her to stay and I told him that.

"Well, just do this for her, Katybug. You'll be asleep and she really just wants to know that you're okay."

I didn't say anything, which he took to mean I agreed. Then he changed the subject.

"Mr. Morgan called me today. He explained everything to me and even said that Mrs. Morgan brought you flowers."

"What do you mean 'explained everything'?" I asked in a hateful tone.

"Oh, about how you liked Max. Katybug, if the fight was about a boy, you should have talked to us about it. We would have understood."

My hateful tone gave way to sadness. Suddenly, I was about to cry. I could expect this from my mother but not Dad. "You have to believe me, I do not like Max. Honestly."

He nodded. "It's okay, Katybug, really."

About that time, a nurse brought in my dinner tray. My stomach felt like lead. I wasn't hungry, but if I wanted to get out of here, I knew I had to eat something.

I just wish that I could make someone believe me. Tiffany was turning all this around and no one knew the truth. And the sad part was that no one cared. The food tray spread out in front of me, I tried to take a bite of Jell-O but even the smell was making me sick.

Dad changed the subject from Max to Nana. He told me how she wanted me to come see her one weekend soon.

"Oh, can I please go home to see her?" I begged. That would be perfect. I could see Jane and all my other friends. I might even be able to stay the night with Jane. Thinking of Jane made me wonder if I had e-mail from her. I couldn't wait to get home to check it. But I knew that if I wanted to get out of the hospital, I had to gain some weight. So I really tried. I ate half of my Jell-O and two bites of my roll. I was so thirsty though, that I drank all my juice. Then I asked for a Sprite on top of that. I was so full that I seriously couldn't eat any more.

"Are you sure that's all you can eat?" Dad asked.

I nodded but I didn't say anything.

Dad looked so sad for a minute. "When did this happen, Kathryn? You were such a healthy child and you never had trouble like this." Healthy, as in fat, was what he was really saying.

"Dad, I'm fine, really. Even the doctor said that I wasn't underweight."

He just looked at me sadly. "You are not fine. Do you know that you've lost thirty-five pounds in just a very short time?" I didn't answer him. "Kathryn, for God's sakes, what do you see when you look into the mirror?"

I didn't know how to answer him. I avoided mirrors most of the time, but it wasn't so much how I felt on the outside. It was what I felt on the inside but I couldn't make him, or anyone else, understand that. "The same me, I guess. I don't know ... I just don't know." I was getting all confused. When I tried on the clothes I had bought for school, I just thought I looked smaller because they were black and because I'd bought them oversized. I never thought it was because I'd lost that much weight. I started to cry because I didn't know what else to do. Caught in a maze of confusion, I felt helpless. Dad sat on the edge of my bed and told me not to cry. Then my favorite nurse came in and gave him a look.

"Why is Kathryn upset?" She was asking like she was accusing him of doing something to make me cry.

"I'm fine," I told her.

She looked at my food tray. "Well, it seems like you're trying and that's what matters, isn't it?" She told me she would leave the tray a little longer, in case I wanted anything else.

I thanked her. As she was leaving, however, she piped in one more sarcastic comment. She asked my dad to try to lift my spirits instead of bringing me to tears. Poor Dad. This wasn't his fault.

# ❧ Chapter Thirteen ❧

Even though I was trying, I didn't gain any weight while I was in the hospital and I had to stay an extra day. But since I also didn't lose any, they went ahead and discharged me on Friday. I heard Dr. Brandt tell my parents that if I continued to lose weight, they might have to put me in a hospital that specializes in this type of illness. I was determined not to have to go to a hospital for mental patients. I wasn't mental. I just wanted to go back to my old life. None of this would have happened if we'd just stayed in Atlanta. My parents couldn't see that though and now I was considered a poster child for eating disorders. In just a few short months, my life had spiraled completely out of control.

The first thing I did when I got home was to check my e-mail. I was thrilled to see that Jane had written back the same day that I'd written her. It had been only a few days, but it felt like forever!

Kathryn, sorry about the problems you're having at school. I was glad to know that you beat up that girl though. She sounds like she needed it. Things here are about the same — the same kids only in a different, bigger school. I'm working on the school newspaper and I love it. I wish you were here with me though. We could do it together, and it would be even more fun.

Kammy is going out with Brent now and she's always hanging all over him. She's always waiting at his locker and they even got in trouble for walking down the hall holding hands. Haha Other than that, there isn't much news.

WE ALL MISS YOU SO MUCH!!!

Kevin had another party last weekend. Jeremy was there, but I didn't talk to him. I kind of hung out with this new guy, Chris. He just moved here from Indiana. He's so cute, Kathryn! He has wavy blond hair and his eyes are blue, and he's tall but not as tall as Brent, and I think we're going to go to homecoming together. I'll let you know! BFF, Jane

I didn't respond to her e-mail because I didn't know what to say. And even if I had, I was just too exhausted to say it. It sounded like she was having fun and although I didn't begrudge her fun, I envied it. Feeling even more down, I went to bed and stayed there until my mother brought lunch up to me. She gave me a peanut butter and jelly sandwich and a bowl of vegetable soup. I wasn't hungry but I had learned at the hospital that hunger wasn't important. I had to eat whether I wanted it or not.

"Do you want to eat in here, Kathryn, or would you like to come and eat in the kitchen?" my mother asked.

I told her that I'd rather stay in my room.

"Where's Dad?" I asked her while I took a small bite of my sandwich. Food seemed to stick in my throat and it was hard to swallow. The peanut butter was worse but my mother insisted I eat it because of the protein. "If you aren't going to eat meat, you have to eat some other source of protein," she repeated over and over.

Mother looked around my room. "Kathryn, I've never seen your room so neat. Everything is in such perfect order. I'm so very proud of you." I rolled my eyes. She mumbled something that I didn't catch, but then she said, "Your dad went to your school to get your assignments. If you feel like it, you can return to school on Monday. In the meantime, we thought that over the weekend you could start on the work you missed."

She was talking as if the only reason I'd missed school was because I was sick. She refused to verbally acknowledge my suspension. Then it hit me; I had been suspended for seven days. Monday didn't make it seven days.

"I can't go back to school on Monday, Mother," I reminded her.

"Why can't you?" Had she lost her mind? Had she forgotten that I was in trouble? She must have read the confusion in my eyes because she said, "Oh, that." She said as if it were nothing. She then strode over to me and sat on my bed. "It's all been taken care of.  Your dad and Mrs. Morgan went to the school and talked it over with Mr. Griffin. He said that under the circumstances, you could return to classes on Monday."

"What does Mrs. Morgan have to do with it?" My voice was really high pitched.

"Well, it was her daughter ..." She trailed off then she started again. "She just wanted to let Mr. Griffin know that it was fine with her if you returned to class."

By that point, I was almost in tears. It wasn't up to Mrs. Morgan and anyway, I didn't want to go back to that school. So much for my fantasy that I would get to live with Nana. I didn't even have the hope of going to a public school. Everyone thought that it was my fault. What's worse, they all thought that this was all over a boy and no one cared to hear the truth.

Then I had a horrible thought. "Mr. Griffin doesn't know I'm sick, does he?"

"Well, Kathryn, it was just easier that way. Dad thought that it would be better if he knew what was going on. He didn't want the people at school to think you're a troublemaker. And we know now that your illness contributed to what happened." I couldn't believe what I was hearing. I just couldn't believe it! Before long, everyone would think of me as a bigger freak than they already did.  Then again, they had already called me that, so why did it matter anyway? Nothing mattered. I just wished that I didn't have to ever go back to that school!

Mom picked up a picture of Jane and me from my bookshelf and said, "You must really miss her." I nodded and she started out of the room, saying, "When you're finished eating, call me, okay?"

Noticing that she hadn't put it back properly, I walked over and straightened out the picture. Then I looked at my food. I couldn't eat all that, but I didn't want to give my mother a reason to lecture me either. So, I opened my window and fed my sandwich to the birds. Instead of eating, I just sat on the window seat and thought about how everything had changed since last year. Last year, school had been so much fun. I couldn't believe things could go so bad in just one short year.

The sandwich taken care of, I then went into my bathroom and threw away my soup. "There," I whispered, "that should make her stop worrying." I didn't know how long it should have taken me to eat all that, so I didn't call my mother right away. I just turned on my TV and started watching talk shows. Before I knew it, I was asleep.

&#x80; &#x3; &#x3;

The weekend went by slowly. I mostly slept and channel surfed. I did some homework, but it was hard to concentrate. Since my parents were watching me so closely, I couldn't run as I had before. So, I started exercising in my room. I did crunches and I jogged in place until I was so tired that I couldn't breathe any longer.

Occasionally, I would hear my parents talking in low voices, thinking I couldn't hear them.

"She seems to be eating, William, but she doesn't look like she's gaining weight. I don't want to ask her to weigh herself, but honestly, she doesn't look like she's getting any better."

"Abby, it's only been a couple of days since she got out of the hospital. Give her time." My dad was silent for a while and then I heard him say, "At least she's eating. And remember, the doctor said she was within her ideal weight range. As long as she's eating, she's going to be fine."

I felt bad about that comment because I wasn't really eating. I didn't like to deceive my dad like that, but I couldn't seem to help myself. Some of the time I threw the food away. Other times, I just took a few bites and sometimes I just fed it to the birds.

# ☙ Chapter Fourteen ❧

Monday morning came too soon. Dreading the thought of returning to those hallowed, horror halls, I asked if I could stay home from school another day. The thought of going back filled me with so much trepidation that it was making me feel bad all over.

"Katybug, you need to get back into the swing of things. Don't you agree?" Dad put his newspaper down and my mother set a plate of eggs and toast in front of me.

I cringed. "But I don't think I'm ready," I pleaded.

"You slept all weekend, Kathryn. I think that you need to get out. A change of scenery would do you a world of good," my mother piped in.

What did she know about it? I didn't say anything else because I knew it wouldn't help. I took a bite of my of toast and it stuck in my throat. In an attempt to dislodge it, I drank some juice and started upstairs. I put on my gray sweater and black jeans. Even though it was almost October, it still wasn't very cool. Despite the warm temperature, however, I stayed cold all the time. The doctor had said that that was because my blood pressure was low as a result of not eating. He had also said that I was anemic and he gave an iron pill to take. But the pills were so big that they were hard to swallow. Most of the time, I just threw them away.

When I walked into school that morning, I felt a familiar tightening in my stomach. As I walked down the halls I tried to make myself invisible, but it was obvious I was being talked about. At first, I didn't know why. I thought it was about the fight, but I was wrong. Apparently, Tiffany had told everyone why I'd been in the hospital and they all stared at me all day as if I was a circus center ring attraction. I couldn't get away from it.

Even the teachers looked at me sympathetically, although they didn't say anything to me. I went through my classes in a daze. My grades were slipping, but I couldn't do anything about it. Even English, usually my best subject, was suffering. I was completely lost in algebra and in history I felt like I was sitting through one long movie that I couldn't follow.

Then right before lunch, I got a note saying I had to see the school counselor. My heart was racing as I walked to her office. I hadn't ever seen a school counselor before, so I didn't know what to expect.

When I arrived, the door was open so I just walked in. She was busy writing something down, so she didn't see me at first. I knocked on the door anyway and she looked up at me and smiled. "Hello! Please come in," she enthusiastically greeted me. She was smiling so big that her eyes seemed to disappear. "I'm Mrs. Porter. I'm assuming you're Kathryn?"

I nodded and started looking around her office. She had a really big picture window that overlooked the back of the school. It had a really nice view and the room was really bright. She had a few potted plants and a bookshelf full of books that were probably all about teenagers and their problems. A poster was taped on the wall that read, "Being a teenage mom is like being grounded for life." That was a depressing thought, although it wasn't really a depressing room.

"How are you today, Kathryn?"

"I'm fine." My voice didn't sound like my own. Then I got right to the point. "Why am I here?"

Mrs. Porter folded her hands and put them on her desk. She smiled at me again. "Please, sit down."

She had two nice oversized chairs in her office and I sat down on the orange one.

"I spoke with your father and he explained to me the problems you're having." I didn't say anything so she went on. "I also asked your teachers about your lunchroom habits and no one has seen you in the lunchroom since school started." She paused again allowing her words time to sink in.

I didn't know if she wanted me to tell her what I'd been doing instead of eating, but I felt embarrassed to explain. So, I just said nothing.

"I'm not going to ask you where you've been, but I am going to have to start making sure that you are in the lunchroom every day. Your teachers will make sure you're in there each day. I know this isn't fun, but we promised your parents we'd keep an eye on what's going on with you."

My first thought was that I didn't know where I would even sit. I didn't know who to sit with because now no one would even want to be near me. My second thought was that my teachers would be watching me eat. It was so humiliating that I didn't think I could stand it.

"Also, I'd like to see you in here once a week."

I hadn't been listening since my mind was running in all directions, so I had to ask her to repeat what she'd said.

"I said that I want you in my office once a week during your study period. We can just talk about things that are bothering you. As I'm sure you know, your grades are something to be concerned about as well. You are really going to have to work hard if you want to pass this semester."

"Nothing is bothering me, Mrs. Porter, and I need my study period so that I *can* bring my grades up." I wasn't about to spend time in this office every week.

She sighed and said, "I can't make you come in, but I am encouraging it."

I didn't say anything else. I just got up and walked out, knowing that I had to go from a bad situation to a worse one— into the lunchroom. The mere thought was more than I could take.

&#8288;&#8288;&#8288; &#8288;

Finally, the dreaded bell rang and I stood in the lunchroom line to get a tray like everyone else. Once again the center of attraction, I saw the stares people were giving me. I knew that if I told Dad about it he would say, "Katybug, no one is looking at you; it's all in your imagination." But he would have been wrong because everyone *was* looking. They hadn't ever seen me in the lunchroom and yet, here I was on the very same day I had gotten back from having been in the hospital for an eating problem.

I picked up my now filled tray, feeling like a large animal begging for food at the zoo and started looking around for a place to sit. While I was searching for a table, Mr. Holden came over to me. I'll forever be grateful to Mr. Holden for what he did next. He asked me to follow him and we walked over to a group of girls I didn't know. They were sitting at one of the round tables on the other side of the room from Tiffany and her clique. "Girls, this is Kathryn Bailey and this is going to be her assigned table for the rest of the year."

They looked at one another, confused, because no one else had assigned seats.

"It seems that Kathryn has been going home for lunch every day because she didn't know our rules for having to eat in the lunchroom." He paused before continuing his explanation. "At her other school, they had permission to eat at home and so she just assumed that she could do it here too." The girls gave each other knowing glances. They knew; everyone knew! Vanguard Academy is small. Everyone knew what was going on with me, but I was so thankful that they were going along with Mr. Holden's story.

One of the girls even said, "Hey! That's a good idea. We *should* be able to go home for lunch."

Mr. Holden just smiled and said, "Since Kathryn hasn't been here for lunch, I thought it would be nice for her to sit here so she could get to know all of you."

Following his lead, the girls started introducing themselves. There were five of them and I knew I'd never keep their names straight, but it didn't seem to matter. Before Mr. Holden walked off, he winked at me and I smiled back at him. I was so relieved to have a place to sit that I didn't care that he'd made up the entire story. Actually, I was glad he had. Even though everyone knew the truth, it gave me a place to sit during lunch and that's all I wanted.

The girls were nice but they asked lots of questions. They wanted to know about my other school and about why I had moved here. They wanted to know if I had brothers or sisters and they asked if I liked it in Sarasota. They were trying to be friends, unlike the rest of the people at this school, so I appreciated the gesture even if I didn't appreciate the hot seat grilling. At least they didn't ask me anything about my eating problems. I was so grateful to them for that.

Here I was, with five girls I'd spent several weeks with yet barely knew existed. I wondered why I didn't know them from my classes. I soon found out that it was because they were in the tenth grade. Despite being a year ahead of me, they accepted me at their table and before long, I no longer dreaded being in the lunchroom.

# ల Chapter Fifteen ౬

Having made some acquaintances, if not friends, for a while, I started feeling better. I didn't dread going to school quite as much. For the most part, Tiffany stayed out of my way and she and Max stopped blocking my locker. Even the other kids stopped staring at me so much. I wouldn't say things were perfect, but they were definitely better.

Then, about three weeks after I had gotten out of the hospital, my dad came home with news about a new ad campaign that his agency was going to launch. We were sitting at the dinner table while he was telling Mom about it. Most of the time, I just didn't listen when he talked about work, but this particular topic of conversation sparked my interest. We were eating Chinese take-out because my mother, who had started volunteering a couple of days a week at the hospital, didn't feel she could work *and* cook. She had gotten the idea about volunteering while I was in the hospital. So now, two days a week, we had either Chinese food or takeout pizza. Mother didn't care when we had Chinese, but with the pizza, she always managed to throw together a salad. That's because she believed no one should live on just pizza. And she always ordered it with everything except anchovies, so there were like a million things on top that I had to pick off. My dad didn't care either way. He just wanted me to eat.

"We're trying to find regular teenagers to model a line of beachwear," I heard him say. "The guy who designed this line of clothing, Stefan Johansson, is new to the industry, but he has very specific ideas. He is really very focused, Abby, and I like working with him." He paused long enough to take a drink of his wine and then added, "The only thing is, he wants the teenagers to be local, and he wants to do the shoot in Miami."

"Well, how are you expected to find the right models?"

"That's the thing—he doesn't really want models. He wants real kids, so they're going to be even harder to find."

I was listening intently but they didn't notice. I started thinking how cool it would be if I could go to Miami to model swimwear. I realized I was too short to be an actual model, but Dad had said they wanted real teenagers. I got excited just thinking about it. I had to admit, even to myself, that I was thinner. I could probably get by with wearing one pieces, maybe not bikinis, but definitely one-piece bathing suits!

Then my mother said, "Oh, William! I just got the best idea. Why don't you ask Tiffany? She's very pretty and she would look great in beachwear!"

Sensing my displeasure at the mention of her name, Dad glanced over my way. He knew that I had issues with Tiffany, even if he didn't know everything. I acted like I wasn't paying attention. "I'll have to have everything approved by Mr. Johansson," he said, not wanting to push the blade of betrayal in any farther. Uncomfortably, I started moving the chicken around on my plate. "He actually wants two girls and two boys."

"Well, I'm sure that Tiffany knows lots of kids who would be perfect for it. And you know, Janet's son"—she rolled her eyes upward as if she was thinking so hard—"I think his name is Max. He's very attractive."

She just went on and on and I felt so hurt. Didn't it occur to either of them that I might want to go to Miami? It would be so much fun, but my mother thought only about the two people I hated most. I knew Dad wouldn't tolerate any more outbursts at the dinner table, so I just told my parents I was going outside for a while. I used the excuse that I needed the air. They didn't seem to even hear me though. They were too busy making plans.

Once I got outside, I started running. I ran until my side started hurting. It felt so good to feel my feet pound the pavement. I blocked everything bad out of my mind and I ran to the beach. Once I arrived, I just sat down on the sand and stayed there until it got so dark that I was afraid I wouldn't be able to find my way home.

# ❧ Chapter Sixteen ☙

By the end of the week, the school was buzzing about the new ad campaign. Anyone who was interested had to schedule an audition at my dad's downtown office. They were required to bring pictures of themselves. They first had to have a short interview with Mr. Johansson and then the final decision would be made during the last week of October. The kids who made it would be in Miami during the first week of November. They were going to spend an entire week there and no one seemed to care that they would miss a full week of school. A learning experience, Mr. Griffin told their teachers and everyone that made it got excused.

And they weren't just modeling beachwear. They were going to do an entire spring layout. They were also going to get to wear casual shorts and T-shirts, Capri pants and even sandals. Everyone was so excited over the prospect. I felt embarrassed because everyone knew my dad was the one heading up the campaign and yet I wasn't a part of the excitement.

I was at my locker one day when I heard two girls talking about it. They were around the corner, so they didn't know I was there. "It's sad Mr. Bailey can't use his own daughter for the swimsuit ad."

"Are you serious, Amber?" The girl laughed. "The girl's a freak? She wouldn't fit in anyway."

They kept talking, but they were walking away so I could no longer hear them. Why wouldn't I fit in? Was it because of my clothes or was it because I wasn't pretty enough? I wish I'd heard the rest of what they'd said. But it didn't matter anyway. In the end, the people chosen to do the ad were of course

Tiffany and some senior girl I didn't know named Lacey. An eleventh-grader named Nick, and of course Max rounded out the elite foursome. It was like a slap in the face.

My dad was so wrapped up in the campaign that he didn't notice my mood. He had to go to Miami too, although I didn't find that out until later. My mother, as excited as ever, decided we should all go along. "It will be like a vacation," she reasoned. We were discussing it over breakfast one morning after the final decisions had been made about who was going to do the modeling.

"Oh, Abby, that would be great!" Dad sounded excited about the idea. "You and Katybug could shop while I work and at night, we could find out what there is to do in Miami." They had to be joking. Anger welled up inside me like a volcano about to erupt, but I decided to keep it under control. There was no way I was going to go to Miami with them. They hadn't wanted me to be a part of the real thing, so I was not about to vacation with them.

"I'm not going," I stated in a small voice.

"What?" Dad asked me as if he didn't understand what I'd said.

I spoke louder. "I said I am *not* going."

"But, Kathryn," my mother wailed, "it will be so much fun. It would be like a vacation in the middle of the year. You'd have to miss school, but I'm sure it would be all right."

I lost my temper then. Didn't they see anything that went on?

I jumped up so hard that my chair fell backward and bounced off the floor. I started yelling, "Do you really think I want to go where the two people who have tormented me the most are going to be modeling while I'm just there for pity?" They looked at each other, and I continued. "There is *no* way I'm going to go and if you try to make me, I'll do something so drastic you'll regret it for the rest of your lives." I had no idea what I was even saying, but I knew that I could *not* go.

"Okay, calm down, Kathryn," my dad said. He and my mother looked at each other with raised eyebrows, startled by my outburst. I'd erupted in front of them before but nothing like this. I'd never threatened anything before. I think it frightened them a little.

"No one is going to make you go. We didn't know you felt so strongly about this," Dad told me.

Of course they didn't. They didn't know because they didn't care enough to know.

"Well, I do." I folded my arms in front of me and suddenly I felt like I was five years old. All I needed to do was stomp my foot and it would be official.

"I'll stay home with her, William. You can go ahead. We'll be fine."

"No, Mother, if you want to go, you can go. I'm old enough to stay home by myself."

My mother insisted I wasn't staying home alone and so it was settled. Dad was going and my mother felt that I'd ruined her vacation. I felt so bad over destroying their excitement that I left for school with a heavy heart.

&#8478;   &#8479;

My next doctor's appointment was scheduled for the day before my dad left for Miami. Despite my parents' attempt at fattening me up, I'd lost seven pounds and the doctor wanted me to go back into the hospital. My mother started crying. That was just so typical of her. It was only seven pounds—nothing to cry about. At ninety-eight pounds, I was still in my ideal weight range. But when I brought this fact up, the doctor said it wasn't exactly what I weighed, but the fast way I was losing it.

My dad then added to the misery by saying that he felt it was his fault because of the trip. They were going back and forth, right there in the doctor's office, about whose fault it was. They even started arguing in front of Dr. Brandt and my mother started crying even harder. I just wanted to disappear. Dr. Brandt took control of the situation and told everyone to calm down. "She would only have to be in the hospital a few days. She just needs an IV and we really need to talk more about counseling."

He looked at my dad. "Mr. Bailey, she isn't getting better. She has to see someone. She needs to talk to someone about what is going on with her."

"No, please don't make me, Dad, please." I was begging him because I didn't want to be analyzed. I simply didn't want to talk to a stranger about what I ate and didn't eat or why. It was just too horrible to think about.

"Dr. Brandt," Dad said, "we'll talk about this at home and get back to you." Dr. Brandt wasn't satisfied with his answer but he didn't have another choice but to agree.

All the way home, my mother cried and Dad tried to calm her. To make matters worse, traffic was backed up and it was making my dad tense. Mother was crying, traffic was horrid and I was just sitting in the backseat, begging him not to make me go to the hospital.

"Here is the deal, Kathryn," Dad said as he changed lanes. "If you start eating the way you're supposed to and gain some weight by Thanksgiving, you can go visit Nana for the Thanksgiving holiday."

I thought about that for a minute and then what he was saying sank in. It would be so wonderful to go back home for the holiday. I would get to see Nana and Jane and all my other friends. Maybe I would even get to see Jeremy. I got so excited thinking about going home for the holiday that I barely noticed the dirty look my mother threw in my dad's direction. I knew it meant that she wasn't happy that he was trying to bribe me into eating, but I also knew that Dad hadn't even noticed the look. For the first time in a long time, I had something to look forward to.

# ❧ Chapter Seventeen ❧

During the week that my dad was in Miami, I had to go into the hospital for two days. Dr. Brandt had told my parents that it would be better if I went in just for some IV fluids. I didn't want to go, but I thought about how much I wanted to go back home over Thanksgiving. If this would help me get better, I would try to endure it. It wasn't easy though. I hated to see my dad leave and I hated to be in the hospital even more. The first day there, I had to talk to a therapist. I was already in the room, hooked up to the IV when she came in to see me. My mother had already been instructed to leave the room while she was there. I didn't mind that part. The entire time she was there she'd been fussing over me and it was making me quite angry.

"Hi, Kathryn, I'm Dr. Carlton." The therapist smiled and the first thing I noticed was the gap between her front teeth. She had this huge gaping hole between her first two teeth, but the others were so close together that you wondered why she didn't get a retainer to fix the problem. "How are you today?"

"I'm in the hospital. Think about it," I sarcastically responded, vowing not to make her job easy. I pulled the covers over me more tightly and looked out the window.

"You're cold?"

I didn't answer her, but I guess it was apparent to her that I was.

"But it's rather warm in here," she said in one of those condescending tones I hated. For emphasis, she took off her sweater and sat down "You're probably cold because you're not eating enough." I noticed that she didn't have a problem eating. She looked about fifty pounds overweight.

I just glared at her.

"I know you don't want to talk to anyone about your problem, but you're not getting any better. Your chart shows that you are ninety-eight pounds and your BMI—that's your body mass index," she explained, "is borderline to being too low." She waited to see if I was going to say anything. When I didn't, she went on. "To complicate things more, you've grown an inch since your last physical. That means you need to weigh more. You have to gain some weight, Kathryn. Once you get home and get a good therapist, you'll do much better."

"But I don't want a therapist," I told her.

"I know, so let's just talk about that for a minute." She pulled out a chart and a pen and started asking me questions about my life; about my parents; about school, friends, my old school; things that basically weren't her business. I think she was disappointed that I wasn't very chatty with her and finally, after what seemed like forever, she left me alone. It seemed like right after she left that my mother was back, fussing and getting on my nerves. I couldn't wait to get home so I could get a moment's peace.

The second day I was there, the doctor said I needed another day to bring my electrolytes up. I hadn't gained any weight, although they couldn't understand why. I was eating, but it seemed like my stomach didn't agree with anything. They still had me on an IV and instead of the two days they'd said I would be there, I ended up staying for four. I was so irritable by the time they let me go that I'm sure the nurses cheered as they released me. I'm also sure that Dr. Carlton was glad I was gone too. Our sessions had proved so unproductive that she'd referred me to another therapist. I was wondering what she'd written in the chart. I'd be willing to bet that the word *difficult* was in there somewhere. But it really didn't matter because I didn't plan on seeing another shrink anyway.

# ❧ Chapter Eighteen ❧

"Can I take tennis lessons?" I asked my mother the day after I got home from the hospital. All I'd done since I'd gotten home was lie around and I was getting very bored. Mother was in her bedroom, sitting on the edge of her bed, rubbing lotion all over her legs and feet. I sat down in the chair in the corner of the room. Settling in, I put my knees under my chin and waited for her to answer.

"I think that's just too strenuous for you right now, Kathryn. You really don't need any exercise. You need to work on eating more." I was watching as my mother applied lotion all over her legs in circular motions. Then she moved down to her feet. I noticed that she was very thorough. Maybe that was why she looked so young—she moisturized her entire body. She put the top back on the lotion and looked at me. "I just don't think it's a good idea." Of course she didn't.

"Can I play with you at the country club? I know I haven't played in a while, but it might be fun."

"Kathryn, what did I just say?" I shrugged and she sighed. "You can't do anything strenuous. You have to work on getting better."

I was just so disappointed but I figured it best to let the matter drop. Instead, I said, "When is Dad coming home?"

"He'll be home tomorrow, but don't think you'll talk him into it because you won't, young lady."

That wasn't even what I had been thinking. Expressing my displeasure, I just got up and stomped out of the room. Then I went into my own room and slammed the door. I would be so glad when Dad came back. Being home alone with my mother was driving me crazy. All she did was fuss over me while I ate and she only let me go outside to sit. I couldn't even sneak away to the beach or for that matter, even walk down the street. She was smothering me without even realizing it.

        &#8678;   &#8680;

    That night at dinner, since it was just my mother and me, we sat in the kitchen instead of the dining room like we usually did. She had made spaghetti and garlic bread and as we were eating, she talked nonstop. I completely drowned out her voice by thinking about other things. I was trying to finish the meal quickly so I could check my e-mail. I'd sent an e-mail to Jane as soon as I'd got home, telling her that I was going to Nana's over the Thanksgiving holiday. I didn't tell her about my sickness or about me being in the hospital though. Dad had decided not to tell Nana since she would only worry. My mother, on the other hand, didn't think we needed to protect her from it. Mother thought that since I would be staying with her, she needed to know so that she would make sure I ate. Dad said that was ridiculous and that almost started another fight.

    Secretly, I've always thought that my mother didn't like Nana. She had always thought that my grandmother was too lenient around me. Mother particularly hadn't liked it when I'd stayed at Nana's when I was younger. But I love my grandmother. She's the only grandparent I have left. Both my mother's parents died before I was born and my Granddad Bailey had died when I was in the third grade.

    "Have you heard anything I've said, Kathryn?" My mother's voice snapped me back to reality.

    "Oh, I'm sorry. What?"

    She rolled her eyes at me. "I really don't know what to do with you anymore. You don't even listen to me and you've barely touched your food."

    That wasn't true. I'd eaten almost all of my bread and some of my spaghetti. I was having a hard time eating my spaghetti because she'd put hamburger meat in it and it was hard to pick it all out. "I'm almost finished, Mother."

"You're *not* almost finished," she said in that tone that I knew so well. "You're going to eat more of your food before you leave this table."

I was so angry with her I wanted to throw the plate right at her. Instead, I just cut my noodles into the tiniest pieces and ate as much as I could. The rest of the meal passed in silence. Finally, after what seemed like forever, I had eaten enough to satisfy her and I practically ran into Dad's den. As soon as I went in, I realized how much I missed my dad. He'd never been gone this long before.

Brushing aside the wave of sadness, I walked over to his desk, sat down and turned on the computer. I had two messages. One was from Jane and the other was from a screen name I didn't recognize. I opened Jane's first.

Kathryn! I'm just too excited about your visit. I can't wait to see you!! I know you'll have to spend Thanksgiving with your grandmother, but please promise to spend the night with me on Friday! I've already asked my mother, and everything is set if you want to come. I can't wait to hear what's been going on in Sarasota. I know that you weren't happy about going but really … the beach being that close has to be kind of exciting!

Chris and I are going out now. I like him so much, Katy! Sometimes we go out with Kammy and Brent but it's when we're alone that is the best. Oh, I can't wait to tell you all about it. And I hope you don't mind but I talked to Jeremy the same day you e-mailed me and told him you were coming to visit. He asked for your e-mail address so he could e-mail you. If you see e-mail from bravesfan2004, don't delete it!!!

BFF, Jane

I looked at the other e-mail. Jeremy must have changed his address since Jane had given me the address book back when we had first moved. I remember his being something about wrestling. I had never e-mailed him though, because I'd wanted him to e-mail me first. But he never had. Until now! I was just so excited; I opened it and read,

Kathryn, jane told me you were coming to visit your grandmother over thanksgiving. I thought it would be kool if we could go out saturday nite. We could either double with chris and jane or go alone. It's your call so let me know what you want to do. e-mail me your phone number and i'll call you since i just got a cell phone. Long distance is free.
Later, Jeremy

Well, it wasn't poetic but I was just so thrilled that he'd asked me out that I didn't even care. I e-mailed Jane back first, telling her what he'd said. I also told her how much I was looking forward to staying with her Friday night. Then I e-mailed Jeremy back.

Jeremy,
I was surprised, but happy, to hear from you. I would love to go out on Saturday night. ☺ Why don't we just go alone though? I'm spending Friday night with Jane, so I'm sure that she won't mind if it's just you and me. My phone number is 941-555-0945. It's awesome you got your own cell phone. I hope to hear from you soon.

~Kathryn~

# ❧ Chapter Nineteen ❧

Thankfully, the month of November passed by quickly. School was the only thing in my life that I dreaded every day now. Two weeks after the Miami trip everyone was still talking about the shoot.

One day during lunch, a girl dressed in yellow came up to my table. My first thought was that she looked like a big banana but no one else voiced that opinion, so I didn't either. She actually had the nerve to come up to me and ask me why I hadn't been chosen since my dad was in charge of everything. The girls that I sat with looked at one another knowingly and then at me sympathetically. I felt so embarrassed that I didn't know what to say. I didn't even know this girl. She wasn't in my grade and she looked big enough to be a teacher. I was about to mumble something when Kara, one of the girls at the table, said, "Don't you know anything? Haven't you ever heard of nepotism? Kathryn couldn't be in the ad *because* her dad was in charge."

Then the other girls started laughing and I felt so relieved. Why hadn't I thought about that? Of course it wasn't the truth, but it sounded good. It put the big banana in her place too because she walked off without saying anything else. After that, no one asked me about it again.

❧ ❧

The Monday before Thanksgiving I had to go to the doctor to be weighed. I was scared because even though I was trying to eat, I wasn't sure if I'd gained any weight. I didn't want my lack of weight gain to be the cause of me missing out on my trip

home. I put on the heaviest clothes I could find and my Nike
Air Max tennis shoes so that I would weigh more. They were the
heaviest shoes I owned. But the doctor was wise to that trick, I
guess, because the nurse made me take off my shoes before I
weighed in. I stepped on the scale and I was ninety-eight
pounds. I hadn't gained any, but I hadn't lost any either.

Although the doctor said he wasn't thrilled with my stagnant
weight, my dad said it was fine for me to go to Nana's for the
holiday. Before we left the office though, Dr. Brandt took my
parents aside to talk to them. I could only guess what he was
saying because I was out of earshot. I was sure he was talking
about therapy again though. It was the only thing he ever talked
to them about. On the way home, I found out I was right. My
mother was agreeing with Dr. Brandt, while Dad said that I was
doing fine on my own for now. They talked about me as if I
weren't even in the car. Mother kept saying that I had dark
circles under my eyes and that she was worried about my hair
falling out.

"Her hair?" Dad asked.

"William, I didn't want to alarm you, but I went into her
room and I saw her pillow. Her hair was all over the pillowcase.
Not just small amounts, but huge clumps. I was terrified." She
was trying to whisper so I couldn't hear but I overheard anyway.
"When I asked Dr. Brandt about it, he said that was just one of
the many symptoms of an eating disorder." When Dad didn't
say anything, she just continued. "She's not sleeping well either.
Always tossing and turning and did I tell you how she wanted to
go play tennis with me? You know she's never liked the game.
She only took lessons because I made her. It's just a way of
getting exercise. Something you and I both know she doesn't
need." Mother went on and on.

Finally Dad got a word in edgewise. "But her weight isn't
below normal." He too tried to whisper.

"William, that isn't the point at all. She's lost so much weight
in such a short amount of time and she still isn't eating. And
didn't you know she's grown an inch? So, that makes it even

more important that she gains weight." She shook her head like she couldn't believe she had to explain all this to him. "Were you even *in* the doctor's office with me?" she finally asked, completely exasperated.

My mother was so dramatic sometimes. When she finally took a breath, Dad said, "Well, at least she hasn't lost any weight. And I promise you, Abby, if she loses any more weight, we'll take her to the best therapist Dr. Brandt can refer us to."

I just sat in the backseat and counted down the hours before I would be away from them, away from the fighting and away from Florida. I knew that it would be strange to be away from my parents on Thanksgiving for the first time ever, but I knew I needed a break.

&#8286; &#8284;

On Tuesday, the day before I was to leave for Atlanta, Jeremy called me. I was sure he'd forgotten because I hadn't heard from him since I'd e-mailed him. It was right after school when the phone rang and I was in my room, getting my things packed. I picked the receiver up on the second ring.

"Hello?"

"Kathryn?" I knew his voice immediately. For one thing, Jeremy has the sexiest voice I've ever heard. And for another, he was the only boy who had ever called me.

"Hi, Jeremy, how are you?" I stopped packing and fell across my bed, ecstatic to hear his voice. I started playing with the phone cord because I was just so nervous. I hoped my voice wasn't shaking. 'How are you?' I actually said that. Who was I, a middle-aged mom?

"I'm good," he answered. He didn't seem to notice that I was such an idiot. "I just wanted to make sure we were still going out Saturday night." He didn't sound nervous at all.

"Oh, sure," I told him. "I'm looking forward to it." Why couldn't I sound normal? Everything I said came out sounding stupid. I wanted to just slap myself. He either didn't notice or didn't care, because he kept on talking.

"Me too. It's just too bad that you can't move back here permanently." He actually sounded like he meant it.

"Yeah, I wish I could move back too," I told him, though he didn't have a clue as to how badly I really wished it. "I really miss it, Jeremy." I rolled over on my back and stared up at the ceiling. The longer we talked, the less nervous I became. We ended up talking for half an hour. When we I hung up the phone, I just lay there thinking about how excited I was. I had so much to look forward to but yet so much to dread once I got back. I had only four days of happiness to enjoy before I had to come back here. I just wished my parents would let me move in with Nana until the end of school. I would miss Dad, but at least I wouldn't be so miserable. Well, I thought, I just won't think about it right now. The next four days are going to be the best days of my life.

# ≈ Chapter Twenty ≈

I thought Wednesday would never come. I was so excited that I barely slept the night before. I was also nervous about flying. Since my parents weren't staying for Thanksgiving, they decided they couldn't drive all the way there and all the way back. It was just too far. At the airport, however, my mother acted like I was going off to war the way she hugged me. We were standing in line to check my luggage and she was acting like she was never going to see me again.

"Now I want you to promise me you'll eat, Kathryn," she kept saying.

I just nodded and kept my head down. I didn't want to make a scene and she was trying hard to make sure she did.

"And don't stay out too late and remember to get plenty of rest. I know you'll be going out with your friends, but please don't sit up all night. You'll just feel worse once you get home."

She was going on and on and on as we walked to the gate. I was about to board the plane when my dad reached over and hugged me.

"Please have fun, Katybug. And call us once you get there." He paused for a minute. "You know we're going to miss you so much, don't you? Thanksgiving won't be the same without you."

"Nothing has been the same lately," I told him. I gave my boarding pass to the airline attendant and got on the plane. I felt so relieved that I was away from my parents that I didn't even care that my seat wasn't by the window. I just read my *Cosmo GIRL* and before I knew it, I was there.

As I was getting off the plane, I heard my grandmother call to me. I turned and saw her standing there and all of a sudden, I knew I'd missed her more than I'd ever thought possible. It felt more like five years since I'd seen her instead of just a few months. I ran to hug her, but she kept looking at me like she'd never seen me before. I thought I saw concern in her eyes, but I wasn't sure. So, I just said, "We'd better get my luggage." As we were walking to the carousel, Nana kept looking at me, like she hadn't seen me in years.

"Kathryn, you've really lost a lot of weight. Don't they have food in Florida?" My father got his humor from her I guess.

"I haven't been feeling well. You knew that I was in the hospital, but I'm so much better now." She just kept looking at me. Finally I said, "What?"

"Well, it's just that I'm worried about you. You look so different from when you left."

"Different how?" I slowed my pace so she could catch up.

"Well, different in the fact that you look like a shell of the girl who left here in August." That was my grandmother. She wasn't one to smooth over words. She said exactly what she was thinking. And it was funny that she used those particular words, because most of the time, that was exactly how I felt.

"I'm fine, really." I started walking faster again and she was silent until we retrieved my luggage. As we were ambling to the car she asked, "Are you happy, Kathryn?"

"What do you mean?"

"You know what I mean. Are you happy in Sarasota?"

I didn't know what to say. No one had asked me that before. We put my things in the trunk of her car and after we got in, she asked me again. "Well?" She was waiting on an answer.

Finally I just said, "It's okay." I didn't want her to worry about me or, worse, go back and tell my parents that I'd been complaining to her. They wouldn't ever let me come back if that happened.

I don't think Nana believed me, but she left the subject alone and told me how Uncle Josh, my dad's younger brother, and his family were going to be with us on Thanksgiving. That included my Aunt Mary and their three kids, who were completely annoying. I guess I'd known all along that they'd be coming since they did every year, but I was hoping that somehow they would skip it this year. I always liked my Uncle Josh and Aunt Mary, but their kids were spoiled and loud. Melanie, the oldest, was eleven. Then there was Sean, who was eight, and then Rebecca, who was five. I didn't want to dread anything about this trip, but I knew that Thanksgiving would be completely ruined with those brats running around. I didn't say that though. In fact, I didn't say anything. I just looked out the car window, thrilled that I was finally back home.

ဆ ☙

Nana's house is a white ranch-style home. It is actually the house my dad grew up in and I've always loved going there.

I ran inside and straight to my bedroom. Ever since I was little, I've used the same bedroom whenever I've stayed at Nana's. It was the one that my dad slept in as a kid, although the entire house has been remodeled since then. Nana fixed up the room especially for me and she even put a TV and a phone in there. But my favorite aspect was the bed. It was a Select Comfort bed and I never slept so well as I did at her house. I always liked to play with the numbers before I fell asleep to figure out which setting was the most comfortable. Usually, I ended up with a different number every night.

I was unpacking my things when Nana peeked her head in. "I'm going to make lunch, so come into the kitchen when you're finished."

After I put my things away, I walked over to the window and opened it. It was so much colder here than it was in Florida, but I loved the brisk weather. I put on a sweater and just stood in front of the window, peering out, wondering when things had gone so wrong and how I could make them right again. I could actually smell winter. Somewhere someone had started a fire in their fireplace and I could smell the familiar scent of smoke.

Suddenly, I missed my old home so much that I couldn't stand it. I never thought I would miss cold weather, but here I was, missing it and missing my home in Atlanta so much that my heart actually hurt.

I knew that Nana was waiting for me to eat lunch, but I just wasn't hungry. I closed the window and curled up on the bed and before I knew it, I was sound asleep. I didn't even hear Nana when she came in to wake me.

"Kathryn, it's time to get up." She had to shake my shoulders a little to rouse me.

I woke up completely disoriented. For a minute, I didn't know where I was, but once I remembered, I felt relieved. I looked at the time. It was already six o'clock. I had slept the entire day away. "Oh, Nana, why did you let me sleep so long?" I didn't want to miss a moment being here, and yet the first day was already gone.

"You looked exhausted. Now, come and have some dinner. Everything is hot. And after you eat, call William. He's already called for you twice and he's on my nerves, fussing over you like a mother hen." I had forgotten to call when I'd arrived like I'd promised.

I got up and she started straightening the pillows and comforter, while Nana mumbled something about how my mother had rubbed off on him. I started laughing. She was completely right about that.

"Oh, I almost forgot. Jane called," Nana said.

I smiled over her casual remark and went into the kitchen.

The thing about Nana is she doesn't know how to stop. She had cooked so much food just for the two of us that we couldn't possibly come close to eating it all. I really couldn't imagine what we were going to have the next day. Since it was an actual holiday, she'd likely triple the quantity. Tonight, a non-holiday, she had prepared chicken and everything that went with it as well as some things that didn't. In my opinion, rice and mashed potatoes didn't go together in the same meal. I still didn't feel too hungry and I had to make myself take some bites of food since my grandmother was already worried. While we ate, we talked.

She asked me about school—I changed the subject. She asked about my new friends (as if I'd made any)—I changed the subject. She asked me about my parents and again, I changed the subject. Finally, she gave up and told me about things that were going on with her. She filled me in on her ladies' bridge club, which she went to every Tuesday and on her charity work at the church she attended. She informed me that she was thinking about joining a quilting bee since she loved quilting so much. Her life seemed so uncomplicated and so wonderful. I loved hearing everything that was going on with her. I just wished that my life was like hers, uncomplicated and wonderful. I didn't want to waste my teenage years being miserable in a place I hated. I just couldn't make my parents understand that concept.

ᘓ   ᘔ

After dinner, I finally called my dad as I'd promised. We talked for a few minutes, during which he said he already missed me and had been worried when I hadn't called back right away. He was about to put my mother on the phone, but I stopped him. I told him that it was getting late and that I had to call Jane. I told him to have my mother call me tomorrow instead. I couldn't deal with her at that moment. It seemed like I had just left her; I didn't want to talk to her so soon.

When I got off the phone with my dad, I called Jane. She was so excited that I had made it back to Atlanta that she actually shrieked. "I'm coming right over," she announced then hung up before I could say another word. Since Jane lives in my old neighborhood, I knew her mom or dad would have to bring her over because it's about a thirty-minute drive. But I also knew she'd arrive in record time, so I jumped up and got in the shower. When I got out, I started brushing my hair and was shocked to see so many strands in the hairbrush. I tried not to think about it and shifted my attention to finding something to wear.

I realized that everything I'd brought was black because everything in my closet in Sarasota fit into that color category. Only here, though, I felt out of place wearing such a dark, drab shade. Before I had time to think about it though, Jane was at the door. I threw on black jeans and a gray hoodie then ran past Nana. When I opened the door, the first thing I noticed was that Jane had gotten her haircut off and it was now really short. It looked so cute, even though I knew I would miss seeing her long hair flopping all over the place. We started jumping up and down when we saw each other. It was just so good to see her. When we hugged, I told her how good she looked. "I love your hair."

She touched it like she was self-conscious about it and said, "I wanted a change, but now I'm not so sure it was a good idea." It was barely touching her shoulders.

"I think it looks cute," I assured her.

"Yours has grown out a lot since the hair disaster," she said and we laughed. "It looks good longer." I took her coat and we headed to my bedroom, dying for some alone time.

After we had shut the door, she immediately blurted out, "You've lost a lot of weight, Kathryn." She kept eying at me up and down, which was making me feel self-conscious.

I just nodded. "It must be something in the Florida air. Everyone there is thin." I kind of laughed, hoping she would see the humor in it and drop the subject.

"You look good. I wish I could lose some weight."

I looked at her. I hadn't really noticed when she'd first walked in, but she had gained some weight. Even her face showed signs of being chubby. I had always been bigger than Jane. For that matter, I had always been bigger than everyone except Kammy. And it wasn't that Kammy was so big; it was that she was tall.

Jane went over to the full-length mirror and examined herself, the self-consciousness obviously catching. "Oh, well," she sighed. "I guess I just like food too much." She started laughing and then I did too.

Jane walked back over to the bed then and flopped on top of it. I sat down on the floor, propped up against a bunch of pillows. With so much to catch up on, we talked nonstop for almost two hours. It was so good to hear about everything that was going on at a school that normal people attended. The phone rang once, but Nana must have gotten it because we only heard it once. When I asked Jane about Chris, she got this look on her face that just made her glow. I'd never seen Jane like that before.

"Oh, Katy, he's just wonderful. I can't wait for you to meet him." She told me how they had met and how she had liked him from the second they had first talked. She talked about him for about thirty minutes straight before Nana knocked on the door and interrupted her.

"Jane, your mom called and she's picking you up in about fifteen minutes."

We both groaned in response. I didn't want Jane to leave, but she reminded me that we had Friday night. "I can't wait," I told her. We talked for a few minutes more and then we heard Jane's mom honk her horn.

I walked her to the door. Outside, it was so cold that a chill ran down my spine. Before I went to bed that night, I took a really hot bath, even though I'd taken a shower right before Jane had arrived. I just felt like I needed to soak for a while. Nana had some lavender bath oil, so I put that in my bath. After that, I went to bed and I didn't wake up until the sun was shining in on me the next morning.

# ❧ Chapter Twenty-One ❧

The first thing I heard when I awoke was laughter radiating from the kitchen. I looked at the clock. It was already after ten. I had gotten plenty of sleep but I was still exhausted and I couldn't figure out why. Even after sleeping over ten hours I was still dead tired. I knew that I had to face everyone and I dreaded it. That might have been why I was just so tired, I reasoned. Dread can completely wear a person out. Hoping to revive myself a bit, I went into the bathroom and splashed cold water on my face. I could smell food cooking and I could hear everyone talking at once. I put on my gray sweatshirt and a pair of gray sweats and went into the kitchen.

When I arrived, Nana was standing over the stove, stirring something and Aunt Mary was seasoning something. No one noticed I was there, so I just stood silently by and watched. I could hear Uncle Josh and the kids in the living room. I think they were watching the parade and that made me wonder what my dad was doing. I missed him, but I was glad I wasn't in Sarasota.

Finally making my presence known, I walked over to get some water out of the refrigerator. Aunt Mary smiled at me. "Good morning, Kathryn!" She came over to hug me. "How are you?"

"I thought I was going to have to come wake you up," Nana told me, though she was smiling as she said it.

I just smiled and told Aunt Mary I was fine.

"The children are eager to see you. They're in the living room."

The two women were both so busy in the kitchen that I knew I would only be in their way. So I started toward the living room to see the brats. As I was walking away, I heard Aunt Mary whisper, "Has Kathryn been ill? She's lost so much weight, and she looks really tired."

I stopped to listen for a minute. I heard Nana say something about how I'd slept so much since I'd arrived and she figured that it was just the change of moving and everything. "She just hasn't seemed herself," Nana said and I didn't listen anymore. Instead, I walked into the living room, only to find it in a state of mess. Uncle Josh didn't seem to know what was going on right before his very eyes. He was watching the parade, but he had a dazed look in his eyes as though he weren't really watching it at all.

"Good morning," I said to no one in particular. Rebecca, the five-year-old, ran up to me and jumped on my legs. I tried to kick her off, but Uncle Josh was looking at me, so I had to just stand there and let her climb my legs as if they were a jungle gym.

"How are you, Katy?" Uncle Josh got up and hugged me so hard that I thought I would break. "How do you like Sarasota?" he asked.

"It's fine," I lied. Finally, I kicked Rebecca off me when Uncle Josh looked back at the TV.

"For someone who lives in Florida, you sure don't have a tan," Melanie, the eleven-year-old chimed in. She looked up from a book she was reading as she voiced the insult and then went right back to it.

I glanced at the book. It was *Blubber*, by Judy Blume. How appropriate, I thought. Melanie had gotten kind of blubbery herself since the last time I'd seen her. I just ignored her remark about the tan and went over to the corner chair and sat down. I felt cold, so I pulled my knees up under my chin and tried to watch the parade. The kids were so loud though, that they were drowning out everything else. I wasn't used to being around noisy kids, but it didn't seem to bother Uncle Josh. However, it made me want to cut out their larynxes until they stopped screaming and running around.

"How are your parents?" Uncle Josh asked.

"They're fine," I answered, raising my voice so he could hear me over the TV and the kids.

"They should have come along. I can't imagine why they would want to stay in Sarasota, without any family, for the holiday."

I wanted to say it was probably my mother's idea. Instead, I told him how they'd been busy getting everything in the house together and how they just wanted to spend some time relaxing. I had no idea what I was talking about, but he didn't ask any more questions because the phone rang.

Nana yelled out to me, "It's for you, Kathryn. It's your mother."

Tricky. She had called first this time so I wouldn't be able to avoid talking to her.

I went to the phone in the kitchen. "Hello."

"Kathryn, are you eating?" I rolled my eyes. Of course, that would be the first thing she would say to me. "Yes, Mother. I'm fine. Happy Thanksgiving to you too." I hoped she'd caught my sarcasm. She didn't.

"We miss you, Kathryn. I wish you'd stayed home for the holiday." I am home, I thought. "So how are your Uncle Josh and Aunt Mary?"

"Fine," I said.

"And their children?" She sighed. "Are they behaving?"

I told her they were acting as they always did and she laughed at that. Then I asked to speak to Dad. I told Nana to hang up the phone, and I went into my room to talk to him. We talked for almost half an hour. It turned out that talking to him that morning was the best part of the Thanksgiving Day. Only I didn't know that then.

ଐ　　ଓ

Dinner was a disaster. The children of the corn acted so badly that I was embarrassed. Melanie ate so much that Nana finally had to say that there *was* going to be dessert and maybe she should save some room. Sean and Rebecca fought and Sean threw some cranberry sauce, which landed right in Rebecca's hair. This started a crying-fest of the variety I hadn't seen since Jane fell off her skateboard when she was six. She had been fine until she saw blood. But this was even worse than that. I mean it was just cranberry sauce! Aunt Mary got up and tried to get it out of Rebecca's hair. Meanwhile, Uncle Josh yelled at Sean and then *he* started crying. For once, it felt great not to be the center of attention at the dinner table. I just watched the circus and felt so sorry for Nana. The kids were making such a mess and all she could do was wring her hands and tell everyone to just calm down. When the cranberry sauce was almost out of Rebecca's hair, everyone sat back down. There was silence for a minute and then round two began.

"Mom," Rebecca started, "Sean is looking at me and he won't stop."

"Stop looking at your sister, Sean," Aunt Mary scolded, in a tired voice.

"*Mom* he's still doing it!" Now Rebecca was whining.

"What is he doing, Rebecca?" Uncle Josh demanded. He took another bite of sweet potato pie and then Rebecca started screaming at the top of her lungs.

"Why is she doing that?" Nana asked in a tone that I knew meant she was losing her patience.

"Because Sean won't stop looking at her," Melanie stated, as if she knew everything.

Having interrupted her gorging only to get in a smart-aleck comment, she started shoveling more food in and I looked at my own plate. I hadn't eaten enough and I knew it, but there wasn't anyone here to get mad about it. It was a relief but I suddenly felt sick for Melanie. She was just a slob and if she didn't stop, she would never be anything but an even bigger slob.

"Stop that screaming right now!" Uncle Josh yelled.

Uncle Josh's yelling didn't even faze Rebecca. She just kept right on screaming. Finally, Nana got up from her chair, picked Rebecca right up out of her seat and smacked her bottom. That shocked her so much that she stopped screaming immediately. Rebecca just looked horrified; as if that were the first time she'd ever been spanked. If, in fact, you'd call a smack on the bottom a spanking anyway, which, of course I wouldn't. She needed much worse and anyway, she had on her jeans.

But that was when the real fight started.

"Mother, what do you think you're doing?" Uncle Josh spoke very sharply to Nana, something my own dad would never do.

"I'm trying to eat Thanksgiving dinner. Your tactics weren't helping, so I had to do something. That child is completely out of control."

"That *child* is not your concern. Mary and I decide how to discipline *our* children and we don't believe in spankings."

"Obviously you don't, Joshua David Bailey. That is exactly your problem! You *don't* discipline the children at all. They control you."

By this point, all eyes were on Nana and Mary's eyes were blazing. "Don't tell us how to raise our children, Margaret."

"Well, *Mary,* I wouldn't have to if to if you would do it properly yourself. Your children are simply out of control. Screaming and throwing food—I've never seen anything like it. And if you don't watch Melanie, she's going to be a handful. She's already got a smart mouth on her." I'd never seen Nana like that. She must have really been angry. I watched Melanie's reaction. She gave Nana a hard look at that comment about the smart mouth but went right back to eating her dinner.

"Well,"—Aunt Mary straightened her back a little—"at least *our* children eat. At least *our* children are being taken care of. Look at this skeleton that your precious William is raising."

"Mary!" Uncle Josh spat the word out at her. He shot a dagger through her but she didn't seem to care. I, however, was stunned at the comment. Having thrown me for a loop, I just sat there until the words sank in.

"Oh, like I'm the only one noticing this. If William was any kind of father, he would have noticed this himself. "And your favorite grandchild, *Margaret*"—she looked directly at Nana when she said it—"would be healthy instead of sitting here picking at her food like a bird."

"That is enough, Mary!" Uncle Josh slammed down his fist and his face turned red. "I've heard enough." He looked at me and his face softened. "I'm sorry, Kathryn. Really I am."

I didn't say anything. I just got up from the table and went to my room. I closed the door and got into bed. I'd never felt so bad in my life.

Shortly thereafter, I heard a knock at the door and then Nana came in.

"Oh, Kathryn, I'm so sorry." She sat on the edge of the bed. "I don't know what got into any of us. Mary is so sorry that she said the things she said."

I shook my head. "No, she's not. And it isn't my dad's fault that I'm sick." I started crying then and I begged Nana to please just leave. I just wanted to be alone. She reluctantly left and before I knew it, I was sound asleep, even without playing with the Select buttons.

# ജ Chapter Twenty-Two ༞

When I woke up, it was dark outside. I looked at the digital clock on the nightstand and saw that it was one thirty. I had no idea what time I'd fallen asleep and for a moment, I forgot about everything that had happened. Then it hit me like a ton of bricks—the entire Thanksgiving disaster. I rolled over on my back and wondered what time everyone had left. I was happy that Uncle Josh lived close enough so that he and his deranged family didn't have to stay overnight.

I flipped and flopped until I finally got up and went to the bathroom. Then I went into the kitchen and got a glass of water. I was so thirsty that I drank two full glasses. Quenched, I then went back to my room. I'd fallen asleep with my clothes on, so I changed into my Atlanta Braves shirt and got back into bed. Now wide awake, I just lay there, thinking about what Aunt Mary had said and it made me feel so bad that I hated her for trying to ruin my weekend. I also felt bad for Nana since she had worked so hard to make Thanksgiving a special occasion. And even though she hadn't said it, I knew she was disappointed that my dad hadn't come.

Nana had always been closer to my dad than to Uncle Josh. That's because right after Uncle Josh had graduated from college, he'd moved somewhere in New England. He hadn't come home until his dad, my grandfather, had died. It was then that he'd decided to move back, but by then he had married and he and my Aunt Mary hadn't wanted to live in the same town where he'd grown up in. So, they moved about an hour away and that's where they had stayed. I think it really hurt Nana even more when we moved to Sarasota because now Dad was even farther away than Uncle Josh. But it wouldn't matter if Uncle Josh lived only two blocks over—he never was one to visit his mother.

I decided not to think about Uncle Josh or Aunt Mary or their horrible children. Instead, I thought about how I was going to Jane's house that night and how I couldn't wait to have someone normal to talk to. It made me realize how much I'd missed having friends.

Then I thought about Jeremy and I started getting a little nervous about seeing him. We still hadn't worked out the details of our date and since neither of us could drive, I had no idea what we were doing or where we were going. I just knew that even though I was nervous, I didn't want to be stuck at some skating rink where everyone would be or at some stupid movie where we couldn't talk for two hours. I wanted us to hang out and I hoped that he had some kind of plan. I smiled at the thought of seeing him and then I reached over and started playing with the Select buttons. After finding the perfect number, I sank even deeper into the bed. The last time I looked at the clock it was two twenty.

*I was walking down the hall at my old school. I felt so happy to be back, but as I walked through the double doors, into the main hall, everyone was staring at me. Then they started laughing and pointing, and I thought, 'No, this is a mistake. This is my old school I have friends here.' I was confused at why my friends were laughing at me. Then I looked down and realized that I didn't have any clothes on. How had I forgotten to put clothes on? I stood frozen and then the bell started ringing. I tried to run but my feet were sinking like quicksand. I couldn't move fast enough.*

That was when I woke up. It was then that I realized that the ringing I had heard wasn't the bell at all; it was just the phone and I felt completely relieved.

I looked at the clock. It was nine forty-five so I got up and started making my bed. I heard a knock on the door and Nana walked in. "How are you feeling this morning, Kathryn?"

"I'm fine," I told her. She walked to the other side of the bed and helped me smooth the sheets. That was always the hard part for me. I couldn't ever get the sheets smoothed out the way she could.

"That was Mary on the phone. She called to apologize. She wanted to talk to you, but I told her you would call her back." We pulled the comforter up and put the pillows on.

"I'm not calling her back." I said defiantly.

Nana walked over to the window and opened the curtains. It was so sunny outside that the brilliant rays almost hurt my eyes. I sat down on the bed and crossed my legs.

"You don't have to, but she really is sorry." Nana paused and then said, "I'm not making excuses for her behavior, but it's those kids of theirs." She raised her eyebrows and sighed heavily. "I know they're my grandchildren, but honestly, they behave like wolves have been raising them. They make Josh and Mary so stressed and you know everywhere they go, people dread to see them coming. If it were me, I wouldn't leave the house with them." She started mumbling about how she hadn't raised her children to act like that and she couldn't understand how her own son could be raising children in that manner.

"You know," she went on, "they all but destroyed this entire house.  After dinner, that Rebecca took out all my toilet paper and rolled it all the way down the hall. Melanie and Sean started running around the house and knocked the curtains off the windows in my bedroom and before I could even get those put back up, Rebecca and Sean started jumping on my bed. The entire time Josh kept yelling, 'If you kids don't stop, I'm going to make you wish you had.' But of course, neither he nor Mary did anything." She sighed again. "It's a wonder you slept through it."

I was just imagining everything she had just described and it made me laugh. I mean, poor Nana, but still, it was like a zoo.

The only difference was instead of wild animals, she had wild children in her house.

"Well, it's good to see you smile." Then she started laughing too.

"What time did they leave?"

"Around nine. Believe me, it wasn't a minute too soon." Nana started toward the door and said, "You need to come and eat some breakfast, Kathryn. You barely ate yesterday."

I told her I would, but first I wanted to get dressed. I went to the bathroom and washed my face and put on my clothes. I then went out to the kitchen, where Nana was busy making breakfast. She had the waffle iron out and I hated to see her go to so much trouble after having dealt with so much the day before.

"You don't have to make waffles, Nana. It's way too much trouble and toast is enough for me."

"Oh, they were your favorite when you were little. And it's not any trouble at all." She busied herself and I asked her if there was anything she wanted me to do.

"Besides eat?" she asked. I just ignored her and sat down at the table. I watched her mix the batter.

"By the way, Kathryn, I've noticed all the clothes you brought were less than colorful." When I didn't say anything in response, she continued. "Is that something that everyone your age is doing?"

"Is everyone my age doing what?" I acted like I didn't know what she was talking about.

"Wearing clothes that make them look like they're mourning the death of a loved one?"

I just rolled my eyes and told her if she didn't need my help, I was going to call Jane.

Jane answered on the first ring. "I was just getting ready to call you."

"So, what's up?"

"I thought we could go to the mall for a while. The day after Thanksgiving sales are really amazing and it will be a fun way to hang out before you come sleep over."

I thought about that for a minute. "How are we going to get there?" I didn't think anyone in their right mind would take us to the mall on the busiest shopping day of the year. I couldn't wait to get my driver's license. Unfortunately, I couldn't even get a permit until March and that was still months away.

"My mother is going to the mall anyway, so she said we could go with her. Of course, she won't hang out with us, but when we're ready to go, all we have to do is call her cell phone."

"That sounds like fun." I thought about how I could get something new to wear for my date with Jeremy. I had packed an outfit, but of course it was black and I was starting to feel self-conscious about it.

"We'll come by for you around eleven."

I told her that was perfect then hung up the receiver and ran to the kitchen to tell Nana I would be going to the mall with Jane and her mother. She said that I had to eat something first, so I took a few bites of waffles and got into the shower. Suddenly shopping sounded like so much fun.

ಲ    ಞ

"Girls, I'm going to drop you off at the main entrance. This is just insane." We'd driven around the parking lot four times and still hadn't found a place to park. The mall was so crowded that cars were actually parking on the lawn. And this was one of the biggest malls in Atlanta, so if it was this crowded outside, we could only imagine what was going on inside.

As we were getting out, I heard Jane's mom say that by the time she found a parking spot, we would be finished shopping. I started laughing but Jane just rolled her eyes.

"Well," Jane said, once we got inside the mall. "I know this is technically Christmas shopping season, but I'm getting something for tomorrow night."

"What's tomorrow night?" I asked.

"Chris and I are going out. We're actually going out with his parents to see *The Nutcracker.*"

"That sounds like so much fun!" I told her.

"Yeah, I love ballet, but of course, Chris doesn't. His family goes every year and this year his mom invited me so I would 'encourage' Chris to go too." She started giggling. "I love how she used the word 'encourage,' when what she really meant was for me to manipulate him into going."

We laughed and I told her that I too wanted to find something to wear for my date with Jeremy. "But since I don't know where we're going, I don't know how to dress."

We started walking toward the food court and Jane said, "Dress casually. You don't want to overdress since he didn't tell you exactly what was going on." I nodded my head.

"Before we shop, let's get something to eat. I'm starving."

I wasn't hungry at all, but I didn't say that. Instead, we stood in line for thirty-five minutes for pizza and then it took us another ten to wait someone out while they finished eating so we could grab their table. In the time it took us to do that, I could have found something to wear and been on my way. But it was more fun to shop with someone else, even if it meant I had to do things that ended up slowing me down.

Once we sat down, Jane started eating like this was her last meal ever. I picked the toppings off, and then I took small bites of my cheese. Jane noticed my hesitation and said that if I didn't like the toppings, I should have told them to leave them off.

"Nana made waffles this morning and I'm not hungry."

"I wish I wasn't hungry. All I want to do lately is eat. Mom says it's hormonal and I'll outgrow it. I think she's wrong though." She took another bite and added, "You know, you're really skinny. I knew that you'd lost weight, but I just realized that you're smaller than Ashley!"

I just smiled. "Well, everyone in Florida is small."

She nodded. "Then it's a good thing I don't live there."

I laughed and I watched her eat. It was making me sick, so I had to look away. It was then that I noticed how pudgy Jane was. It didn't seem to bother her though, because once we left the food court, we spent another fifteen minutes waiting in line for a cookie at the Cookie Company. This time I didn't even bother ordering anything. I thought it was disgusting that Jane was eating again so soon after just stuffing herself with so much pizza.

&#x9C;   &#x3;

It was hours before we finished shopping because of all the lines and our indecision about what to wear. When we finally got to the car, it took us another half-hour to get out of the parking lot.

"Girls, remind me to never do this again. I thought I would find sales. Instead, I find out that the real sales start at six o'clock in the morning." By that point Mrs. Hunter was actually out of breath and she looked like she'd been in a war zone. "Who gets up that early to come to the mall?" She adjusted her rear-view mirror and looked at us. We were both sitting in the backseat and Mrs. Hunter commented that she felt like a chauffeur. She then asked why one of us couldn't sit up front.

Neither of us said anything and the rest of the drive was silent except for the Christmas music that spilled forth from the radio. The day after Thanksgiving, on certain radio stations, all they play is Christmas music the entire day. Wouldn't you know Jane's mom would be one of those who would listen to *all Christmas, all the time*?

On the ride home, Jane didn't talk much because she was upset. The dress she'd fallen in love with only came in odd sizes, which she'd always worn up until now. But she was now an even size because of her weight. She ended up getting a black velvet dress that was cute but not as cute as the one she wanted. The sleeves were too puffy and it was a little longer than she wanted, but she bought some really nice shoes to match. I thought that would make her happy, but she was still pouting.

'Keep standing an hour in line for cookies and that's what happens,' I was thinking, but of course, I would never actually say that.

I had ended up getting a new pair of jeans since my others were black. I got a pair of Guess because they fit so well and lately I'd having a problem finding clothes that fit.

"Look how tiny they are." Jane had looked at them in disbelief.

I had just shrugged and found a red cardigan pebble-washed sweater to go with the jeans. It was softer than a regular cardigan and it looked really nice. I just wasn't used to wearing such colorful clothing. I had almost gone with blue, but Jane said that the red looked nice and I should get it. I also bought a pair of Wallabies since my parents had given me their credit card and told me if I needed something to get it. And I desperately needed new shoes. We also found new earrings, and I felt like I'd really gotten something accomplished, even though at the beginning of the shopping trip it had seemed like we'd never even get into a store.

Since I had to go back to Nana's to pack my things for the night, Jane's mom dropped me off and I told them that Nana would bring me over later.

"Thanks for letting me to go with you. I had a good time," I told Jane's mother. Then I told Jane I would see her later. I just hoped that she would be in a better mood.

# ೞ Chapter Twenty-Three ೕ

Nana dropped me off at Jane's and when she greeted me, her mom told me Jane was up in her room. I went upstairs only to find her on the phone. I put my things down and she smiled at me. She put up one finger, telling me to wait. By the look on her face, I could tell she was talking to Chris.

I looked around her room. It seemed like forever since I'd been there. In my absence, she'd rearranged her furniture and I liked where she'd put her bed. It was near the window. I always thought Jane's bed was kind of childish, though. She had a white iron daybed with pillows all over it, and right in the middle was her favorite teddy bear, which she'd gotten when she was five, I think. I would have thought starting high school would have made her change that, but obviously I was wrong.

Killing time while she finished her conversation, I walked over to her desk. On it, she had a picture of her and Chris and I wondered who had taken it. They were just sitting on a blanket out at Woodland Park and they were infatuatedly staring at each other. It was almost like they didn't know anyone else was around. I wanted to gag. I've liked Jeremy for a long time, but I hoped I would never get that look on my face over him or any boy.

I also saw that she had a picture of her and Tori on top of the desk. In it, they were in Jane's backyard, sitting on the grass and they were laughing at something. It was a cute picture. The other pictures were the same ones she'd always had. I was about to sit on the bed when her cat, Puff, jumped out at me. I've always hated her cat. Don't get me wrong, I'm not an animal hater, but Puff is just evil. She sits and waits for someone to get comfortable and then she lunges. Besides, I'd always thought Puff was a stupid name for a cat anyway. When I'd mentioned this to Jane, she'd explained to me why they had named her that. Way back, when Jane's parents were in school, they had learned to read from books that had characters named Dick and Jane. And the Dick and Jane children had had a cat named Puff. So, I guess the Hunters thought they were being clever. Only no one our age ever gets the joke since we never learned to read from those books.

I put Puff outside the bedroom and sighed loudly. I was getting tired of waiting for Jane to get off the phone. I guess she took the hint because I heard her say, "I'll see you tomorrow night." Then it was silent and she started giggling. "No, you hang up first." And then she started laughing again, "No you." Then she started laughing too loudly. "No, you, Chris." By this time, I was just about to throw up. She was still giggling when I went over to the phone and hung it up myself.

She looked startled and immediately stopped laughing. "Why did you do that?"

"Because if I hadn't, you never would have gotten off the phone."

She looked a little disappointed. "Now he'll think I've hung up on him."

"Oh, puh-lease, Jane." I rolled my eyes.

"Well, you just don't know what this feels like." She flopped back on her bed and sighed loudly. "I am *sooo* in love with him, Kathryn."

"Really?" I said dryly. Suddenly I was sorry I'd come over. I didn't want to talk about Chris all night. I just wanted to hang out the way we used to. That wasn't the plan though. For the next hour I had to hear about everything they did; everything he said to her; everything she said to him and everything she felt as they were saying it. I don't know why it was making me mad, but this night was supposed to be about us, not about her and Chris. She would see him tomorrow night. Tonight, we were just supposed to hang out like we had before I moved.

After she finally ran out of breath, she said, "Let's order pizza."

"We had pizza for lunch," I reminded her.

"I could eat pizza for every meal." She laughed. "What do you want on it?" Apparently she was over her dress depression.

"I don't care. Anything I don't want, I'll just pick off."

She called the pizza place and then we ran downstairs to tell her parents that we'd ordered it and asked them to let us know when it got there.

"Do you want to watch a DVD?" Jane asked me while we were still downstairs.

I shrugged.

"We can watch *Drive Me Crazy*."

"We've seen it like ninety-seven times."

"So we know how it ends." She took the movie from her parents' DVD collection and we went back upstairs.

Wanting to make myself more comfortable before settling down in front of the TV, I went to the bathroom and changed clothes. When I came out of the bathroom, I discovered that Jane had also changed and was writing in her diary. She stopped long enough to put the movie in and then returned to writing. I felt bored. I wanted to talk to Jane. I wanted to *really* talk, but she only wanted to talk about Chris and I realized that we really didn't have a lot in common anymore. She was into boyfriends and although I liked Jeremy, he wasn't my entire life.

When the pizza came, Jane's mother brought it up to us. At the sight of food, Jane stopped writing and dove right in. I took a piece and started picking at it.

"I'm starving," she said, although I couldn't see how she could be. "So, have you heard from Jeremy?" she asked in between bites.

"No, not since I got here. I think he'll probably call tomorrow. I just hope he hasn't forgotten about our date."

She shook her head. "No way. He wouldn't do that. I think he really likes you, Kathryn. I just wish you didn't live so far away."

I didn't say anything and we finished watching the movie in silence. She ate three more pieces of pizza while I picked at my same slice. That was the nicest thing about being away from my parents. They weren't hovering over me, although my mother had called twice. Fortunately, I hadn't been home either time. I'm sure she was wondering about how much I was eating, but I didn't care.

After the movie, we decided to give ourselves facial masks. I'd never done it before, but Jane said she did so once a week. "It's supposed to keep your face from breaking out," she told me. We went into the bathroom and she showed me how to put it on.

"It feels strange, very tight on my face," I told her as the gloppy mess hardened against my skin.

"That's the way it's supposed to feel."

We had to let the stuff stay on our faces for fifteen minutes before we could rinse it off, so we talked while we waited. Making ourselves more comfortable, we went to her bed and sat down. Struggling for a way to escape the silence that seemed to keep popping up between us, I picked up her yearbook from last year and started flipping through it. I found Jeremy's picture right away and he looked so cute that I got butterflies in my stomach just thinking about seeing him.

I felt Jane staring at me, so I looked up from the book.

"You know, that shirt swallows you whole," For some reason that statement made me mad. It was just something that my mother would have said and the whole point of this trip had been to get away from my mother.

"I've had this shirt forever and it's always been big." It was my Atlanta Braves shirt, the one I slept in every night.

"Why don't you eat, Kathryn?" She just blurted it out so quickly that I almost didn't hear her.

"I do eat." I didn't take my eyes off the yearbook.

"No, not like you used to. And you've lost so much weight. I overheard my mother talking to your grandmother. I think everyone is really worried about you."

Why would she bring this up? This was supposed to be a fun night, not a night during which I had to sit and explain myself. I felt the anger inside me grow worse.

"Well, they need to *stop* worrying about me because nothing is wrong."

"Don't get mad, Kathryn." She was talking in a small voice. "It's just that, well, you look tired and I thought you might be sick."

"I'm not sick. I just haven't been hungry." I was just so angry that I lashed out at her. "Maybe it's just my hormones out of whack. Like your mother said about yours."

"What did my mother say about my hormones?" she demanded.

"You told me that your mom said your hormones were just out of whack, which was why you were overeating." Instantly, I was sorry I'd said that because she looked like she was about to cry.

"I may overeat but at least I'm not starving myself to death."

She stomped into the bathroom and started rinsing her mask off. I waited until she was finished then did the same. Then I brushed my teeth. Jane was already in bed by the time I came out of the bathroom. The lamp was still on, but she was under her covers. I took my sleeping bag out and unrolled it on the floor. Usually when I slept over, we talked until her mother had to come in and remind us to be quiet. No one would have to remind us of anything this time. She reached over and turned off the lamp.

"Goodnight," she snapped.

I didn't say anything. I just rolled over and tried to fall asleep. I had looked forward to this weekend so much and now that it was here, I wasn't having fun at all.

# ✌ Chapter Twenty-Four ✆

Saturday morning, I woke up to the sound of rain. I looked at the clock and saw that it was only seven forty-five. Jane was still sleeping so I started thinking about my date with Jeremy. If in fact I still had a date with him. He hadn't called and I was worried. Pellets pounding against the window, I sat up and looked outside. It was raining so hard that I couldn't even see across the street. I wondered how I would get home. Since Jane and I weren't even talking, it didn't seem right to ask her parents to take me home.

Deciding to take matters into my own hands, I went to the bathroom and got dressed then I went downstairs. I didn't know if anyone else was up, but when I went into the kitchen I found a note on the counter. "Jane, Dad and I went to Grandma's. We'll be home by lunch. If you need us, call the cell phone."

I went over to the phone that was attached to the kitchen wall and called Nana. She answered on the second ring. "Did I wake you up?"

She started laughing. "Of course not. I've been up since six, same as any other day."

"Would it be too much trouble for you to come get me?"

"Come and get you?" She sounded startled.

"Yes." I sighed. I didn't want to explain, but I knew she would want to know why.

"I'll come and get you but it's early. Are you feeling all right?" She sounded worried.

"I'm fine. I'm just ready to go."

"I'll be right over."

I told her I'd be watching for her so she wouldn't have to get out. Then I went back to Jane's room and got my things together. Jane is a very sound sleeper, so she didn't even move while I noisily gathered up my stuff.

Willing the time to pass quickly, I went to the front door and watched for my grandmother from the window. As soon as I saw Nana drive up, I ran to the car and got in. I was soaked and immediately started getting chills. It was really cold and I started sneezing. I guess I'd gotten used to the weather in Sarasota more than I'd realized.

"So, you *are* sick!" she accused.

"No, I just sneezed. I feel fine. I think I'm just cold."

She turned up the heater. "Did you and Jane get into a fight?"

"Not exactly," I told her, figuring a slight stretching of the truth wouldn't hurt anything. I don't think Nana fell for it though.

"Do her parents know you left? The house was dark, like no one was up."

"They were up. Jane's parents went to see her grandmother today." I didn't say anything else so she didn't ask anything else about it.

Once we got back to Nana's house, I went to my bedroom and put on some dry pajamas. Still shivering, I got back in bed. I was still very tired and the rain was making me even sleepier. The last thing I remember was Nana asking me if she could make me some breakfast. I think I fell asleep before I could even answer her.

ЪО    ♋

When I woke up, the sun was shining and I felt like the entire night had just been a bad dream, like it hadn't happened at all. I wished that it had been just a bad dream and I wished I were waking up on Friday morning so I could have it to do all over again. Only this time, Jane and I wouldn't fight. Since I'd been in Sarasota, all I'd wanted to do was come back for a visit but now that I was finally in Atlanta, nothing was going right.

As I always do when I first awake, I instinctively looked at the clock. It was already twelve thirty in the afternoon. Half the day already gone, I got up and found Nana in the kitchen, where she was talking on the phone. Not wanting to interrupt her, I walked over to the refrigerator and helped myself to some bottled water.

"Oh, here she is, Abby." Nana handed me the phone.

At the mere mention of my mother's name, I wanted to run away but there wasn't anything I could do. I had to take the phone.

"Hello?"

Nana went to the stove and started stirring something.

"Did you and Jane have a fight?" Mother always seemed to get right to the point.

"Not exactly," I told her, feeding her the same line I'd fed Nana.

"Well, I *exactly* got a phone call from Mrs. Hunter. She was worried about you."

"Why?" I took a long drink of water and leaned against the wall, bracing myself for her lecture. "For leaving without even saying anything. You didn't even leave a note, Kathryn Ann. That's just so rude."

"Jane was still asleep and her parents were gone," I tried to explain. I hadn't even thought about leaving a note though.

"Well, you just call and apologize for worrying them."

I didn't say anything, but one thing was for sure: I was not about to call anyone and apologize for anything.

We were quiet for a minute and I was about to ask to talk to Dad when she said, "Are you eating?"

I sighed. "Yes, I am."

"Are you feeling well? Nana said you were sneezing."

Since when was sneezing a sign of terminal illness? "I'm fine, Mother. I only sneezed the one time."

"Well, you have a doctor's appointment on Tuesday."

"Because I sneezed?"

Nana looked at me for a minute and I just shrugged. Returning to her task, she went to the pantry to get something.

"Dr. Brandt wants to see you," my mother said. "It has nothing to do with your sneezing."

"Will you put Dad on the phone?"

"He's at the club, playing golf, Kathryn."

The club. That phrase always made me cringe—'the club,' like we were important. It was just so snobby and I couldn't understand why I was the only one who could see that. "Well, I have to go now," I said, trying to bring the pointless conversation to a close.

"Just make sure you eat and also, call Mrs. Hunter. And whatever is wrong with you and Jane, please make it right again. You know you'll regret it if you don't."

I just mumbled "whatever" and we hung up.

"Is everything okay?" Nana asked. I nodded. "I'm making chicken stew. It should be ready in a little while. I'm sure you're hungry."

I was just about to say that I didn't like chicken stew when the phone rang. Oh, please don't let it be Mother again, I thought. I answered it though, because Nana was busy slicing onions.

"Hello?"

"Kathryn, it's me." It was Jeremy!

"Hey, Jeremy." Nana looked at me and smiled. I told Jeremy to hold on and whispered to Nana that I would take the call in my bedroom.

"So, are we still going out tonight?" he asked me when I got back on the line.

"Sure."

"My parents went out of town today and they won't be back until tomorrow afternoon. I thought we could just hang out here and watch DVDs or listen to music."

His voice sounded so lazy and I could just picture him lying on a comfortable couch, talking. I got tingles just thinking about him.

"My parents made the basement into a room for my friends and me to hang out in. It's really cool." He paused for a second and when I didn't say anything, he said, "I know it's not like a real date, but I didn't think it would be fun to go to a movie when we could just watch one here. And I'm not about to hang out in some skating rink with a bunch of junior high geeks."

I started laughing because that's exactly how I felt about it. "I think it sounds fun, Jeremy." I loved saying his name. It gave me goose bumps all over my arms.

"One thing though. Do you think your grandmother could drive you over?"

"Sure. She won't mind. Though I think I'll tell her other kids are going to be there."

"Yeah, good thinking." He started laughing. "It's what I told my parents too."

"It's cool that they'd let you have company while they're away."

"I think they expected it."

I started laughing. I was happy that he called, but I was even happier that we were going to spend time alone together.

After we got off the phone, I asked Nana if she would take me over to Jeremy's around six o'clock.

"Aren't his parents out of town?"

*How would she know that?* I wondered.

"I think so, but he's having a few people over. His parents know about it."

She acted like she was thinking about it and I had to know. "How did you know his parents were out of town?"

"Because Edward always goes to his parents' house on the Saturday and Sunday after Thanksgiving. He's been doing that for years. Your grandfather and I always got a laugh out of it because we figured he was just doing it on principle, not because he really wanted to." This area that we live in is really too small.

Too many people know too many small details about each other's lives.

"Why would he do that on principle?" I got some water and drank it while she explained. Then she started laughing. "Because when he and Joan married, on their first Thanksgiving together they spent the entire weekend at her parents'. He griped about it for an entire year and after that, he decided two days with hers, two days with his was how they'd spend future Thanksgivings."

I was sorry I had asked. It was a silly story, but Nana thought it was funny. And the more she talked about it, the more she laughed. I wasn't finding it funny.

"So, will you take me?"

She stopped laughing and after a moment said, "I'm not sure it's a good idea, Kathryn. What would your parents think?"

"They'd think I was just out having fun with my friends, Nana," I told her.

"Well, I don't really like the idea, but I guess it's all right. I'll pick you up around ten, so watch for me."

I was relieved. For a minute, I was scared she wasn't going to let me go. But still, ten o'clock was kind of early. I would have argued, but ten was better than nothing.

I went to the phone and almost called Jane to tell her about Jeremy, but then I remembered our fight and put the phone back down. I felt bad and wished she hadn't brought up that food thing. Why was everyone so determined to talk about food?

# ❧ Chapter Twenty-Five ❧

After Nana dropped me off at Jeremy's, I got really nervous. My heart was beating too loudly and I thought I might pass out. When I finally got to the door, I paused. I wasn't sure if I should knock or ring the bell. I didn't have to worry though, because while I was standing there debating the issue, the door opened and Jeremy was standing in front of me. *How cute is that?* I thought. He was watching for me.

He looked so good with his Levi's and a dark blue Tommy shirt. I was glad that I'd decided to go shopping. Otherwise, I would have looked morbid compared to him. When I walked in, he didn't move so I had to squeeze by him. As I did so, we were really close. He smelled *so* good, like a combination of soap, laundry detergent and shampoo. The ends of his hair were still wet from the shower, which made him look even more adorable. I wanted to reach out and touch him, but I didn't.

"I'm glad you came over, Katy." He looked me up and down. "You look really good."

"Thanks, Jeremy. You look nice too."

"Do you want something to drink?" He walked toward the kitchen, and I followed him.

I nodded. "Water?"

He looked in the refrigerator and handed me a bottle of Evian. "Are you sure you don't want something else?" He took a Pepsi.

"I'm sure," I assured him.

Drinks in hand, we went downstairs to his basement. I was impressed. His parents had made it into this amazing room for him. He had an entire entertainment system with a CD player, a

DVD player and a big screen TV. He even had these huge speakers with surround sound. In another corner a pool table had been set up. He bragged that he was getting pretty good. "You want to play later?" he asked me.

"No thanks. I don't know how."

"I could teach you." But I just shrugged.

The room had a sectional couch and a couple of chairs that looked very comfortable. Jeremy went over and sat down on the couch. For an awkward moment, I didn't know if I should sit beside him or if I should sit in one of the chairs. I decided to sit on the couch but I sat at the other end. I felt so nervous that I was afraid to sit too close.

Jeremy retrieved the remote control from the coffee table and turned on MTV2. We watched videos for a while, but neither of us said anything. I felt very uncomfortable. I didn't know what to say and I wondered if we were going to spend the entire night watching TV

"I know I said this before, but you look really good, Katy," he told me again when the Incubus video, "Megalomaniac," ended. "You've lost a lot of weight."

"Thanks." I wondered what he'd thought of me before. That statement, "You've lost a lot of weight; you look good," made me wonder if he'd thought I *hadn't* looked good before.

"You look like you've been working out." It was all I could think of to say.

"Actually, I'm on the wrestling team this year, so I *have* to work out."

"Cool. I didn't know you were into wrestling."

"Yeah, I love it." He tried to tell me about some of the moves he'd been working on, but it was hard for me to follow since I'd never actually seen a wrestling match.

We got silent again. I didn't know what else to say. He muted the TV, got up, put in a Linkin Park CD and sat down on the floor. The basement carpet was very thick and looked extremely comfortable. Throw pillows were tossed all around, so he kind of leaned back on one of them. He stretched his legs way out then pulled up his shirt up a little. When he did so, his stomach showed. He really had been working out because I could tell from his abdominal ripples. They looked amazing. I think he knew it too because he kind of looked at me with a confident gaze and I felt my knees grow weak.

I felt silly sitting so far away from him. Unable to resist the distance any longer, I went over and sat down cross-legged beside him. He reached over and he took my hand. We then just sat there, staring at each other.

"What are the chances that your parents would let you move back here?"

I looked away. "Not much of a chance."

"Do you like it there?"

I sighed. "I hate it there, Jeremy." This was the first time I'd ever felt like I could talk to anyone about it. Jane wasn't listening, I couldn't talk to my parents (they only heard what they wanted to hear) and if I'd talked to my grandmother, my parents would be mad at me for complaining. "The kids there are so snobby."

My confession bridged the intimacy distance between us. He pulled me down on one of the pillows and we lay really close together. I told him about Tiffany and about the trouble I had gotten into fighting with her. I loved how he listened so attentively. I could tell because of how his facial expressions changed with what I was saying.

"You ... fighting?" He looked impressed. "Wow, Katy, I wouldn't have ever pegged you for a fighter."

I started laughing. "Until this year, I wouldn't have thought I could do it." I even told him how I hit Max and how I'd gotten suspended for it.

He started laughing. "You've turned into a real wild child. A Katy Rebel."

We both started laughing at that thought and he reached over and started tickling me. I hate to be tickled because it mostly just hurts; only when I laugh, people think I like it. I tried to tickle him back, but he was too fast for me and evaded all my moves.

Finally, I was gasping for breath and couldn't take it anymore. I stood up to get some air and I felt so dizzy that I almost fell over backward. Jeremy noticed and got a worried look on his face. "Are you okay?" he asked in a concerned voice.

I felt funny for a minute. "Yeah, I'm fine."

"But you looked like you were going to pass out or something."

"It's just that I got up too quickly, that's all."

"Maybe you need something to eat. Are you hungry? My mom left a bunch of food in the kitchen since she thought I was having lots of people over."

"I'm not hungry. I ate before I came over."

"Well, okay," he reluctantly gave in, "but if you get hungry we'll see what she left us."

I nodded and he sat back down. I settled myself down beside him on the floor and we talked some more about Sarasota and Vanguard Academy. He seemed so interested that it made me feel good that finally someone was actually listening to me. I told him everything except about being in the hospital. I didn't want him to know that, so I just left that part out. But it felt wonderful to get out all my feelings about school, about my parents and about how I just wanted to come back home.

"I wish that your parents would let you move back. I think you'd like high school with us, Katy."

"I know I would," I told him.

We got quiet again then and he went over to the CD player to put something else in. This time it was an old Nelly CD. He went straight to the slow song, "Dilemma." Rifts from the song floating through the air, he lay back into the pillows and pulled me to him. My heart was beating too fast as he did so. I wasn't sure what to do next. He played with my hair for a few minutes, twirling it around his fingers and I was getting tingles from him touching me. I reached over and stroked the ends of his hair. I loved how his hair felt. I loved how this moment felt even more.

We were sitting so close to each other that I was scared to breathe. His eyes looked more beautiful than I'd ever seen them. I was so mesmerized by them that I couldn't look away from him. And then he reached over and kissed me. When he did so, it literally took my breath away. It was much more romantic than being in Woodland Park surrounded by all our friends. I felt so grown-up because we were alone. Then his hands started moving crazily over my body and I pulled away.

"What's wrong?" he whispered.

"Nothing," I told him. I didn't want to make him mad. So we kissed again, only this time his hands were diving under my sweater. He touched my bra and I pulled back again. "Don't," I told him.

"Sorry," he mumbled. But he didn't seem sorry because he did it again.

"Stop, Jeremy." I grew insistent this time and he got defensive in response.

"I'm not *doing* anything, Kathryn."

He sounded irritated and that wasn't what I'd wanted. I decided to let it go and we kissed again. The next thing I knew my bra was undone. It's the kind that snaps in the front, and he had undone it within two seconds flat. I had to wonder how much experience he'd had to figure that out so quickly.

"*Now* you're doing something" I pulled back and put my clothes back in place.

"I didn't realize you were such a baby, Kathryn." His eyes, which had looked so beautiful before, had a very mean look to them and I was hurt.

"What do you mean, a baby?" Why was he acting like this? We had been having so much fun and he was ruining it.

"I thought we were having fun," he told me.

"We are. It's just that I don't feel comfortable with my clothes half off," I told him.

He rolled his eyes and got up. He turned off the CD player and flipped MTV2 back on. Then he sat down on the couch and sulked.

"Do you want me to go home?" I finally ventured.

"Do what you want." He wouldn't even look at me. He just kept his eyes glued on the TV.

"Jeremy!" I yelled at him, wanting his full attention again. "Is that why you wanted me to come over? So we could have sex?" I was just amazed at how this night had taken such a wrong turn. I jumped up from my spot on the floor and just looked down at him.

"We weren't having *sex*, Kathryn. We were just fooling around a little. Everyone does it."

Everyone? So that meant that I was right and he *had* done this with other people. That was just great. And I thought I was special. I really was an idiot.

"I'm calling my grandmother and having her come get me." I started walking to the stairs, but he ran in front of me to stop me.

"Don't go, Katy. I'm sorry."

I wanted to cry. I had mixed feelings. I wanted to stay so badly, but I didn't want him to think he could just touch me like that. And knowing that he'd done that with other girls was just too much for me to bear. "I really should go, Jeremy."

"No, I was being a jerk and I'm sorry."

I didn't say anything.

"We can do whatever you want to do, or don't want to do." He smiled and, as always, his smile lit up my entire life. My knees grew weak underneath me and he looked so cute that I just nodded my consent. He then took my hand and we walked upstairs to the kitchen.

"We have so much food here. If we don't eat some of this, my mother will know for sure that I didn't have people over."

I started laughing as we pulled out sandwiches, a chocolate cake and Pepsis from the refrigerator. He even found a dip that his mother had made from sour cream and it looked good. He took out chips and some pretzels from the cabinet. Satisfied with the feast he'd rounded up, he put everything on the table and started eating right away. I just looked at the food and started thinking how many calories he was consuming.

"Come on, Katy, you have to eat something."

I was so tired of those words. Deciding the only way to stop the lecture was to just join him, I picked up a pretzel and nibbled on it. I went to the refrigerator and got water then sat down at the table beside him.

"You should try this dip. It's really good."

I shook my head. "No thanks." I kept nibbling my pretzel.

"No wonder you've lost so much weight—you never eat."

No matter how many times people said it, I couldn't see it. I still felt like the same girl I always was. I didn't feel small, even though everyone said I was bony and skeleton-like.

"I'm not that small. It must just be the clothes. They're hiding my real size." I giggled.

"Well, we can always take them off and see for sure." He laughed at his own joke.

I just rolled my eyes. "Real cute, Jeremy."

He looked at me for a long time and said, "Yes, you really are cute, Kathryn."

ဆ    ૭

True to his word, Jeremy kept his hands off me for the rest of the night. We just hung out in the basement playing XBOX, even though I didn't have a clue as to what I was doing. It was a graphic-intensive game called Mortal Combat and I was terrible. We had fun though. In fact, Jeremy was making me laugh because I played so badly. Time went by too quickly because before I realized it, the clock from upstairs was chiming ten and I knew that Nana was probably outside, waiting for me.

Jeremy walked me to the front door. "I'm glad that you came over and I'm sorry about before."

"It's okay." I reached up and kissed him. He kissed me back and after about a minute of lip play, I heard a horn. I couldn't believe my grandmother would do that. "I'd better go," I told him.

"The next time you visit, we should hang out again."

"Yeah, next time." But inside I wondered if there would ever be a next time. With my parents, you just never knew. "Call and e-mail me sometimes, Jeremy, okay?"

He nodded and kissed me again. Then I ran down the walk to Nana's car. When I looked back, he was striding through the door and I suddenly got the weirdest feeling that I would never see him again.

# ೫ Chapter Twenty-Six ಐ

My plane wasn't due to leave until six o'clock on Sunday. Around ten that morning, Ashley called and wanted to come over to see me. I was excited because I really wanted to see her too. Making it a small celebration, she brought Kammy and Shelly with her. When we saw one another, we just shrieked and started jumping up and down, just like Jane and I had, only this time we were louder.

"Just look at you!" Kammy said. "You've lost so much weight! You're even smaller than Ashley." Ashley flashed her a dirty look and Shelly gave her a nudge then said, "Let's go somewhere so we can talk."

It was unseasonably warm outside, considering how cold it had been the last few days, so we walked out to Nana's backyard. We sat on the patio furniture and after a few minutes Nana brought us some cookies and Cokes, hoping to make us all feel at home.

Kammy got right to the point. "Jane is very upset, Kathryn." She took a cookie and explained how I'd hurt her feelings by just leaving without saying anything. "And what's worse is that you haven't even called her."

"She hasn't called me either, guys and anyway, she started the fight."

The three of them just looked at one another, and I knew that they weren't saying everything they'd come to say.

"Okay, what's really going on?" I demanded.

Ashley hesitated and then said, "Well, it's just that Jane said she was concerned about your weight."

"There isn't anything to be *concerned* about," I spat out. By that point, I was getting angry. I didn't like being ganged up on like that.

Shelly's voice was softer. "It wasn't Jane's fault. She was just worried because she overheard her mom talking to your grandmother. And look at you, Kathryn ... you *have* lost a lot of weight."

"So what if I have?" I was fuming. "If that's all you came over for, then I guess it's time for you to leave."

"But we're your friends," Shelly whined. "We just want to help."

"Help what?" I was getting angrier by the second. "What is there to help?"

No one said anything for the longest time. It was like they were just waiting for the right thing to say, but no one knew what it was.

"Just call Jane before you leave," Kammy finally said. "You two have been friends for so long that you don't want to ruin that over some silly fight."

"She can call me if she wants to. I'm not calling because I didn't do anything," I replied stubbornly.

"Look," Ashley started, "we're really worried about you. I know you don't think there's anything to worry about but we can see you and you look really unhappy. You don't look like yourself and you really don't act like yourself either. You have an entirely different attitude. You seem so angry, Kathryn and you've never been angry with us. Not *this* angry, not even when Kammy ruined your hair." Kammy flashed her a dirty look, but they started nodding in agreement with one another. That was making me even angrier.

"Jane is over at Tori's," Kammy informed me. "Why don't we call them and let's meet at the mall before you have to go home?"

I felt too tired to go anywhere. I didn't want to even think about seeing so many people at once and I wasn't ready to talk to Jane. I wasn't sure I even wanted to be around these three anymore. I didn't want to talk about my weight anymore and I didn't want to be fussed over. I just wanted to take a nap.

"Thanks, guys, but I'm really tired. I didn't get to bed until late last night and I just really want to rest before I go home."

They looked disappointed, but before they left we all hugged and they promised to write and keep in touch. I watched them leave, knowing that it could be the last time any of us were ever really friends again.

ℬ    ℭ

At the airport as my flight's boarding was announced, Nana hugged me hard and I knew I'd miss her so much. "Come back again soon, Kathryn. Maybe you can come again for the Christmas holidays?"

I knew that my parents wouldn't let me but I didn't say that. "That would be great," I told her instead and I meant it. It was only once I'd gotten on the plane that I realized I had actually left without saying anything to Jane. I had mixed feelings about that, but I decided not to think about it.

I didn't want to go back to Sarasota; the thought of returning to school the next day filled me with dread. But I did miss my dad, so that was something to look forward to. I was so exhausted that I slept the entire plane ride and before I knew it, I was back in Florida. There I was, having to face everything bad all over again.

ℬ    ℭ

My parents were waiting for me the minute I got off the plane. I hugged Dad first and he kept telling me how much they'd missed me. "The house was just so empty without you, Katybug."

When my mother hugged me she practically yelled, "Kathryn Ann!"

I jumped back. "What?"

"How much weight have you lost?" Oh, not again, I thought. "It's just that I can feel your bones under your shirt."

"You're exaggerating, Mother." I rolled my eyes.

"Well, we'll see when you go to the doctor's, won't we?" She was just so smug.

On the ride home, I told them about Thanksgiving and about how Uncle Josh's kids had torn up Nana's house. I also told them about how rude they had acted and about how they had started throwing food during our meal. Dad started laughing at that.

"I don't think it's anything to laugh about," my mother snapped at him. "Your brother really needs to take better control of his children." My mother straightened her back a little, kind of like Mary had that night when she'd said those horrible things about me. But I didn't tell Mother or Dad about that. I figured it would just cause a serious fight! But Mother kept raving. "Kathryn was always so well behaved even at that age. I don't see why Josh and Mary let their children act like that."

Dad didn't say anything, but I could tell he thought it was funny. When he looked at me in the rearview mirror his eyes were twinkling, but I didn't think Mother noticed.

I decided to change the subject. "What did you two do for Thanksgiving?"

"We had a nice quiet dinner, just the two of us," Mother told me.

"We missed you though, Katybug," Dad looked at me again in the rearview mirror. "Nothing seemed the same while you were gone."

"We're glad you're back, Kathryn," Mother chimed it. "It's just that you promised to eat and you come back looking like one long bone."

I gave the back of her head a dirty look, but she couldn't see it. And suddenly, I felt tired again. I couldn't wait to get home so I could fall into bed. I knew that I had school the next day and I needed to rest up for it. I already dreaded returning to that hateful prison.

# ❧ Chapter Twenty-Seven ❧

On Monday, Mrs. Jamison informed us that we had a term paper due right before Christmas break. "It's going to count for more than half your grade and if you don't do well, you might have to take this class again next semester." As a final warning, she told us to pick our topics carefully and then we reviewed the proper way to write term papers.

I was determined to do well. At the beginning of the year, my English grades were good, but lately they'd fallen. I knew that I could do well on this paper and I knew that if I set my mind to it, I could even get an 'A' in the class. It became my goal to do well. I decided on the topic of animal rights. Since I'd been avoiding eating meat, this was something I thought would be interesting to me. Even though I wasn't a complete vegetarian, I knew that I might be one day. My parents thought it was just a phase I was going through and that was reason enough to keep pursuing it. For the first time in a long time, I felt excited about something going on at school.

❧    ❧

On Tuesday, I had to go see Dr. Brandt, so I didn't go to school that day. When I weighed in, I knew I was in trouble. I was down to eighty-five pounds.

"Most people gain weight over the holidays." Dr. Brandt tried to keep his voice light when he came in the room holding my chart. I ignored him.

"I've talked it over with your parents and we've decided to put you on a low-dosage antidepressant."

"But I don't want to take medicine," I defiantly replied.

His voice was no longer soft. I could tell he was losing patience with me. "You don't want to see a therapist, you don't want medicine. Kathryn, all I hear from you is what you *don't* want. Why don't you tell me what you *do* want?" He put the chart under his arm and looked at me.

"To be left alone." I narrowed my eyes at him and he took the chart and wrote something down. As he clicked the pen shut he said, "Well, young lady, that's not going to happen." He handed me a prescription and told me to start taking the pills right away. "A half of one every day for a week, then one every day after that."

I looked at the prescription, but I couldn't really tell what it was. I wasn't familiar with antidepressants or any other medicine, but obviously that was going to change.

"But I'm not depressed," I told my mother in that car. Before we left, Dr. Brandt had talked to Mother in private, although I had tried to overhear what they were saying. All I could make out was something about if this medicine didn't help, then therapy would be the next step and maybe even hospitalization.

"Well, something is going on with you and if this medicine doesn't help, we're going to find something that does." We pulled into McDonald's after we'd gotten the prescription filled and we went inside to eat. My mom ordered a chicken sandwich and fries and I got a side salad and water. She reminded me to take half of my medicine.

"That's pressed chicken, Mother," I informed her. "It's not even real."

I ate just a few bites of salad then told her I was ready to leave. She sighed and said that she really hoped the medicine worked.

ᙡ　ᙒ

The rest of the week I spent every minute I could at the library doing research. I also spent time on the Internet, reading stories about animals in unnecessary laboratory experiments where they endure physical pain before they are "sacrificed." I learned about other "lab animals" that are used in the testing of toxic chemicals, cosmetics and almost every kind of household product on the market. The more I read, the more interested I became. I decided that from then on, I was going to be more aware of what was going on around me. I was going to be careful about things like makeup, because it might have been tested on animals first. For the first time in a long time, I felt I had something else to focus on besides food and it felt good.

I took my medicine just as I was supposed to. I tried to eat, but it was harder than I thought it would be. At first, I had thought I was in control of what I was eating, but now I realized that my throat just didn't want to swallow food. I had a hard time with everything I ate. And if I did manage to get food down, my stomach hurt horribly since it hadn't held food in a while. I was scared because for the first time since all this had started, it occurred to me that I couldn't just simply turn this around at the drop of a hat.

Because solids were so hard for me to handle, I started having to put food in the blender. I drank a smoothie almost every day, but the fruit hurt my stomach so much that I would double over in pain. When my mother talked to Dr. Brandt about it, he said that I was going to have to learn how to eat all over again. I needed to start with things that were bland and soft. He even suggested that I start out on baby food. I was appalled by the thought. I just was no longer sure I could do this. My weight wasn't really changing but for the time being, no one said anything.

ᘿ    ᘾ

The second week in December I got e-mail from Jane. I'd been thinking about her, but I couldn't bring myself to e-mail her. I'd talked to Jeremy twice on the phone since I'd been back and he'd e-mailed me once. We weren't keeping in touch as much as I would have liked, but at least he hadn't forgotten about me completely. Anxious and reluctant all at the same time, I opened Jane's message.

Kathryn ... I just wanted to say that I was sorry for the way we left things. I never wanted anything to get out of control like that. We'd never had an argument like that before so I wasn't sure how to handle it. I should have called you, but I was angry that you left without saying good-bye. I don't know what has happened to us. We used to be so close. I just wanted to let you know that everything I said was just because I was worried about you.  I hope that we're still friends. Jane

She didn't use her regular ending, BFF. That kind of bothered me but it was just a small thing and I knew I should just let it go. I didn't respond right away because I didn't know what to say. I felt so bad about our fight, but I wasn't sure how to say I was sorry. Instead, I went back to my term paper. I worked on it every day. I had never worked so hard on anything in my life. My parents didn't know what I was doing because I wanted to surprise them with my grade once I was finished. I knew they thought I was going to fail and I was going to show them how well I really was doing. But *telling them* I wasn't going to fail wasn't enough—I wanted to *show* them the final grade. Just the thought of making them proud of me made me excited.

଼ଠ    ଔଃ

On Friday, a few days after I got Jane's e-mail, I finally wrote her back.

Jane ... I'm sorry about the way I left. I wanted to call you, but I wasn't sure what to say. And of course we're still friends. You have no idea how many times I wanted to pick up the phone and talk to you. I also wanted to tell you about my date with Jeremy. It was great, though it didn't start out that way. I'll have to tell you about it sometime when we're on the phone. When I left his house though, it was all good and he's called me a couple of times since then. We even e-

mailed, but I really wish I could see him again. If you talk to him, tell him I said hi and to e-mail me soon. I really miss you, Jane. I wish that I could visit Nana over the Christmas holidays, but I'd be more likely to win the lottery. My parents aren't letting me out of their sight lately. Talk to you soon!
 ~Kathryn~

I spent that entire weekend working on my term paper. It was almost finished, even though it wasn't due for another week and a half. I was staying in my room so much that my parents started worrying about that too. They didn't give me too much grief about it because at dinner, I was trying to eat better. Everything had to be put through the blender, but I was eating more bites and I wasn't throwing up. I was also taking my medicine, but that wasn't what was putting me in a good mood. It was the term paper and the 'A' I was sure I was going to get.

80 03

"Katybug, do you want to go get some ice cream?" Dad knocked on my door and poked his head in. It was Sunday night and I was exhausted from working. I was already in my nightshirt and it was barely seven o'clock.

Ice cream? I wasn't sure I wanted that. It was just so high in fat and I was already scared I was gaining weight too quickly, although I knew that's what I was supposed to be doing. I just wasn't sure I was ready to turn into another beach ball with legs.

"I'm kind of busy now," I told him.

He walked over to my desk. "What are you working on?" he asked me, eying my paper.

"Just homework," I replied noncommittally.

"Oh, you can take a break. Come on, it'll be fun. It'll be just the two of us."

"I really don't feel like it, Dad. I'm so tired," I explained, trying to weasel my way out.

He looked disappointed and I felt bad about that. But I couldn't eat ice cream and I knew that if I went, I would be forced to. He left the room disappointed and I felt so guilty that I just lay down for a while. I didn't realize how tired I was because before I knew it, Mother was waking me up, saying it was time for school.

# ❧ Chapter Twenty-Eight ❧

"How is your paper coming along in English?" Jared, a friend of Tiffany's, asked her that morning at school. I was standing by the lockers and I overheard them talking. Jared was tall and lanky, not really Tiffany's type. He was more of an 'in-group' wannabe.

"Actually, not so good." She sounded worried and she lowered her voice. "I haven't really even decided on a topic."

"Are you kidding me?" Then Jared whooped. "It's due in like a week."

"I know, I know. Just shut up," she said hatefully. "I'll think of something. It's just that I've had a lot going on lately." She sounded worried and I couldn't help but watch them while they talked. "Max and I are thinking about breaking up. Have you already heard?" She kind of tilted her head up at him, like she was flirting. But really, she was just messing with him. That's how Tiffany was. She was mean. She wanted all the guys to like her, even if she'd never consider dating them.

Jared looked a little amused. "Why are you two breaking up?" He shut his locker and they walked off together. I didn't hear anything else they were saying.

I didn't know why Tiffany and Max were thinking about breaking up and I didn't care. I just got some kind of interior happiness from knowing that Miss Perfect was having trouble with her paper. It helped that I just had a little more to do on mine and then I would have it completed.

I walked down the hall, feeling good about myself for the first time since I'd started school here. Maybe the medicine was helping some. The girls at lunch noticed that I was feeling better.

I still didn't eat so much, but at least I would join in on their conversations. We joked around and laughed a lot, which was, for me, a personal milestone.

That day at lunch, Allison, one of Tiffany's friends, came over to our table.

"Hi, Kathryn." She pulled up a chair. I must have looked surprised because she said, "I'm sorry to just bother you like this, but Tiffany is in real trouble with her paper. I know you two haven't really hit it off, but she would be really grateful if you would help her out with it."

"Help her?" I was skeptical. What did she really want?

"Sure, she just needs some help and we all know how well you do in English."

"I don't think she wants my help, Allison. We're not exactly friends."

Alison shook her head, "No, she really does want your help. She *needs* it, only she was scared to ask you herself."

"Why would she be scared to ask me?" I picked at my food, waiting for her to say something.

"Don't you get it?" Alison asked me as if I was mentally challenged. "This is so important to her. If she fails this class, she's in major trouble. Not only with her parents, but she'll be off the cheerleading squad and she just can't afford to lose everything she's worked so hard for. She was scared that if she asked you, you'd say no." Her voice sounded edgy but I didn't care.

"And she would be right. I'm not helping her."

"Oh, please, Kathryn. Really, she's desperate."

"Then you help her," I suggested.

The other girls were eating, trying to ignore the fact that we were having this insane conversation. Since I'd started at this school, all Tiffany and her friends had done was torment or ignore me and now they were asking for my help. They had so much nerve.

"I'm not as smart as you are. I don't think I could help her get a good grade," Allison said.

"Well, I'm not worried about her grade and I don't care if she fails."

With that, I got up and threw my tray of food away. I walked out of the lunchroom and into the library, where I sat until lunch was over, working on my paper. Then I went back to the library during my study period and worked until I finished it. I had never felt so good about completing something in my life. I'd accomplished something big and with time to spare and I was so happy with myself.

At home, I put the paper in my desk drawer until it was due. I couldn't wait until we got it back so I could show my parents how hard I'd worked. I knew I'd done a good job, so I was positive I would get a good grade. The paper wasn't due until right before the Christmas holidays and we wouldn't get them back until after the break. I didn't want to wait that long, but on the other hand, it gave me something to look forward to.

&#8359;   &#8360;

"Kathryn," my mother yelled for me that night. "Someone is on the phone for you."

My heart leaped—it had to be Jeremy. I excitedly picked up the phone in my room. "Hello?"

"Kathryn?" It wasn't Jeremy. It was a girl's voice that I didn't recognize.

"Yes?"

"Hi, it's Allison."

My heart fell. Why would she be calling me? "If this is about Tiffany, I don't want to hear it."

"Actually, it's not. I just thought I would see if you were having trouble with your term paper? I've been calling around, and it seems like everyone is having trouble finishing theirs."

"No, I'm not having trouble. In fact, I'm finished with it," I told her arrogantly. Usually I hate arrogance, but in this situation, it seemed to fit.

"You're actually finished with your paper?" She sounded happily surprised. "All of it?"

"Uh-huh."

"Well, I need a break from mine. Do you want to go to the mall and do some Christmas shopping?"

My mind was whirling. Why would she want to hang out with me? "Thanks, but I don't think so."

"Oh, why not? It'll be fun and besides, I haven't gotten anything for anyone yet and I'm really behind."

I knew that I needed to go shopping too, but I didn't want to go with her. "Actually, I'm busy tonight."

"Well, um, okay, if you don't want to go shopping, I understand."

She sounded disappointed for some reason. We awkwardly said good-bye and then hung up. That was the strangest conversation and I had to wonder what was really up.

# ≈ Chapter Twenty-Nine ≈

When the last day of school before the Christmas holidays arrived, the same day the term papers were due, I couldn't find mine anywhere. I searched in my desk where I'd left it, but it wasn't there. Then I looked around my desk. I tore apart my closet; I tore apart my entire room. "MOTHER!" I yelled for her.

She came running into my room, looking worried and frazzled, do I guess I must have frightened her. "What on earth are you yelling about?"

"Have you seen anything that looked like a term paper? It was in my desk drawer."

"What are you talking about?"

I was breathing so hard that I couldn't catch my breath. "My paper, have you seen it?" I gasped.

"I haven't been in your room, Kathryn. Lately, you've kept everything in such neat order that I haven't had a reason to come in here."

"But I can't find my term paper and it's due today." I knew I was hysterical, but it didn't make sense that it was missing.

"I didn't know you had a paper due. And I haven't seen it." She helped me look around my desk, but it wasn't anywhere to be found.

"Has anyone been in my room besides you or Dad?"

She shook her head. "Not that I know of, Kathryn. Maybe you just left it at school."

I shook my head in a crazy motion. "I wouldn't do that. It was just so important. It counts for over half our grade and I left it here, in this drawer." I pointed to where I'd left it. By that point, I was near tears. I couldn't imagine what had happened to it.

My mother looked at me skeptically. "I don't remember you working on a paper."

"I've been working on it every day since we got back from Thanksgiving break." To make matters worse, I couldn't even find my notes that I'd kept on the paper. Everything was gone and nothing made sense. I couldn't go to school without that paper.

"Did you type it on the computer?" she asked.

"Oh! You're right!" I squealed. "I saved it on Dad's computer."

I ran downstairs and turned on the computer. There it was, just as I'd left it. I had never felt so relieved in my life. I knew I would have to get another cover for it, but at least the work was there. My mother came into the den as I printed out the paper.

"I wanted to surprise you and Dad when I got my grade," I told her, "but since I don't know where the other one is, I'll show you now."

She took it from the printer and looked at it. "This is really good, Kathryn." I could tell she was genuinely impressed.

"I had no idea you had worked this hard. I'm so proud of you."

I was beaming by the time I left for school. It was still a mystery as to where my first printout had gone, but I figured it would matter as long as I had another one to hand in.

୫০ ଓଃ

During the last period of school that day, Mr. Griffin announced over the loud speaker that he wanted to see both Tiffany and me in his office. The entire class went, "Ooooh!" I just rolled my eyes. I wasn't sure what the conference was about, but I knew I hadn't done anything wrong so I wasn't too worried. When I got to his office though, I saw that Mrs. Jamison was also inside. At the sight of her, my stomach kind of knotted up. Tiffany was already there, so the meeting got under way.

"It seems, girls, that we have a problem," Mr. Griffin said.

I looked at Tiffany for clues, but she just looked away.

"What's wrong?" My voice was shaking by then. My heart was racing and I felt it beating in my ears.

Mrs. Jamison looked down at me accusingly. "It seems that you and Tiffany turned in the same term paper."

My mind was whirling. I thought I had heard her wrong because that would be impossible.

"I don't understand," I said, finally finding my voice.

"Well, the papers you both turned in are exactly alike. And we were just wondering how that happened."

To back up her claim, Mr. Griffin stood up and handed us both our papers. It was all hitting me now. Tiffany was the one who had taken my paper. How she got in my room, I didn't know, but that's what the phone call was about—the one from Allison. I was certain of if. She had somehow found out that I was finished and was trying to get me out of my room so Tiffany could get in. That was why she had wanted to go shopping with me. Only I didn't go, so how had Tiffany gotten a hold of my paper? My mind was spinning in an attempt to figure it all out.

"Look, this term paper is my own. I've worked on it since Mrs. Jamison gave out the assignment," I asserted, but no one seemed to listen.

"This is very good work, Kathryn," Mrs. Jamison said in a stone cold voice. "And I hate to say it, but your work hasn't been this good since the beginning of the year."

She didn't believe me.

I looked at Mr. Griffin. "You have to believe me; I did this work." I tried to tell them how I had to print it again this morning because my copy was missing, but they didn't say anything.

"I've worked very hard, Mrs. Jamison," Tiffany chimed in. "I'm against the cruelty of animals and I was very excited about getting to express my opinions. I picked this topic the very day you assigned it. I believe in this paper. You can ask Allison. Every word of it is mine, and I can prove it."

I couldn't believe what I was hearing. How could she prove it?

"Well, it's just one girl's word against another's and until we figure out who is the plagiarist, you'll both get Fs," Mr. Griffin said in an icy tone.

Tears welled up in my eyes. I'd worked so hard. This was just unbelievable.

After Mr. Griffin dismissed us from his office, I didn't go back to class. Instead, I just went home. I had to talk to my mother. She had to believe me. *Someone* had to believe me. I defiantly walked home, knowing full well that I could get in trouble for skipping the rest of the class period, but not really caring because, to me, this was much worse.

When I got home, my mother was in the kitchen, leafing through cookbooks. Not expecting me yet, she looked at the clock. "What are you doing home so early, Kathryn?" She looked concerned. And suddenly I couldn't help myself. I just started crying. "My paper, the one I couldn't find—" I couldn't finish the sentence.

She came over to me and hugged me. "What about your paper? You printed it out this morning, right?"

"Yes, but Tiffany turned in the same paper and now no one believes me and we're both getting Fs." By that point, I was crying so hard that she could barely make out what I was saying.

"Tiffany did what?" She walked over to the refrigerator and took out a Sprite. She handed it to me as she might a peace offering. "Take some sips of this and calm down."

I obediently drank some of the Sprite and it burned going down. I took deep breaths to calm myself down. It didn't work though because I was so upset that I couldn't stop crying.

"Now Kathryn, tell me what's going on."

I told her everything in between sobs. When I was finished, she looked quite concerned and went over to the phone. I didn't know what she was doing. I was just too worn out to care. I went into the living room and fell on the couch, utterly spent. I just curled up in a ball, wishing that all this would just go away.

"I need to make an appointment to see Mr. Griffin." Then there was a pause. "Yes, right away." Another pause. "No, after the Christmas break is too late. I need to talk with him immediately." Another pause. "This afternoon at four thirty will be fine." Then she dialed again. "Hi, Sally, this is Abby. Could you come over for a moment? I think we have something to discuss." Those were the snippets of conversation I overheard from the living room.

After she got off the phone, my mother came into the living room.

"I cut you a piece of cake and there's another Sprite on the table. Try to eat something, okay?"

Obeying her command, I went to the kitchen, got the cake and took it up to my room. I put the cake on my desk then strained my ears to hear what was going on downstairs. When I heard the doorbell ring, I tiptoed to the top of the stairs.

"Thanks for coming over, Sally," I heard my mother say.

"Is there a problem? You sounded upset." I couldn't see what they were doing, but their voices faltered a little. So, I could tell they had moved their conversation into the living room. I walked down a few steps and strained my ears harder.

"Well, yes, there does seem to be a problem. It seems that our girls wrote the same term paper."

"What?" Mrs. Morgan sounded genuinely confused.

"Well, Kathryn has been working on an English paper for about a month and suddenly it disappeared. Thankfully, she saved it on the computer, but it seems that Tiffany turned in the same paper. They're both getting Fs and I just want to know how this mix-up came about."

"I'm sure I don't know what you're talking about, Abby. I haven't seen any term paper."

Mother sighed. "I didn't want to bring this up, especially in front of Kathryn, but a few days ago while Kathryn was running errands with William, Tiffany came over to borrow some colored pencils for a poster she said she had to do for a history assignment. I sent her up to Kathryn's room to get them and didn't think anything else about it."

So *that* was how Tiffany had gotten into my room.

After a pause, my mother said, "I didn't think anything about it until this paper came up and now I'm just wondering ..."

"Are you suggesting that Tiffany took Kathryn's paper?" Mrs. Morgan interrupted, her voice very strained. "Because if that's what you're saying, Abby, you couldn't be more wrong. My Tiffany has always made good grades. It's Kathryn who hasn't been doing well at school."

"That's what I'm trying to get to the bottom of. I want to know what happened, and I have an appointment with Mr. Griffin at four thirty this afternoon so I can do just that. I thought it would be good if we both went with our daughters."

"I'll discuss this with Tiffany," Mrs. Morgan abruptly replied, stomping out of the house. The juicy gossip over, I went back up to my room.

Tiffany had said that she could prove the paper was hers, but how? I couldn't imagine how she could do that, but my head was hurting too much to think about it. I went to the medicine cabinet and took some Tylenol then decided to take a bath. Needing the relaxation, I even used some scented bath beads. I soaked in the luxuriousness until my mother knocked on the door, wondering if I was okay.

"It's almost time to meet with the principal, Kathryn. You need to get out of the bathtub!"

I jumped out and hurried to get dressed. I was downstairs in record time and my mother and I were in Mr. Griffin's office by four twenty-five. We were told to wait by his secretary. As we were waiting, I kept wondering if Tiffany and her mother would show up.

"Good afternoon, Mrs. Bailey." Mr. Griffin came into the office and greeted my mother with a handshake. To me, his tone was cold. "Hello, Kathryn, I guess I know what this is about."

"Well," my mother started, "I know that this isn't a pleasant situation, but I thought it was something that needed to be cleared up. I realize that Kathryn's grades haven't shown her best work lately, but I know that she did this paper. The work was on our personal computer."

Mr. Griffin sat his things down and walked over to the edge of his desk. He leaned against it. "Mrs. Morgan called after she spoke to you, Mrs. Bailey, and said that same thing about Tiffany's paper. I'm afraid that's just not enough proof. Anyone could get access to work on a computer. It just doesn't prove anything.

"But I did the work," I said. "I worked on it for weeks."

"That may be," Mr. Griffin said, "but we can't accuse another student of cheating unless we have solid proof. So, until something comes up, we have to fail both of you."

I thought I was going to cry, so I bit my lip so I wouldn't. Then I had a thought. "Call Jared!" I exclaimed. "He'll tell you! I heard Tiffany tell him just a week ago that she hadn't even picked out a topic!" My heart was racing. This was my only chance.

"I really don't think it's fair to fail them both," my mother said. "Can't they do it over or even have a test instead?" She wasn't even listening. No one was. I tried again.

"Call Jared into this office and he will explain to you that Tiffany couldn't have possibly done the work. A week ago she hadn't even picked out a topic yet, so how could she have done all this work?"

"Jared Martin?" Mr. Griffin asked and I nodded. This was a small school, and there was only one Jared that I knew of. He hesitated for a minute and then looked up Jared's phone number in the student directory. When he got him on the phone, he asked him some very pointed questions. While he was talking to him, Tiffany and Mrs. Morgan knocked on the door.

"We're sorry we're late," Mrs. Morgan said. They strolled in and took seats on the other side of the room.

"It's quite all right." Under his breath, Mr. Griffin explained that he was on the phone with Jared Martin and that he would only be a minute. Tiffany paled for a moment, and then she looked at me like she could kill me. I'd never before seen such hatred in anyone's eyes. It was so glaringly obvious that even my mother noticed it too. Wanting to offer reassurance, she just patted my hand and whispered for me to ignore her.

Apparently Jared was doing most of the talking because everything was so quiet that I was getting nervous. I could hear the clock ticking and the sound of the janitor's vacuum cleaner turning on and off. It seemed like forever had passed but it was only a couple of minutes before Mr. Griffin said, "Thank you, Jared, you were very helpful."

"Well, I've been enlightened about a few things." Mr. Griffin nodded knowingly, turning toward Mrs. Morgan and Tiffany. "Jared just told me that what Kathryn has said is in fact the truth."

He looked pointedly at Tiffany. "Tiffany, did you have a topic picked out from the beginning as you told us earlier today in the office?"

Tiffany turned a purplish red color then stammered, "Well, um, yes, well ..."

"Jared just told me that not only did you not have a topic picked out but that you also said that you would 'figure something out.' Did that mean that you would simply steal another student's work?"

"Jared is a liar!" Tiffany spat out with such hatefulness that both our mothers looked shocked. I'd seen her angry before, so it didn't faze me, but finally my mother could see her for what she was.

"Jared is just getting back at me for not going out with him. It's his way of getting revenge."

"I don't think so, Tiffany and I'm sorry to say that with this information, I'm going to have to let Mrs. Jamison know. You will receive an F for this paper."

"You cannot fail my daughter, Mr. Griffin." Mrs. Morgan stood up. She looked as angry as Tiffany had been. "Tiffany is a good student and you won't destroy that just because some anorexic nobody comes in here with wild stories. And who is Jared anyway? He might just be some friend of Kathryn's who's ready to frame my child." Mrs. Morgan took a deep breath and started again. "Mr. Morgan and I contribute a great deal of money to this school, Mr. Griffin and I will NOT have my Tiffany fail a class because of someone else's word."

In response, my mother's eyes flashed such anger that I knew she was about to snap. I could tell she was about to say something, but Mr. Griffin intervened. "Actually, I didn't think about it until now, but there is another solution. We can look at both computers, yours and the Baileys' and see what date these documents were created." Tiffany let out a gasp at that, knowing she was busted. Mr. Griffin knew it too. He went on. "And I think it's inappropriate to talk about another child like you just did. That isn't the example you need to set for your daughter," he scolded Mrs. Morgan.

Mr. Griffin looked at Mother and me. "Mrs. Bailey, I'm so sorry that we've caused you all this trouble. You do realize I was only doing my job."

She nodded. "Yes, I do realize that. I also now realize that everything Kathryn has been telling us from the beginning was true." She looked at me apologetically. "We'll be taking Kathryn out of Vanguard and placing her in public school after the holidays are over. Please have her records ready for us."

With that, she marched out of the room and I followed her. I had never felt such relief wash over me as I did that day. It was like having a really bad nightmare then waking up and realizing that it was just that—a nightmare.

# ❧ Chapter Thirty ☙

During the first week of Christmas vacation, I went to the beach almost every day. It gave me a lot of time to think. I thought about my parents and how distant we'd become in the past year. Mother told Dad everything that had happened in regards to the term paper and he said he felt so bad about not noticing there was a problem that big. They both promised that they would listen to me from now on about things that were bothering me. I wasn't sure I believed them, but I could hope.

I was just glad that they finally saw Tiffany for what she was. Her eyes opened to the true Morgans, Mother decided that she and my dad were going to quit the Country Club and that she was going to start working more hours at the hospital. She enjoyed it and she no longer wanted to be associated with anything that the Morgans did. My mother was still quite angry over the way Mrs. Morgan had talked to me. Although Mrs. Morgan called a few days after the incident, Mother was still too upset with her to accept any kind of apology.

I also thought about Jeremy a lot. I realized that it had been a while since I'd heard from him. Jane and I had talked a few times, but she never mentioned him. I couldn't help wondering what had happened.

I thought about my health too. I wondered if I was getting better. I was still taking my meds like I was supposed to, but my weight hadn't changed much. Dr. Brandt was giving my parents a hard time about it. He kept insisting that I needed more help than just the antidepressants. I fought it though and my parents didn't push me.

Even though the beach was scattered with people who were walking or jogging ... or even just sitting and talking to their friends, I felt like I was on the only one there. I felt invisible to everyone around me. Entrenching myself in that solitude, I climbed onto a huge, lonesome rock that provided a great vantage-point to watch the waves crash onto the shore, then withdraw back into the ocean and go back just to do it all over again ... it was almost hypnotic. Then suddenly, I felt someone touch my shoulder. Not expecting it, I jumped a mile into the air.

"Oh!" I yelled and spun my head around to see the cutest guy I'd ever seen since I'd moved here. I was instantly embarrassed for yelling out like that.

"Sorry, I didn't mean to scare you. I said hello, but you didn't hear me."

"I guess I was in my own world or something," I admitted to him then realized what a stupid thing that had been to say. *'In my own world'?* What did that mean anyway? He probably thought I was an escapee from a mental institution. Which according to Dr. Brandt, I wasn't far from it.

"I'm Jason Neely," he told me.

"I'm Kathryn Bailey." I scooted over to make room for him on the rock. "Do you want to sit down?"

He sat down beside me, but we didn't say anything for a minute. I just looked at him, losing myself in his incredible gorgeousness. He had light brown hair that almost looked blonde in the sun and greenish-gray eyes. He was probably about five foot nine and he was thin, but it was the kind of thin that worked for him. His arms looked bigger though, as if he worked out. I couldn't be sure, though and I didn't want to ask. He was also very tan, even though it was the dead of winter. But of course, this *was* Florida after all and most people were tan all year around.

I didn't realize I was staring until he said, "Why are you looking at me that way?"

I looked away, embarrassed all over again. My face was hot and I was just sure he would notice me blushing. "Sorry, I didn't realize I was staring." That wasn't the truth but what else could I say?

"Are you new to Sarasota?" he asked me, steering the conversation into safer territory.

I shrugged. "Kind of. We moved here in August."

He then asked me where I had moved from and we talked about that for a while. I explained to him about my dad's job and how we had to come here.

"Where do you go to school?" he asked me.

"Well, when school starts again, I'll be going to Beach Valley High."

"Really? That's where I go. What grade are you in?" I liked how he looked when he asked a question. He gazed right into my eyes, like he was really listening.

"Ninth," I told him.

"Oh, cool. Me too." Then he thought for a minute. "But you said you moved here at the beginning of the school year. Where were you going before?"

"Vanguard Academy." I was almost embarrassed to admit it.

"Ooooh ..." he responded, a knowing look on his face.

"Yeah, don't make a big thing out of it. I didn't fit in and so now I'm finally getting out of there."

He smiled and I noticed that his teeth were perfectly straight and so white that he could have been in a toothpaste ad. But even more impressive were the dimples he had in his cheeks. For a minute, I wanted to reach over and stick my finger in one of them. I decided not to though. I didn't even know this guy and I didn't think poking my finger into his cheek would leave a great first impression.

We spent the rest of the afternoon talking as if we'd been friends for a while. Jason had a funny sense of humor and he made me laugh. It was the first time I'd laughed like that in a long time and I hated that I had to leave.

"Will you be back tomorrow?" he asked me.

"Sure. I come here almost every day."

"Great. Meet me here tomorrow at noon then."

I smiled. "Okay, great."

He got up and started to walk away. "See you tomorrow Kathryn," He winked at me as he descended from our perch and I smiled all the way home.

ఴ   ౽

That night, after dinner, I went to the computer to check my e-mail. To my surprise, I discovered that Jane had written. I was excited to see what she had to say, but I was even more excited to tell her about Jason and the beach.

Kathryn,

I hope that you're having a great holiday. I know that you're excited about not having to go back to private school, but I wish that you could still move back here. Things here are good. Chris and I are still seeing each other, though I still don't know what to get him for Christmas. I'm sending yours tomorrow priority, but don't open it until Christmas. I really hope you like it!

I wanted to call you and tell you this over the phone, but I was kind of scared to. I hate giving bad news, so I'm taking the easy way out ... e-mail. You've asked me about Jeremy, but I've avoided telling you because I didn't think it would last. Now I guess it is, so here goes: Jeremy has been seeing Alyssa Atwood. I hope that you're not going to be upset. I would have told you sooner but like I said, I didn't think it would really last. Unfortunately, they seem to like each other, and I wanted to tell you before you did something like send him a Christmas card. I hope you're not too bummed out. I don't know what he sees in her anyway ... she's not even pretty and her personality sucks. None of us like her, Katy ... we just can't figure out why he does!

E-mail me back ... BFF, Jane!

So that was why I hadn't heard from Jeremy! I didn't know how to feel. I knew that he and I wouldn't keep in touch forever, but I had hoped we would still be friends enough that if he wanted to see someone else, he would tell me. Furthermore, I didn't like the idea of being replaced so easily. I actually thought he liked me!

I didn't e-mail Jane back. Instead, I went to my room and tore up the card I was going to send him. I was glad that Jane had told me because I would have been completely mortified about mailing him something when he was dating someone else. I'm sure that he and Alyssa would have gotten a huge laugh about that. Then I got Jane's gift out and wrapped it. I would ask Mother to take it to the post office the next day. I had gotten her a Jewel CD that I knew she loved, even though it was an old one and a Nike watch that was too cute. It was pink and yet sporty, the perfect combination of feminine yet athletic. After our misunderstanding, I'd wanted to somehow make things up to her. It was a little pricey but I'd had Mother's credit card with me when I bought it and I doubted that she even noticed. I couldn't wait for her to get it. I would tell Mother to mail it priority, like Jane had mailed mine, whatever that meant.

ᴆ    ᴂ

The next day, I met Jason at the beach at noon as planned. True to his word, he was already sitting there when I arrived. After I climbed up on the rock, I realized that he'd brought us a picnic lunch. I started laughing and yet when I saw that he'd brought so much food, I felt a terror in my heart. I wasn't sure I could eat in front of him. I was just getting used to eating small amounts and even then, it was still hard. He'd made sandwiches and he'd brought pickles and chips and grapes and sodas and even a box of doughnuts for dessert.

"How did you get all this to the beach?" I asked as he pulled out a blanket and spread everything out. He nodded toward his bicycle and I just started laughing. It had a basket in the front and I could just imagine how geeky he looked driving down the road on a bicycle with stuff in the basket.

"Hey!" He pretended to be offended. "Don't laugh. I had to borrow that ugly thing from my ten-year-old neighbor. But I got everything here and aren't you glad I did?" He grinned at me then and I fell over laughing.

"Yes, I'm very glad," I told him truthfully. "How far do you live from here, Jason?" I realized I didn't even know where he lived.

"My dad and I live about two miles that way," He pointed in the opposite direction of where I live. I'd never been down that way, so I didn't know what was there.

"I live about a mile that way." I pointed in the other direction.

He rolled his eyes. "Of course you do. You live in the richy part of town." His eyes were twinkling so I knew he was teasing. I had only been around him a couple of times but I already picked up on the fact that when he teased, his eyes danced. It was so cute.

But for me, my neighborhood was nothing to joke about. Of course he didn't understand my contempt for my affluent neighbors and I didn't expect him to. "Oh yeah, right. As if I wanted to live there. Believe me, you can have it."

He playfully nudged me. "No thank you. When you talk about it, I wonder what all the hype is about."

My eyes kind of narrowed. "Well, I don't know either," I responded in a small voice then reached over and picked up a grape.

He started eating a sandwich and I just watched him. He seemed so relaxed just sitting in the sun, eating picnic food and not thinking about how many calories he was consuming. I continued to eat a few grapes, but I left out the other stuff.

"You don't eat a lot, do you?" he inquired observantly.

I just smiled at him and shrugged. If he only knew, I thought. That was all he said about it though and I was glad. Changing the subject, we talked about other things. I found out that he was already fifteen—he'd had a birthday in November. It was then that I informed him that I didn't turn fifteen until March.

We talked about school and the music we liked and I told him about Jane and how I missed my friends at home.

"Do you have any brothers or sisters?" I asked him.

"No, I'm an only child."

"Yeah, me too."

"You said you and your dad live here. Where's your mom?" I knew I was being nosy, but I was curious.

"She's in Los Angeles. My parents aren't officially divorced, but they're separated because my mother is an actress and my dad got tired of her drama-filled life. So we moved here about a year ago. He wanted to get as far away from her lifestyle as he could. And since Mom is on the West Coast, he picked the East Coast." He tried to laugh but I could tell he didn't really mean it.

My eyes widened. "Is she anyone I know?"

"Do you know Vanessa Randolph?" he asked me as he bit into a doughnut.

"Of course!" I shrieked. "Everyone knows her." Vanessa Randolph was famous for starring in a nighttime drama. "Is she your *mother*?" I was completely impressed.

"No, my mother is Elizabeth Neely. Vanessa Randolph is someone she wants to be like." His eyes were twinkling again and I realized he was teasing. I burst out laughing. I'd fallen right into that.

"Actually"—he got serious again—"my mom has been in a few commercials and she played a small part in a daytime soap opera, but right now she's trying for a pilot in a sitcom." He paused for a minute and looked at me. "She really wants this, but I know that if she gets it, most likely my parents won't ever get back together." He got quiet then and we just sat and watched the waves crash on the sand.

# ꙮ Chapter Thirty-One ꙮ

Thanks in large part to my friendship with Jason, Christmas
vacation flew by and before I knew it, school was starting again. I
had wanted to go to Atlanta over the holidays to see Nana but as
I'd predicted, my parents wouldn't let me. Over break, I had to
see Dr. Brandt only once and that hadn't gone too well. I had
lost a few pounds and Dr. Brandt reminded me that if I lost any
more weight, I would end up in the hospital. He talked again
about therapy and he told me that it would get to a point where I
wouldn't have any choice. He stressed to my mother that he was
really concerned, pointing out that I didn't seem to be getting
any better. The whole time we were there, my parents wore
worried expressions, but they kept thinking a miracle would
happen and I would be fine. I guess I thought the same thing.

We had a quiet Christmas, just the three of us and although
I dreaded seeing the holiday end, I mostly dreaded going back
to school. I was scared to start all over again since my last
experience had been so bad. But at least this time when I started
school, I would have a friend. Jason and I now talked on the
phone almost every day. Sometimes we would meet at the beach
to just hang out and talk. Other times we would go to really bad
movies and make fun of the plot and acting. It was so much fun
... more fun than I'd had since I'd moved to Sarasota. Of
course, he still saw his friends from school and he even asked
me to come along and meet them. I wasn't ready for that
though. I knew that he had a lot of friends and I wasn't ready to
surround myself with people yet.

My parents hadn't actually met Jason but they knew about
him because I talked about him a lot. Most of the time, I just
met him places. If it was the beach I could walk, but anywhere

else Dad had to drive me. I think he was just glad that I was getting out of the house and being more like a normal teenager. Mother didn't think the same way though. She worried about what I was up to. She was never happy, no matter what I did. She always found something to worry about.

&#8734; &#8518;

On Christmas Day, Jason came by to seem me. When I answered the door, I was surprised to see him but I was also excited. His dad was sitting in the car waiting on him, but I acted as if I didn't notice.

"I hope you don't care that I just popped over without calling." He looked a little embarrassed. He was dressed in a blue sweater and khaki pants. He looked nice and I told him that.

"You look nice too, Kathryn." I was just wearing my old jeans and a gray hoodie. I couldn't look nice but it was sweet that he said so.

I walked outside and stood on the porch. It was very typical Florida weather—too warm for December.

"You have an amazing house, Kathryn. I found your address in the phone book. I knew you lived in a nice neighborhood, but I had no idea it would be like this."

I shrugged. "It's an okay house, but it's just a house." I wanted to know why he had come over, so I shifted the subject. "I'm glad you came by. It's good to see you," I told him. "My parents are in the kitchen—do you want to meet them?"

"Maybe some other time. I only have a few minutes." He nodded toward his dad by way of explanation. "And I wanted to see you before I had to leave."

"Leave?" I asked, confused.

"Yeah." He started shuffling his feet around. "I have to go to LA to see my mother. I'm not looking forward to seeing her though. I haven't really talked to her since the separation, but my flight leaves tonight so I have to go." He paused for a minute.

Then added, "I also wanted to give you this." He then handed me a beautifully wrapped box.

I took the box from and opened it, fumbling with excitement. Inside lay a beautiful pair of earrings in the shape of dolphins.

"They're beautiful, Jason. Thank you so much." I reached out and hugged him.

"Well, I saw those and the first thing I thought about was you. Since we met at the beach, it just seemed like it fit you perfectly."

"Wait right here," I told him and I ran upstairs. I was back before he could even ask me where I was going. I handed him the gift I'd been saving for him and he opened it right away.

"Oh cool! Thanks, Katy ... you knew I wanted this!" I could tell he really liked it and that made me even happier. I had gone to every store in Sarasota trying to decide on the right gift. Finally, I just took the easy way out and chose a Green Day CD, *American Idiot.* I just didn't know him that well but I knew that he liked Green Day. Now I felt bad though because his gift had more personal meaning than mine.

While we were standing on the porch, talking, a really horrible thought occurred to me. "You'll be back in time for school, right?"

"Yes, I'll be back," he assured me. "I'll actually be back the day before, so I'll call you as soon as I get home."

I smiled at him, glad that he understood how nervous I was about school starting back.

I thanked him again for the earrings and I told him I couldn't wait until he got back. "Don't forget your autograph book," I teased him and he laughed as he ran to the car.

                              ဢ     G3

True to his word, Jason called me the minute he got home. With so much to catch up on, we talked for over an hour. He told me about LA and how wonderful the weather was. I didn't want to ask him too many questions about his mom because I didn't want to come across at nosy since he never seemed to want to talk about her. But after a few minutes, he opened up to me on his own. He told me how strained it had been being there and how he blamed his mom for the separation. He also told me that he thought his mother was selfish to choose acting over her family. I could relate to him in some ways since I blamed my mother for most of the things that went on in my life too. We talked about that for a while then he told me that he would wait for me at the office entrance the next day at school so I wouldn't have to find my classes alone. I let him know how much I appreciated the help and then we hung up.

Playing over the various possibilities for the next day in my head, I didn't sleep much that night and was up two hours too early the next morning. It was a good thing I'd allowed myself some extra preparation time, however, because I was just so indecisive about what to wear. For Christmas, my parents had bought me clothes, *colored* clothes, so I had a lot of things to choose from. I was slowly getting out of my Hot Topic phase, but I still kept what I'd bought there hanging in my closet for comfort. After trying on five different outfits, I finally decided on a floral drawstring skirt that was really comfortable and a wine colored blouse that matched the skirt. I critically looked at myself in the full-length mirror and decided that it would just have to do. I felt strange inside, unlike the way I usually felt and I decided that it was just nerves.

At breakfast, my mother tried to make me eat. In fact, she practically chased me around the table, offering me food.

"Mother, honestly, I can't eat this morning."

She and Dad gave each other a glance that I didn't like.

"It's not like that," I tried to assure them. "I'm just really nervous this morning and if I eat anything, I'll throw up."

"Well, at least eat a yogurt." Mother went to the refrigerator and handed me a strawberry banana yogurt and I took it just to keep her quiet. I knew I couldn't eat it though, so I just put it down and got some juice. I only took a sip because it felt funny going down.

"Are you driving me to school this morning?" I asked my dad.

"Yes." He put his newspaper down and took a sip of coffee. "I'm taking you on my way to work."

"Then can we please go?" I was impatient. I couldn't walk to the new school; it was too far so I had to rely on my parents. It wasn't something I liked but I didn't care, as long as I didn't have to go back to Vanguard.

"Why the hurry, Katybug?" He looked at his watch. "It's only seven fifteen. You have plenty of time."

He didn't understand. I wanted to get there early so I could get my schedule and still meet Jason. I sighed. "It's my first day. I have to get my schedule, I have to find my locker, I have to do a lot of things before eight o'clock—so, could we please go?"

Dad drank the rest of his coffee in one gulp and got up. "Well, Abby, I guess we'll see you later."

"Don't forget, Kathryn," my mother interrupted, "I'll pick you up right after school, so please watch for me."

I sighed heavily. "I'll watch for you, Mother." Geez, what did she think I was going to do?

"I just wanted to remind you, that's all."

I didn't want to get into anything with her, so I just said fine and went to the car. Outside, across the street, we saw Mrs. Morgan and Tiffany getting into their car to leave. Spying us, Mrs. Morgan ran across the street to us and stopped my dad. I just got in the car, not at all in the mood for the scene she would undoubtedly create.

"I'm so sorry about everything, William. I know it's been a hard year and I feel terrible about everything I said and everything that Tiffany did to make things worse. Please be forgiving."

"Sally, it's not about forgiving. Your daughter put Kathryn through hell and we didn't even believe her. It's more like Abby and I need to forgive ourselves."

"Well, at least reconsider coming back to the Country Club. So many people were asking about you. I just didn't know what to say ..." She trailed off and Dad interrupted her.

"It's not the place for us, Sally. I'm sorry. I really have to go." Mrs. Morgan peeked her head into the car and took her chances with me. "I hope you're feeling better, Kathryn, really." I didn't say anything and Dad slowly backed the car out of the driveway, leaving Mrs. Morgan's half-hearted apologies hanging in the air.

On the way to school, my dad tried to make me feel better by starting funny conversation, but for some reason, I just couldn't shake the strange feeling that I had. I tried to convince myself that it was just nerves and that the encounter with Mrs. Morgan hadn't helped, but I couldn't be sure.

When he pulled up to Beach Valley High School, I noticed the difference immediately. The school was big with a large Eagle in the middle of building where the entrance to the school was located. I deductively guessed that they were the Beach Valley Eagles. Much friendlier than Wildcats, I thought.

"Have a great day, Katybug," Dad said and I furtively looked around hoping that no one heard him call me that. Making my escape before he could embarrass me further, I just shut the car door and walked toward the building.

The school was just one level but it was shaped in an L. I wondered if I could get lost, but I remembered that I had Jason to help me so I tried not to worry. When I walked through the double doors, I could feel my heart beating heavily in my chest. I felt like it was beating too quickly and I didn't know how to slow it down.

Turning my attention back to the task at hand, I found the office right away. It was the first thing you noticed when you walked in because there was a huge sign that said, "All visitors must report to the office."

When I walked in, I saw a lady who was probably in her forties sitting behind a desk. I hoped my voice worked because she asked me if she could help me. For a minute, I just looked at her blankly. Then I stammered out, "I'm Kathryn Bailey. I'm new."

She smiled at me reassuringly, but didn't seem to be expecting me like they had at Vanguard. She started shuffling through piles of papers. It took her ten minutes and two phone calls to find out where my records were. Finally, she found what she was looking for.

"Here is your locker number, your combination and your schedule. If you have any questions, remember you can come in anytime. Also, we have a wonderful bunch of students who would be glad to help you." She smiled at me again and I tried to smile back, but I think I just got my papers and walked out.

"There you are!" I heard a voice behind me say. I turned around and there was Jason. It was so good to see someone familiar in such a big, unfamiliar place. He looked really nice too. He had on cargo pants and a dark green shirt that matched his eyes. He was a really cute guy and for the first time, I worried that since we were at school rather than alone at the beach, he might ditch me to be with his friends. We were becoming really good friends, but I hadn't had to share my friendship with him. What if he decided he didn't want to hang out with me now that he was back with all his school friends? But then I realized how fuzzy I was feeling and I figured it was just nerves messing with my mind.

"I'm so glad that you're here! I have no idea where I'm going," I gushed

He reached out and took my schedule. "Oh sweet!" He smiled. "We have homeroom together. We also have third-period algebra and our lunch period is the same."

I felt relieved about that. We could eat lunch together and maybe he could even help me get caught up in algebra.

I sighed. "Well, where do we go for homeroom?"

"First, let's find your locker." His locker was farther down the hall from mine, so he showed me where mine was first and then helped me with the lock. I was so grateful for his assistance. My new morning ritual out of the way, we walked over to his locker and got his books then walked to homeroom together.

As we walked in the door, some of the kids looked up and a few yelled out, "'Sup, Jason!" Or, "How's it going, Neely!" No one really acknowledged me, but I didn't care. I wasn't alone and that was all that mattered. For the first time since I'd been in

Sarasota, I wasn't alone. I just dreaded the classes I had to go to without him.

"In this class we can sit anywhere, so we kind of switch up daily. Mrs. Whitman is really laid-back and she doesn't mind." The classroom was large and we walked over to two seats that were empty and sat down. Jason sat behind me and I turned around so we could talk until the bell rang.

"So, this must be who you've been hiding out with all winter break, Neely!" Some guy with a spiky haircut and an earring in his eyebrow came up and sat at the desk on the other side of Jason. He looked at me, up and down and said, "Well, at least you have good taste."

I didn't know what to say so I just ignored him.

"Shut up, Pitman. I haven't been hiding, though I don't remember seeing you the past couple of weeks. Where've you been?" Jason asked.

"I had to go to Indiana with my parents. My mom's mom lives there."

"So you went to your grandmother's?"

"Okay." This Pitman guy wasn't very bright. Jason didn't mention that he'd been to Los Angeles and I felt special for knowing something that personal about him.

"Kathryn, this is Craig Pitman." Jason introduced us and I smiled. Craig hurriedly said hi but then quickly turned his attention back to Jason.

Craig and Jason talked until Mrs. Whitman came in and told everyone to settle down. She had a piece of paper in her hand and after reading it, she smiled and said, "Class, we have a new student joining us. Her name is Kathryn Bailey and she just transferred from Vanguard Academy."

I immediately wished she hadn't said that. I would rather she'd just said I'd moved here from Atlanta. Now people were going to get the wrong idea about me. I started to feel dizzy again, seeing all those eyes on me. I tried to look away, but there was nowhere else to look. I felt Jason's hand on my shoulder. He squeezed it a little to let me know it was okay. I turned and smiled at him, grateful for the reassurance. I felt good knowing he was there.

After homeroom, Jason showed me where my first-period class was. He had to go way out of his way to do so because it was down past the gym, all the way into a small hallway that looked like nothing was there. I'd have never found it on my own. I thanked him and he ran off to his own class.

I found out that first period was a Family Dynamics class that I really hadn't wanted to take, but because I didn't get to discuss my schedule with anyone, I was stuck with it. I didn't even know what Family Dynamics was until I got in there. Turned out, it was just a fancy name for Home Economics.

When I walked in, everyone was already sitting at tables. I felt so stupid just standing there, but then I heard, "Hey, Kathryn, do you want to sit with us?" A girl I had never seen before was talking to me. She had long brown hair and big brown eyes and was sitting at a table with three other girls. "We have an empty seat."

Grateful for the offer, I walked over and sat down at the only seat left. I guess I looked confused because she said, "You don't know me, but I'm Kelly Kephart. I saw you hanging with Jason. He told me to look for you." I should have been embarrassed about having someone look out for me like that, but I was so grateful to him for the protective gesture.

"So, are you two dating?" A really pretty girl with long spirally blond hair asked me in a vile tone of voice.

I shook my head. "No, we're just friends."

"You looked like more than that to me," she shot back at me. She looked very unfriendly the way she was frowning at me, but her eyes were electric blue. I just stared at her, unable to speak. I had to wonder if she wore colored contacts but decided that she probably didn't and I wouldn't dared have asked anyway.

She had on a belly shirt and low rider jeans that showed off her curves. I noticed that she had a belly button ring, and for some reason, she made me feel like a little girl. She looked so much more grown-up but it was more than that ... she had an attitude that made me kind of scared and yet amazed all at the same time.

I finally found my voice. "No, we're just friends, really. I met him during winter break."

Then she said, "Well, I've known him since he moved here and I've never seen him hanging out with any girls just as friends."

I shrugged. "I guess there's a first time for everything, huh?" I didn't know what she was getting at, but I was feeling very uncomfortable. I started shifting in my seat.

The teacher, Mrs. Laraby, walked in then and told us that this semester we were going to be introduced to managing a family and a career. We kind of laughed at that, but she was serious. We were only in the ninth grade! What did we need to know about families and careers? But Mrs. Laraby went on to say that we would learn to budget money, to balance a checkbook and we'd even learn time management. I was wondering how we would learn that when she pulled out a computer disc.

"Are any of you familiar with the Sims House Party?" She held up a computer game that had these weird-looking people on it. It looked fun but I'd never heard of it. I looked around and most of the kids in the class had their hands raised. Of course, the blonde girl had her hand raised and again, I blamed my utter cluelessness on my parents for not letting me have a computer in my room.

"Well," Mrs. Laraby went on to explain, "For those who don't know, this game will teach you how to manage time, money and a family. For those of you who have played it before, there will be no cheats." She paused for a minute. "That's right, no rosebud." Everyone laughed, but I didn't get it. "We're going to play correctly and I'll monitor your progress. We only have enough computers for half the class, so while the first half plays the Sims, the other half will work on balancing checkbooks and budgets. Then in three weeks, we will switch up. Does anyone have any questions?" No one did. "Well, since this is the first day back, I'll let you talk quietly and we'll start fresh tomorrow."

The blonde girl started in right where she'd left off. "Do you think he's cute?"

"Jason?" I asked, knowing of course that was exactly who she meant.

"Yes, of course, Jason, duh! So, do you?" She made me feel so stupid that I didn't know what to say.

"He's okay." I shrugged. But of course I thought he was cute. Who wouldn't? I just didn't think that was the answer she was looking for.

She looked at me kind of funny then. "Okay, this is the situation." She looked over at Kelly and then back at me. "I have had a major thing for Jason since he moved here. We've gone out a couple of times and right before school let out for the holidays, things looked good between us. But then suddenly he just stopped calling. I'm assuming you're the reason he stopped calling me."

"I'm not the reason for anything," I shot back at her. "He hasn't mentioned anyone that he's gone out with. In fact, I don't even know your name." I was being over-sensitive but I didn't care.

"I'm Breeana Blake," she said in a snotty tone, as if that was supposed to mean something. "And I just wanted to give you the 411 because now that school is in, you better back off."

What was this girl talking about? And why was it that I always met the worst kinds of people. The other two girls just sat silently by and watched us. So, this was what I was stuck with first period every morning: a drama queen who thought I was messing up a relationship between her and Jason that didn't even exist. Or maybe it did. I had no idea since he hadn't told me about her. But I didn't care; I just didn't want to see her every morning.

After class, Kelly cornered me before I got out into the hall.

"Don't worry about Breeana," she told me. "She comes across as the devil's spawn but she's basically harmless." She smiled when she said it and I smiled back at her because that was a good word for her ... devil's spawn.

"I hope so," I told her. "I don't want to spend every morning with her being like that." And despite the fact that Kelly and Breeana were friends, I kind of liked Kelly. She reminded me of Jane in some ways.

"It'll be okay. I'll talk to her." She leaned in closer. "If Jason had liked her that much, he'd have called her by now." We both started laughing and I walked out of the room feeling a little better.

ஐ    ௧

I couldn't talk to Jason during third period because the teacher seated us in alphabetical order. Because I was a B and he was an N, we were halfway across the room from each other. He caught my eye, though and I smiled at him. Then he winked and I felt better—special even. This was the guy some girl was ready to cause physical harm over and he was my friend.

The class seemed to go on forever, but when it was finally over, Jason came up to me and walked me to my locker. "You have a worried look on your face, Katy."

"It's just math. I can't get caught up." I didn't tell him about Breeana. I didn't know how to bring it up.

"Oh, I can help you with that," he told me. "I got an A in algebra last semester."

"I barely got by with a C," I told him truthfully.

"Well, don't worry. We can start studying today after school if you want."

"Um, okay." I thought for a minute. "My mother is picking me up from school. Do you want to ride home with us?"

"That's great." Then it occurred to me that he would be the first friend I'd had over since we moved to Sarasota.

ஐ    ௧

Despite the excitement I'd felt when I first learned I'd share it with Jason, lunch proved uncomfortable. Having met up in the hall, Jason and I got our trays and found a table where no one was sitting. The lunchroom was twice the size as the one at

Vanguard and the tables weren't tables at all. Rather they were booths like the variety you see at McDonalds. It wasn't long, however, until Breeana came over to us and sat down, Kelly trailing right behind her.

"And where have you been hiding yourself, Jase?" Breeana had a flirty voice that made her seem too obvious. She set her tray down beside Jason, and Kelly sat beside me.

"I was in LA for a while during the holidays." Jason took a bite of his pizza and he didn't explain further. "How was your Christmas, Bree?"

He looked at her and I hated to even admit it to myself but I felt scared. What if she talked him into not hanging out with me anymore? And the way he called her Bree—it sounded like they were really close.

"It was okay." She kind of shrugged then touched his arm. "I really missed you though."

At that, he looked over at me kind of embarrassed.

She didn't seem to notice, however, and went right on rambling, saying something about a party over the weekend. She was asking Jason if he wanted to go and I suddenly realized I didn't feel well. I looked at my food and everything started spinning. I felt funny—lightheaded and nauseated. I'd felt bad all day, but I kept assuming it was just nerves. Suddenly I felt like I was going to faint.

"Are you okay, Katy?" Jason got up from his seat and was beside me in a minute. "You look really pale."

Kelly asked if she could get me some water, but Jason said no, that he was taking me to the school nurse. Breeana muttered something that I couldn't make out and then I tried to stand up. It was the last thing remembered.

# ❧ Chapter Thirty-Two ❧

I woke up in the clinic on a bed with Jason standing over me. The nurse was on the phone while I tired desperately to figure out what was going on.

"What happened?" I asked him.

"You fainted."

"How did I get in here?"

"I carried you." He smiled like he was so proud of that. But all I could think about was that I was the new girl who was being carried out of the lunchroom by a guy. What was worse, I was wearing a skirt! I felt mortified and the room started spinning again.

"Yes, Mrs. Bailey, she's awake now ... Yes, I'll tell her ... Okay, thank you, good-bye."

Having hung up the phone, the nurse came over to me. "Kathryn, I just got off the phone with your mother. She's coming to get you. Are you feeling better now?"

I tried to sit up but everything was still spinning.

"Just lie back and don't try to move. Jason,"—she motioned for him—"go get Kathryn a Coke." He was gone within a second.

"So, what's going on? Do you know why you fainted?" the nurse asked me.

I shook my head. "I just felt kind of dizzy, but I've felt bad all day."

"Have you had problems in the past?"

Before I could answer, Jason had come back. He handed me a Coke and I sipped it slowly.

The door opened then and a girl came in complaining of a headache. The nurse went to her and Jason sat at the edge of bed, a worried look lining his face.

"I know you said you were nervous about school starting, but I didn't know it was worth fainting over." He was trying to make a joke about the situation, but I could tell he was still a little shaken up that someone had just fainted right in front of him. I wanted to make the situation lighter so I kind of laughed, but I didn't have a response. I was too tired to think of one.

The nurse peeped around the curtain to see if I was okay.

"I think so," I told her.

"Don't you think you should get back to class, Jason?" she hinted.

"I'm still at lunch and if it's okay, I'll wait with Kathryn until her mom comes." The nurse looked at me and I pleaded with my eyes to let him stay. I didn't want to be left alone.

"I really shouldn't let you, but just this one time I will. Don't forget to get a pass back to class." She then walked back to her desk, leaving us alone in the small room with the curtain opened this time.

"So what made you faint, Kathryn?" Jason asked, serious this time.

I wanted to tell him how sick I'd been since we'd moved, but I couldn't. I just looked at him and told him I would be okay.

"Well, I guess we'll just have to put that algebra lesson off, huh?"

I was so disappointed, but I didn't get a chance to answer him because at that very moment my mother came rushing in like a maniac. Before I could even say anything to Jason, she'd swept me out of the room and into the car. She didn't even bother signing me out of school.

"Where are we going?"

"To the hospital. I've called Dr. Brandt and he's meeting us there."

"Don't you think you're overreacting, *Mother*?" I asked her.

"No, I certainly do *not* think I'm overreacting." Her voice was in a panic and I knew that I'd better not say anything else.

She was speeding through the streets like a woman possessed. Only then did I get really scared. I knew that my mother was kind of a worrier, but she'd never taken me to the hospital like this before. While I was evaluating her demon-like behavior, she picked up her cell phone as though she'd suddenly remembered something important. "William, it's me. Yes, I'm taking her now. Yes, I'll meet you there, in Emergency."

She hung up and I said, "Emergency?"

"Yes, they're admitting you through the emergency room."

"Admitting me?"

My mother urgently changed lanes. "Kathryn, would you please stop parroting everything I say? Yes, they are putting you in the hospital. You're sick and although we thought that changing schools would help, you're not getting any better." She started speeding through the downtown area.

"I've been feeling better," I told her.

"Would you please get a mirror and look at yourself?" She got completely turned around when we saw the exit for the hospital. She wasn't sure which way the emergency room was so she went down a one-way street (the wrong way, I might add) and almost caused a head-on collision.

"Well, look at it this way, we almost made it to the ER without having to drive another minute," I said sarcastically. She gave me a hard look in response.

"This is not the time to make jokes, Kathryn Ann." Knowing she was dead serious, I didn't say anything else.

Finally, she found the arrows pointing to the emergency room and drove to the ER entrance. Someone must have known we were coming because a person with a wheelchair started moving immediately toward the car.

"I don't need a wheelchair," I told her.

"Kathryn," she warned, "don't argue." Something about the seriousness in her voice told me that she wasn't in the mood for me acting like a brat, so I obediently got in the wheelchair.

"I'll be in after I park the car," she told the person who had brought out the wheelchair. And to me she said, "I love you, Kathryn." It was the first time in a long time I'd heard her use those words. I didn't say anything back though and before I knew it, I was being wheeled in through the automatic double doors.

❧ ☙

It was about an hour before I got into a room. They did more tests on me than I've ever had taken in my life. Throughout it all, I felt like a pincushion. I had an IV in my arm, but this time I wasn't as scared of it coming out. I was feeling better by the time Dr. Brandt walked in. In the meantime, Dad had gotten there and taken Mother to get some coffee. They had been gone only a couple of minutes when he arrived.

"Hi, Kathryn, how are you feeling now?"

"I feel a little better," I told him.

"Do you know why you fainted?"

I shook my head.

"Well, we're waiting for your test results, but I can tell you now. It could be a number of things. Your weight loss is still an issue, your blood pressure has dropped since you were here last and your electrolytes are really low."

"What are electrolytes? You talk about them all the time but you never say what they are." I couldn't help but have an edge to my voice. I was angry. It was like he expected me to just know this stuff.

"Electrolytes are important because they are what your cells, especially your nerves, your heart and your muscles, use to maintain voltages across their cell membranes and to carry electrical impulses, nerve impulses and muscle contractions across themselves and to other cells." He kept talking but I had lost him at cells. I didn't understand a word he was saying.

"In English please," I begged. He kind of smiled at me and said, "Basically, electrolytes are ions in your body that you need to stay alive. They're body fluids and ions like sodium, potassium, calcium and other vitamins and minerals like that. Things that you haven't had in your body because you haven't been eating or drinking enough." I still didn't get it and I was sorry I'd asked.

"Am I going to be okay?"

He looked at me for a moment. "That is going to be up to you, Kathryn. You have an eating disorder, and it's up to you to help yourself. We're going to do everything we can, but you have to know that we can only do so much." I nodded because for the first time I really understood. I wasn't getting better and I was finally getting scared.

"What do I have to do?"

He wrote down some stuff on my chart and then said, "You have to stay here for a few days and then we're going to get you a really good therapist."

"But I don't want—"

"Remember when I told you that there would come a time when you wouldn't have a choice about a therapist?"

I nodded and bit my lip so I wouldn't cry.

"Well, the time is now. And then we're going to put your parents in touch with a good dietician. She's going to tell them what to feed you and how much you should eat each day." He paused for a minute so I could let everything sink in. "You're going to miss a lot of school, so I'm going to talk to your mother about a homebound teacher coming in a few days a week to help you stay caught up. Your teachers can give your assignments to her and she'll help you be able to pass this school year."

"So I won't go to school?"

"No, it's too much for you right now. You're going to have to concentrate on getting better." With that, he walked out of the room.

I thought about no school for a minute. On the plus side, I wouldn't have to deal with Family Dynamics, with Breeana, or with anyone else. But then I thought about Jason and I realized that he was the negative side of being out of school. I would miss seeing him. He would be in school, hanging out with friends, dating and going to school dances. And I would be at home, doing homework and watching *The Young and the Restless.* Then I realized that show fit me perfectly ... I was young and would soon get very restless staying home all the time. I wasn't sure which was worse. I tried not to think about it because either way, I couldn't do anything about it. That was my last thought before I fell asleep.

൪ ൫

I woke up to someone calling my name. "Katy?"

I was really dazed and I couldn't remember where I was. As my eyes fluttered open, Jason was standing there and I thought it was all a dream.

"How are you feeling?" He was almost whispering and I tried desperately to figure out what was going on. Then I remembered that I was in the hospital.

"What time is it?" I asked him.

"It's after seven. I had my dad drive me over. He told me to call him when visiting hours are over."

I sat up. "Did you see my parents?" I wondered where they were.

"Yes, they just went to get something to eat. They said they'd be back in awhile." He paused for a minute. "They seem okay."

"Yeah, well you don't live with my mother." I instantly regretted having said that because he didn't live with his mother either. He didn't seem to notice my slip-up, however. To be on the safe side, I changed the subject anyway. "Thanks for coming, Jason."

"Well, I wanted to check on you. Why do you have to be here? Why are you so sick?"

I decided I had to admit it to someone. I hadn't admitted anything to anyone about my sickness. Not even to Nana, who knew but was too nice to say anything. And not even to Jane, who was my best friend and would completely understand. But for some reason, it seemed okay to talk to Jason. "I have an eating disorder," I whispered.

He nodded and didn't look surprised at all. Sensing his understanding, I went on. "I've been sick since we moved here, but lately I really thought I was feeling better."

He didn't say anything for a minute and I got scared. Maybe he thought I was just too much of a freak to hang out with now. But I figured since I'd gone this far, I might as well tell him everything. When I was finished, I looked at him. His face wasn't showing any sign of expression. Most people would look shocked, but not Jason. "You don't seem surprised," I said to him.

"I'm not. I figured it was something like that. Every time we're together, you never eat. You always look tired and you're really skinny."

"Then why didn't you bring it up?" I couldn't believe he had suspected I was sick and hadn't said anything.

"I figured you would talk to me when you wanted to. I didn't want to pry and make you mad at me."

I was about to protest and tell him that I wouldn't have gotten mad at him but the truth is, I probably would have. Just like I had gotten mad at Jane for bringing it up.

"Thank you for being so nice to me, Jason. Since I've moved here, you're really the only one who has been."

"No worries, Katy. Just get some rest and feel better so I can teach you algebra." He smiled as he said it and I knew I had to tell him. I dreaded it. It was ironic though. The very thing I hated about moving was starting school and now I had an 'out.' The only problem was, now I wasn't sure I wanted one.

Amazing how one person could affect an entire situation so that it appeared so different.

"I'm not going to be going back to school this year, Jason." I explained to him about the homebound teacher and about getting a therapist and even about the dietician. I told him everything and it felt so much better just saying it all out loud.

"Well, we can still see each other after I get home from school. We can still do homework together and when you're feeling like it, we can go to the beach again."

I smiled because it didn't seem like he was going to forget about our friendship after all. It felt good to know that I had someone there for me, someone other than my fussy Mother and my worried Dad. Someone other than friends who lived almost nine hours away. He turned the TV on then and we sat and watched MTV together until visiting hours were over.

# ഓ Chapter Thirty-Three ൚

It took a little over three weeks for me to get home. After I got the IV out, my doctor sent me to an inpatient hospital for people with eating disorders. The hospital was right outside Sarasota, about an hour away. That was the closest one, although I didn't want to go that far. Unfortunately for me, I just didn't have a choice.

That's where I learned how to eat all over again. I stayed sick almost an entire week in an attempt to get used to food again. It took a lot of time and I got frustrated quite a few times along the way. In fact, I think the nurses labeled me as the most unpleasant, most disagreeable person there. I didn't care though. I wasn't there to make the nurses happy; I was there to get better. It was just much harder than I'd thought it would be.

I also had to attend group therapy because it was mandatory. It was a situation where kids sat in a huge circle and talked about what they were feeling. I never actively participated. I just sat back and watched everyone else whine about how pathetic their lives were and about how they were just so scared to eat because it was like losing control. I just didn't see myself like that, so I didn't talk in a group setting.

But I did talk with my therapist. In fact, I actually liked her. She really listened and she helped me straighten out my confused thoughts. During the course of our sessions, I came to realize that I was using food as a tool to hurt my parents and to gain control of my own life. I hadn't understood that before. I guess I just felt that if I told myself I wasn't hungry, I would believe that was the only reason I wasn't eating.

While at the inpatient center, I couldn't have visitors, except for my parents, but Jason sent cards and we talked on the phone once a week. He told me about school and about what was going on in the outside world. He also told me how baseball was about to start and that he was going to try out.

Once, when my parents came, I gave them a letter to mail to Jane. In it, I told her about my sickness and about how I was in the hospital. I also admitted to her how right she had been about everything and about how sorry I was for getting mad at her over the Thanksgiving break. I felt better after I'd written that letter.

ଡ଼    ଔ

The only good part of the hospital stay was my roommate, Leslie Ross. We hit it off so well that we became friends right away. She was fifteen, but she looked older. Mother always says that when someone looks older than they actually are, it means they've had a hard life. In Leslie's case, Mom was right.

Leslie was taller than me, about five feet nine inches and weighed about eighty pounds. She was so thin that I could see her bones beneath her clothes. She had short dark hair and her eyes seemed bigger than her face. They were dark like her hair, but they were kind of washed out like the rest of her. She was so pale that she made me look like I had a tan. Like me, she hated talking in a group, but she later told me in private that she didn't like talking to her therapist either.

"It's not like she can do anything. Since I've been here, I haven't felt any differently."

I wondered how she felt but I didn't ask. I didn't want her to think I was playing psychiatrist. For a short while, I'd thought we didn't have anything in common. I wasn't as thin as she was and we didn't have the same problems. Her parents, she told me, were divorced and she and her younger brother were being fought over for custody.

"It's really messy," she told me one night.

We were in our room and it was supposed to be lights out. We still talked though while we were lying in bed. Our twin beds were separated by two nightstands and although we couldn't see each other in the dark, we talked a lot ... maybe even more sometimes *because* it was dark. Under the cover of blackness, we didn't have to see each other or each other's reactions.

"My mom wants us to live here, but my dad wants to take us to live with him in Arizona," she confessed to me one night.

"What do you want to do?"

She was quiet for a minute and I imagined that she was thinking. "Actually, I don't care. Either way it's the same. Neither of them really wants me or my brother. They're just doing it to hurt each other."

I didn't say anything because I didn't even know how to respond to that comment. I couldn't believe that a parent wouldn't want a child. No wonder Leslie had so many problems. It made me wonder what I had to complain about. But Leslie never said anything like that to me and she always listened to my problems as if they were as serious as hers were. She told me that it didn't matter if problems seemed big or little to other people; the only thing that mattered was how they made us feel inside. She seemed to understand me in ways no one else ever could. Sure, Jason was understanding, but he couldn't know what I was going through. Leslie, on the other hand, knew because she was living it.

Over time, Leslie and I became like sisters. I'd never had a sister and I'd never shared a room with anyone, which made me hesitant at first. Initially, I hadn't thought I would like it. Over time, however, it grew almost fun, except when Leslie got in her moods. Sometimes she would become so angry that she would throw things. A few times, she ended up having to stay in a room alone until she had calmed down. Those were the loneliest times for me because I wasn't close with anyone else. It seemed like there wasn't anyone else at the hospital I could relate to. I felt that together, Leslie and I could get through this entire ordeal and emerge from it much stronger and better. We even made plans for when we got out of high school. We would go to the same college and be roommates. But of course, we would laughingly joke, under much better circumstances.

We would sit around and talk about the future like it was going to start tomorrow. Leslie confided in me that she secretly wanted to become a therapist some day. She wanted to help girls like us who had problems that no one else could fix. She said she just wanted to do a better job than the therapists she'd had in the past.

Then one day, out of nowhere, Leslie came in and told me she was leaving.

"You're what?" I was astonished at her casual attitude about it.

"Leaving," she told me while she started packing.

"But why?"

"I've been here a month and it's time to leave."

"But you're not better."

"Better is relative," she replied, but I didn't understand what she meant. All I knew was that I was going to miss her and I had to hurry and get better so I could leave too.

"Why are they letting you leave? You haven't gained any weight since you got here, Leslie. In fact, I think you've lost some." I didn't want to bring that subject up, but it was painfully obvious.

She was busy folding her clothes. "I think it has something to do with our insurance. It only covers a month, so I'm out of here."

I felt so bad that bureaucratic (that's a word that I've heard from my dad over and over ... I think it has something to do with the unfairness in the world) standards were getting in the way of her recovery. More selfishly, I didn't want her to go. I didn't think I could be in this place without her. I would feel completely alone. What's more, I was genuinely scared for her. She wasn't ready to go.

"So, what will you do now?" I asked, still in a state of distress over her leaving like that.

She shrugged. "I guess go home. I've decided to go ahead and live with my mother. I don't like her any more than I do my dad, but at least she's not as strict."

I wasn't sure what she meant by that, but I just hoped she would be okay. Before Leslie left, we hugged one last time and she promised to write me. I gave her my phone number and told her to call me soon. We also exchanged e-mail addresses and promised to keep in touch. I told her I hoped to be out soon too.

After she left, I felt so empty and alone, although I got a new roommate right away. Her name was Cassidy Chambers, but I didn't like her. She was one of those chatty girls who seemed happy to be in a place for problem people. When I asked her why she was there, she just shrugged and said, "I'm like you; I have an eating disorder."

She wasn't anything like me, but I didn't voice that opinion. In fact, after that, I never asked her anything else again. From that point forward, we were just two girls sharing space. I couldn't wait to get out of there!

# ❧ Chapter Thirty-Four ❧

The day I came home from the hospital, I weighed one hundred ten pounds and I felt more alive than I had in months. I wasn't tired and when I looked in the mirror, I noticed that I didn't have circles under my eyes anymore. Even though I couldn't wait to get out, I was a little scared to go home because I didn't know how things would be. I was scared that I would end up the way I was before, since I hadn't had one well day in the new house.

As soon as I walked through the door, the phone started ringing. I ran to answer it.

"Hello?" I watched my parents take my things up to my room as I anticipated the voice on the other end. I motioned for them to wait so I could help, but they were already carrying everything themselves.

"Hi, Katy."

It was Jason and the minute I heard his voice, I realized how much I'd missed him.

"I know you just got home, but is it cool with your parents if I come over?"

"Yes, I'm sure it'll be fine. I'm just going to shower, so I'll see you in about an hour?"

"Sweet. Later, Katy."

We hung up and I went to my room, where my parents were putting my stuff away. "Jason is coming over for a while," I told them.

"It's already three o'clock, Kathryn and you just got home. Are you sure you're ready for visitors?"

I rolled my eyes. Mother was back to her normal self. She started busing herself ... sorting all my dirty clothes and putting away my shampoo and other things I'd packed in my cosmetic bag. I just wanted to yell for her to stop, but I knew she wouldn't.

"Yes, I'm sure and besides, all I've done is rest and I haven't seen Jason in weeks. And just so you know,"—I flipped my head around as I was walking out of my room, "I wasn't asking. I was telling you he was coming over."

"Well, our Katybug is back to normal," I heard my dad say as I went into the bathroom to take a shower.

&#8276; &#8259;

"Kathryn," my mother yelled up to me, "your friend is here." I looked at the clock wondering if a whole hour had already passed. As usual, Jason was right on time. After I'd dried my hair, I'd thrown on my blue hoodie and a pair of jeans. I wanted to look causal for him and the outfit seemed to work. I looked at myself once more in the mirror and put lip-gloss on as a finishing touch.

I then ran downstairs, where I heard my parents talking in the kitchen. I excitedly burst in on their conversation and the minute I saw Jason, my stomach started fluttering. He looked better than he had the last time I saw him. His hair was lighter because of the sun and his eyes seemed greener. He had on a short-sleeved shirt that made his arms look great. Given the muscular ripples, I was sure he'd been working out. He and my parents were sitting at the table and when he looked at me, he smiled. Elated to see me, he got up from the table and hugged me. We stayed in each other's arms for a long time, until my dad cleared his throat. Taking his hint, we broke the hug then and Jason just looked at me.

"You look amazing, Katy!"

I could tell he meant it. "Thank you, I feel better." I smiled at him. Realizing they were intruding on an intimate moment, Mother and Dad took their coffee into the living room and left us alone to talk. Jason and I then sat at the kitchen table and I offered him something to drink.

"No thanks, your parents already asked. I'm good." Then he got quiet for a minute. I started to say something to break the silence, but he said, "I'm so glad you're better, Katy. I've been worried about you. I've really missed you."

"I missed you too," I told him truthfully.

"See if your parents will let you go to the beach and hang for a while." I nodded and we walked into the living room to ask their permission. They were sitting on the couch and my mother had her feet in my dad's lap. She was reading a novel while my dad was channel surfing. They looked so comfortable with each other and for a minute, I wondered if I would ever have that kind of relationship with anyone. They looked so young and *so not* parental. I wished that they were always like that.

"Mother, Dad ... I'm going to take a walk to the beach. I'll be back for dinner." Upon hearing my plans, Mother put her novel down and sat up from her comfortable position. The moment passed and she was back to being parental, full force.

"What?" She looked frantic.

"I'm going to the beach," I told her again.

"I think it's too soon for you to go out of the house." She looked at Dad for backup, but he hadn't taken his eyes off the TV.

"Oh, right." I rolled my eyes. "I've been cooped up for almost a month. I'm getting out," I asserted.

Finally, Dad spoke. "Oh, leave her alone, Abby. Let her get out for a while. Fresh air is good for her." That said, he went right on channel surfing.

"Thanks, Mr. Bailey," Jason said. "My dad is picking me up at six, so we'll be back before then."

"That's fine." Dad handed Mother her book and told us to have a fun time. My mother just stared at him, her mouth agape, realizing she'd just been overruled.

ဆ ဆ

The weather felt wonderful. It was sunny and warm even though it was February. I took deep breaths just to get the salty air into my lungs. The walk to the beach didn't take long, but we were quiet the entire way.

When we got there, we sat on our rock and I asked Jason about the baseball team. "I didn't make it," he confessed.

"But why?" I was stunned. I thought he would have made it without any problem.

"I don't know. I think because I'm too thin." We both started really laughing at that. "Really though, I think it was because I wasn't focused enough. It's not a big deal. I just thought it would be fun. Instead, I changed my schedule and I'm taking weight-training." I knew he'd been working out and I wanted to tell him he looked great, but I was too embarrassed to admit that I'd noticed.

So, I just changed the subject and asked him about school.

"It's fine. Nothing new."

Then I asked, "How's Breeana?" I couldn't believe I'd asked that, but it had been on my mind for a while.

He looked at me sideways and smiled. "She's good. She's been kind of hinting around that we should start 'going out'. You know, it sounds silly but she wants everyone to know that we're a couple."

"Yeah, she made that kind of clear to me too." I giggled a little. "Do you want to?"

"I don't know." He shrugged.

I looked out into the ocean, amazed at how it never seemed to end. No matter how many times I came here, the beauty of it all always mesmerized me. I had really missed coming to the beach while I was in the hospital. Then I realized Jason was saying something.

"I'm sorry. What did you say?" I felt embarrassed but he was nice about it.

"Oh, nothing really. What are you thinking about?"

"Just how great it feels out here. I'm so glad that I'm home." And then it hit me, for the first time ever, I considered Sarasota home.

"Yeah, I'm glad too. I just wish that you could come back to school."

"I never thought I would want to, but I really think I'm going to be bored sitting at home all the time."

"Well, I'll come see you when I can."

"Oh, I know you will! I'm going to make you." We started laughing and, feeling more comfortable with him, I asked him about his parents. He told me about how his mom and dad were talking more often but that she was still trying for this part in the sitcom. He said they seemed to miss each other, so he didn't know what was going to happen. He also told me about Kelly dating a friend of his, Jake Ryan and how he and Breeana all went to the movies together a few weekends ago.

"I just wish she was more like you though," he told me.

"How do you mean?"

"You know, more ... well, I wish she'd listen sometimes instead of talking so much. And not just that, she's so pushy. Everyone has to do what she wants or she gets mad and pouts." I started laughing. I could definitely see that about Breeana.

"I don't really know her, but that sounds like her, from what I've seen anyway. But other than that, she's okay, right?" I still didn't like her but if Jason did, what could I do about it?

"Well," he said after thinking for a minute, "she's pretty." He started laughing and I tried to too, but it came out weak. That was just the problem with the Breeana's of the world. They were just so pretty and I was so plain that it was agonizing. No matter how much weight I lost or how much I changed myself, I would still just be plain, boring Kathryn. And the Jasons and the Jeremys of the world would always end up with the beautiful people—the Alyssa's and the Breeana's—and it wasn't fair.

We spent the rest of the time at the beach talking and watching the seagulls soar over our heads. In my life, I'd had lots of friends, but never one like this. I'd even had friends who were boys before, but something about Jason was different. He was special ... I just hoped that he felt the same way about me.

# ෨ Chapter Thirty-Five ଔ

Katy … Chris and I broke up. I knew it was over right after Christmas. He got me a Hello Kitty doll, one of those with the really big heads that I'd just like to punch. I got him a sterling silver bracelet with these really amazing rectangles on it. I went into every jewelry store in the entire state of Georgia almost, and he got me a Hello Kitty doll. I didn't say anything right then, but it was like he completely didn't get it. When I asked him why he thought a doll would be appropriate for me, he said that he thought it would look 'cool' in my room. It was over for me then. I guess for him too 'cause the past month he's just been distant, and now I find out that he's been hanging out with Holly Paxton between classes. I think they like each other now. At first it hurt my feelings because he could have at least told me, but I've been talking to Kevin a lot anyway. I never told anyone, but I've always thought he was cute. He and I have talked on the phone a few times, and we went to the Valentine's dance together, but just as friends. I'll keep you posted on what happens between us, if anything.

And by the way, Kammy and Brent broke up too. Kammy has been in a really bad mood since they did. Brent likes some girl, who's in the tenth grade, and she's going around acting like its no big deal, but I can tell that it is. I'm glad to hear that you're feeling better. I knew something was wrong, but I didn't know how to help you. I'm glad that you finally found your way out, and I'm really glad it's working. I also want to hear more about Jason. He sounds adorable. And speaking of adorable ... Jeremy is available again! Alyssa moved to the other side of town, and she's going to a different school. He didn't seem to think that it would work with her being so far away. What a jerk, huh? E-mail me back and let me know what's going on with you.
BFF!! Jane

After I read Jane's e-mail, I just stared at the computer screen for the longest time. I couldn't believe how much could change in just a few months. When I thought about it, I realized it had only been like seven months ago that we were all friends, hanging out at Woodland Park: Me with really bad hair and Kammy and Brent just deciding that they liked each other. How could so much change in just a short amount of time?

Jane ... I remember the night at Woodland Park when I saw you and Kevin talking. I wondered if you liked him. I think that you two would make a great couple. And you better keep me updated! haha
What was the dance like? How do you go to a dance as just friends? Did you dance with other people?
I'm also feeling much better. My weight is still at 110, and the doctor said that was fine for my height (I've grown an inch), even though he thinks I could stand to gain a few more pounds. But I think he'd say that if I weighed 210. LOL I'm also eating better and my therapy is going well. I still have moments when I feel like I'm going to relapse, but I just talk to my therapist and I feel better.
I can't believe that about Jeremy ... . You think you know someone, huh? E-mail me again soon.
~Kathryn~

Having school at home was a different experience. I felt like I could go back to real school, but everyone was against it. They wanted me to wait until next year. I didn't particularly like my teacher, Mrs. Bell, but she was all that was keeping me from failing. I just looked forward to when the school day ended, when Jason would come over. We would hang out every afternoon that Breeana wasn't monopolizing his time. Soon, I was so caught up with my algebra that even Mrs. Bell was impressed.

Jason and I walked to the beach sometimes after school and when we did, we talked about everything. He told me about Breeana and him and I told him about things that Jane wrote to me. Ever the tactful one, he didn't ask me about food or how much I was eating and I was glad.

"Do you still like that Jeremy guy?" he asked me one day at the end of February. We were sitting on the same rock we had always sat on and out of nowhere, he just asked me that. I shrugged. I'd told him about Jeremy and me and about what Jane had told me in her e-mail.

"He's a jerk and anyway, if he doesn't like someone who moved across town, he certainly wouldn't like someone who lives states away."

"What if you moved back to Atlanta? Would you like him then?"

I kind of laughed at that question because I didn't know what Jason was getting at.

"I don't know, Jason. I don't think I'll have to worry about that happening anyway."

"Yeah, I know. But I'm just saying, if you did move back, would you two get together?"

I sighed. "Why do you care?" After all, he had Breeana, so why was he asking me about someone who lived in Atlanta. But with his eyes intensely looking at me like that, my stomach felt flutters inside it.

He shrugged. "I don't know. I just wondered." He grew quiet then and his mood shifted. I just couldn't figure out why. Sometimes Jason was just like that. Most of the time he was in a great mood, but if anything ever happened and his mood became dark, you couldn't tell if he was angry or sad.

Most of the time, the mood shift stemmed from his problems with his mother. If she called or she and his dad fought, he would get kind of distant. But that day, nothing had happened with her, so I couldn't figure out what was going on.

When it came time to return to my house, Jason and I waited for his dad on the porch. We sat on our porch swing, not talking, just listening to the creaking sound of the swing as it rocked back and forth. It was then that I asked him, for the thousandth time, if everything was okay. He assured me that it was, but I didn't believe him.

In an attempt to lighten his mood, I reached over to him and started playing with his hair. I'd never done that before but I had always wanted to touch it. He had amazing hair. Taking advantage of the intimate moment, he kind of leaned over into my lap and put his legs on the swing. I felt so comfortable being with him like that, but my heart was racing, although not in a scared way. It was more exciting than scary. I then started scratching his head lightly with my fingernails.

"God, that feels good, Katy," he told me quietly. "Don't stop." And I didn't. I lightly went over his head, his face and his arms with my nails. He closed his eyes and for the first time, I just wanted to reach over and kiss him. But I couldn't do that. He liked another girl and anyway, Jason and I were just good friends. I had to keep reminding myself of that. His dad then pulled into the driveway, interrupting my thoughts and Jason sat up.

"I guess I have to go." I nodded. Then, as he was leaving, he reached over and kissed me on the cheek. He'd never done that before but I liked it. I smiled at him and he was gone. I sat outside just thinking about what had just happened. I had felt tingly all over when he'd kissed me like that and the uncontrollable sensation scared me.

I had the hardest time sleeping that night. My mind was racing and I kept thinking about Jason. I was really confused. I knew I was having feelings for him that went deeper than just a friendship, but I also knew that he liked Breeana. And even if it was for no other reason than just because she was pretty, the fact was ... he still liked her. I also knew that liking him could change things between us and I didn't want anything to mess up our friendship. Besides, I decided right then that I had to stop thinking about him in that way. The only problem with that was that it was a lot easier said than done.

ᛦ ᏣᎦ

That same week, I heard from Leslie. She'd moved in with her mother and they were living in Chicago. Her brother had decided to live with their dad in San Francisco. I asked her how she was doing, but she always said the same thing, "Fine." She didn't sound fine though. She sounded sad, but I didn't push her to talk about it. I knew how that was and I didn't want to be that kind of person. I just told her that I wished she lived closer so that we could hang out. I knew she wished the same thing because she sounded really lonely. Although we had talked a few times on the phone and e-mailed each other sometimes, it wasn't the same. I tried to sound cheerful whenever we talked, but I didn't think it helped. I worried about her but I didn't know how to help her. I only hoped that her mother was getting her the help she so desperately needed so she could feel better like I was.

# ൭ Chapter Thirty-Six ൫

February quickly turned into March. One late winter afternoon Jason and I were sitting on my bedroom floor doing homework. As we did so, talk turned to my birthday, which was coming up in a couple of weeks—March fourteenth to be exact. Despite the fact that my mother was old-fashioned when it came to such matters, she didn't mind us doing homework alone in my room as long as the door was open at all times. I thought that rule was funny, but we left it open anyway.

"What are you going to do for your birthday, Katy?" Jason asked, closing his history notebook.

I just shrugged. "I don't know. With the way things have been going this year, I just feel lucky to see fifteen."

"All hail to the drama queen." Jason laughed and I kicked at him, but since we were sitting down, it didn't make contact. "So, you have no plans at all?" He asked in surprise after he stopped laughing.

My mother peeked her head in then. "How's it going, kids?"

"Fine," we said at the same time. I rolled my eyes. She always had that knack for being around at the wrong time.

"Well, I wasn't trying to listen in or anything"—Jason and I gave each other a knowing look, but she was completely clueless to it—"but I happened to overhear you say something about Kathryn's birthday. Actually," she looked at me, "your dad and I thought it would be fun if we took you to Le Bordeaux. We were going to talk to you about this anyway but we just hadn't gotten around to it. We thought you might want to invite Jason along." I was kind of embarrassed that she would ask me like that, in front of him. It just kind of put him on the spot since he was dating Breeana. And besides, Le Bordeaux might not be a place Jason would want to go to.

"Isn't Le Bordeaux that new French restaurant?" Jason asked Mother. She nodded, looking excited.

"We've never been there before, although I hear it has an amazing view, outdoor dining if you want it and even a dance floor." She was telling him all this like he had asked for additional details. He hadn't and I felt really embarrassed.

"That sounds so nice, Mrs. Bailey. Thank you for inviting me and I would love to come."

"Great! Kathryn will fill you in on details once I talk with Mr. Bailey." Finally, Mother walked out of the room and let us get back to our homework.

I waited until I knew she was downstairs and then I asked Jason, "You mean you want to go?" I asked kind of surprised, but happy.

"Well duh, Katy. Of course I do."

"What about Breeana?" I was playing with my fingernails as I posed the question. I didn't want to look at him. I felt embarrassed and when I get like that, I start peeling off my fingernail polish.

"What about her?"

"Well, won't she mind if you go with me?" I couldn't look at him, so I kept my eyes focused on my nails.

"You're my friend, Kathryn and she knows that. And anyway, I don't care if she gets mad. She'll get over it." I had mixed feelings over his response. On the one hand, I was happy that he didn't care what she thought, but on the other hand, it was just the way he'd said it ... 'you're my friend.' It kind of made me feel like he would have gone no matter who it was that had invited him. But for the most part, I was excited he'd agreed to come along. I was just having a hard time controlling my feelings for him and I just wished that he felt the same way.

80 cg

The weekend before my birthday, my mother and I went clothes shopping together. She thought I needed something nice to wear the night of my birthday. We browsed through several different stores before we finally found the perfect dress. It was so pretty but really expensive and I didn't know if Mother would let me have it. She told me I could try it on though, so I took that as a good sign.

I went into the dressing room and tried it on. Once I'd zipped it up, I came back out to where Mother was waiting, so she could give me her opinion. When she looked at me, she actually gasped. "You look beautiful, Kathryn. You even have color back in your face. "

I rolled my eyes; of course she would bring that up. Nothing like a backhanded compliment to ruin the moment. I looked at myself in one of those three-way mirrors, the kind where you can see every angle. "The dress, Mother, what do you think about it?" I asked focusing her attention back on the matter at hand.

I loved it, but I wondered what she was thinking. It was a light pink silk dress, with spaghetti straps that tied at the shoulders. The skirt portion came up above my knee, though and I thought for sure my mother would say it was too short.

What I liked about it most, however, was the way it felt against my skin. I felt pretty and I instinctively wondered if Jason would think so too. Given that I looked nothing like Breeana, I wasn't sure what he would think. She was taller and had amazing hair and he had already told me that he thought she was beautiful. I couldn't compete with that. Since the chestnut color had grown out of my hair, I was back to basic brown and it was so plain that I almost asked Mother if I could color it again. On second thought, I figured why would it matter anyway? I could change myself as many times as I wanted, but inside I'd still be just me ... mousy Kathryn Ann Bailey.

"I love the dress, Kathryn. But it's just more than that. You're beautiful; the dress only enhances what you already have. You're so pretty, but you've just gotten it into your head that you aren't and I can't understand it." I didn't expect her to understand it but when she said I could have the dress, I felt like my heart was going to burst. I couldn't wait for Jason to see me in it. I knew that he had a girlfriend, but I couldn't stop thinking about that night on the porch. Even to that day, it still gave me tingles.

Since then, Jason and I hadn't had any more moments like we had on the porch swing that night and although I really wanted to be close to him like that again, I knew that he had a girlfriend and we couldn't. For a minute, I felt jealous of Breeana, but I quickly decided I didn't have that right. So again, I pushed the feelings aside.

During our shop-a-thon, my mother and I also found some matching shoes. They were strappy with enough of a heel to make me feel taller. I loved them! Mom even let me go into Abercrombie and Fitch, a store that I'd never before been allowed to shop in because it was just too pricey. That day, however, she relented and let me get a few pairs of shorts for spring and a couple of shirts that were too cute, but as she put it, 'entirely overpriced.' When I asked her why she had let me get them, she just sighed and said, "I'm just glad that you're not wearing black."

After we were finally exhausted from shopping, we went to lunch at a sushi bar, even though I'd never tried sushi before. Mother loved it, but I almost threw up. Making sure I didn't get away with skipping a meal on her account, on the way home, she stopped and got me French fries from McDonald's. On the return ride, we didn't talk about anything in particular. In fact, it turned out to be one of those rare days when she didn't get on my nerves. She didn't even bug me about eating and we didn't talk about doctor's appointments or therapy or anything else that would spoil the moment. We were just together—like a normal mother and daughter. And for the first time in a long time, I was genuinely happy to be with her.

# ❧ Chapter Thirty-Seven ❦

That night, after dinner, Jason called me. "You want to come over and hang out for a while?" I'd been to his house a couple of times and had even met his dad. Mr. Neely seemed nice enough. He was a lot like Jason and they even looked alike. Seeing him gave me a peek into what Jason would likely look like once he got older. It was a nice thought because for an old person, Mr. Neely was really nice looking.

"Where is Breeana tonight?" I asked. It came out kind of catty even though I didn't mean for it to. I just couldn't help myself. Even though I was trying to push my feelings for Jason aside, it wasn't working as well as I'd hoped.

He didn't seem to notice though. "She's got cheer camp this week. They're learning new cheers and stuff. It's almost time for cheerleader tryouts or something."

"I thought she was already a cheerleader," I said sarcastically.

"She is ... it's for next year." I rolled my eyes and I was glad that he couldn't see me because my attitude about Breeana was getting worse and worse. "Anyway, why does it matter?" he went on. "Do you want to come over or not?" He sounded impatient and I didn't know why.

"Sure," I told him. "I'll have my dad drive me over in a few minutes." When I got off the phone, I brushed my teeth and ran a hairbrush through my hair. My hair had grown way past my shoulders now so I was glad for that, but it was straight, not spirally like Breeana's. For good measure, I also put on some lip-gloss. After all, I didn't want to go over there looking like I was trying too hard. At the same time, however, I wanted to look nice, so I even changed clothes. The weather was nice so I put on my new pair of light khaki shorts, the ones I'd gotten that day at Abercrombie and Fitch. To top them off, I also put on the navy tee that had **AMBERCROMBIE** written across it. I had to admit that I almost looked nice. I even put some Tommy Girl perfume on my wrists before running downstairs to ask Dad to take me over to Jason's.

My dad was in the living room with Mother, watching some movie on American Movie Classics. They watch those old movies a lot and it always drives me crazy. I hate to see a movie that's in black and white. It seems so depressing. I mean, everyone in those movies that once looked so beautiful and handsome is dead now. Either that or they're so old that it doesn't even matter anymore. Like I said, it's depressing.

"Katybug, do you have to go over there this late?" my father chided.

"Really, Dad," I said impatiently. "It's only seven and anyway, it's not like you're busy." Dad looked at Mother and she rolled her eyes.

"That's not nice to say that we're not busy, Kathryn." But she nodded and said to Dad, "Just hurry up, or you're going to miss the best part." I had no idea an old black and white movie had a best part.

When Dad dropped me off, he told me to call him when I was ready to come home. I told him I would, then I ran excitedly to the front porch. I knocked a couple of times before Jason finally came to the door. He was wearing denim shorts and no shirt. I'd never seen him without a shirt on before, but I had to admit, he looked amazing. He had abs and I could see why Breeana was so possessive of him.

"How's it going?" he asked me once I was inside the house.

"Great. Thanks for asking me over." I was kind of nervous and I just blurted out, "Where's your dad?" We were standing in the middle of the living room and I realized that I hadn't heard any noises coming from any other places in the house.

Jason and his dad live in a cute, little one-level brick house. It has three bedroom, two bathrooms, and a nice-sized kitchen.

It even has a big backyard, with a huge deck that his dad built. Jason told me that when they first moved here, the neighbors came over a lot and they had big barbeques. That was another thing I liked about Mr. Neely; he was very sociable and seemed to like everyone.

"He's out with some friends. He should be home later." I hadn't known that would be the case when I'd agreed to come over. Now I felt even more nervous. I'd never been alone with Jason in his house before. In fact, I didn't even know if my parents would want me over here without his dad being present.

It was as if Jason could read my mind. "Don't worry about it, Katy. He'll be home soon." I didn't know what he thought I was worrying about, but I just kind of shrugged like I didn't care.

Leaving it at that, he walked into the kitchen then and opened the refrigerator. I followed him.

"You want a Pepsi?" he asked me.

"No thanks, do you have water?" Granting my wish, he handed me a bottle of Evian.

"So, what do you want to do?" he asked, the welcoming mechanics out of the way.

"I don't know." I shrugged.

"Want to listen to CDs?" I nodded. "Let's go to my room, I have a kick-ass system in there. Dad's isn't so great. I felt funny about going into his room alone with him but I didn't want to be a goody-goody priss, so I followed him there like an overanxious puppy dog. Once we got into his room, he sat down on his bed. Not knowing where else to sit, I sat down beside him. He didn't have any furniture except for his computer chair and I thought that would be rude to sit all the way across the room from him. So, sitting on the bed seemed like the only thing to do. He didn't turn any lights on and the only illumination in the room came from the moonlight streaming through his window.

He handed me about a million CDs to go to through. "Here, you pick something to listen to."

I fingered my way through some of them. We sat with our legs crossed on his bed, flipping through CDs but not really talking.

"Jewel?" I asked him. "That doesn't sound like you."

"It's not. That's Bree's." I put it back and kept going. Then I found an Alanis Morrisette CD. I didn't want to know if that was hers too and I didn't want to ask because I liked it. So, I just put it in. He didn't seem to mind, so I sat back down on the bed to enjoy the music. Then, out of nowhere, Jason said, "Dad is going out to LA to see my mother."

"When did he decide that?" I asked, mildly shocked because the way Jason had talked about his dad, I didn't think he'd go back out there.

"I don't know. He just told me a couple of days ago that he was going. My mother starts shooting the pilot for that sitcom in a couple of months. I guess that has something to do with his decision to go."

"Why would he go because of that?"

He got an edge to his voice. "I don't know, Katy."

I looked at him with concern but he turned on his side so I couldn't his face. Making myself more comfortable, I took off my Birkenstock sandals and lay down beside him. We were facing each other and we were really close. My heartbeat quickened just from sitting so close to him. Quietly, I said, "Actually, I didn't know that your mother got the part in the sitcom. You didn't tell me."

"Well, I didn't want to talk about it." Even though he was looking at me, it was almost as if he was looking right through me, like he wasn't really even aware I was beside him.

"What are you thinking about, Jason?"

"Nothing, everything. I don't know. I'm so confused." I nodded like I understood but I wasn't sure I did. I didn't really know what any of it meant. So what if his dad was going to see his mom? I would have thought he'd been glad. I wanted to reach out and play with his hair again but I was afraid he wouldn't want me to.

"Do you want to talk about it?" He shook his head and then closed his eyes. I didn't know what to do. I wasn't sure if I should leave or stay. I didn't know if I should just lie there and act like everything was okay—because it wasn't okay. And it's really hard to pretend that something is fine when it's not.

Putting an end to my internal torture, he reached over to me, his eyes still closed and put his arm around me. He pulled me even closer, then whispered in my ear, "I'm so glad that you're here."

"I'm glad I'm here too, Jason." We stayed like that, curled up beside each other for the longest time. We didn't talk; we didn't move. We were just together. And then we fell asleep in each other's arms.

The next thing I remember was a ringing sound, although I didn't know where it was coming from. Then I felt a stirring beside me. I opened my eyes, completely at a loss as to where I was.

"Oh, man!" I heard Jason's voice break the silence of the room. The CD had gone off and I sat straight up. It hit me hard where I was then. I was at Jason's house, on Jason's bed and no one was home but us.

"What time is it?" I asked in a frantic, high-pitched voice.

"It's only ten o'clock. Everything is okay," he reassured me, reaching over and hugging me close to him. "I'm sure that was your parents calling. Do you want to call them back?"

"Are you kidding me?" I shrieked. "They're going to freak out. I was supposed to call them before now. They're going to kill me."

"Chill girl, you're shaking." And I realized that I was. I got up and found the phone on Jason's bedroom floor. I dialed home and it rang once. Dad answered.

"Kathryn Ann, your mother and I were worried about you!" was the first thing he said to me. "I was just about to come over there."

"I'm sorry, Dad. We were just watching a movie and we fell asleep."

"Fell asleep?" he yelled at me, something that he'd rarely done before. "But I've been calling since nine twenty. Where is Mr. Neely?" I was trapped. I knew that if I lied, I would get caught. But if I told him the truth, I would be in even more trouble.

"He's not here," I reluctantly admitted.

"I'm on my way to get you, Kathryn, so you'd better watch for me. We're about to have a long discussion."

I hung up the phone, slipped on my shoes and then ran my fingers through my hair. We hadn't done anything wrong and yet, I felt like the worst person in the world.

"I'm so sorry, Kathryn. I know it's my fault. I'll talk to your dad if you want."

"No, it's okay. That might make things worse. And anyway, he'll get over it." I walked into the living room and watched out the window for my father's car. Jason followed me.

"He just sounded so mad." My voice sounded strange, even to me. I guess I still felt a little out of it. Sensing my discomfort, Jason came up behind me and put his arms around me. I realized then how tall he'd gotten since we'd first met. I was standing under his chin, my back to his stomach and we were both just stood there, watching for my dad.

"Are you going to be all right? You're really shaking," he observed. I nodded. Then I saw my dad's headlights.

"I have to go," I told him. But as I was walking to the door, he stopped me and kissed me lightly, very lightly, on my lips. It was almost like it hadn't happened because once I got to the car, Jason was back inside and I wondered if I hadn't just made the entire thing up in my head.

# ৪৩ Chapter Thirty-Eight ৪৩

"You are never to be in a boy's home without parental supervision. Do you understand any of that, Kathryn Ann?" Dad and I hadn't talked all the way home, but once we got inside, he no longer seemed lost for words. Dad and I were sitting at the kitchen table and Mother was standing up, pacing back and forth like a caged animal.

"I understand," I responded bitterly. I was looking down at my hands and I felt like crying. I hadn't done anything wrong and yet they were acting like I'd committed one of the deadly sins.

"And what's worse is that you didn't even tell us that Mr. Neely wasn't going to be there."

"Dad, honest, I didn't know until I got there."

"Then you should have called us right away, Kathryn Ann Bailey," my mother lectured through clenched teeth. "We didn't raise you to hang around in boys' houses and do God only knows what."

That was it ... the last straw. I jumped up from the table. "We weren't doing ANYTHING! Don't you understand that? Can't you understand *anything*? Jason doesn't even know I exist like that. He doesn't look at me like a girlfriend. If I were beautiful like Tiffany or Breeana, you'd have to worry about me being in a boy's house without parents, but I'm just a plain, ugly nobody. And believe me, nothing would happen if we stayed in that house a month together. So just get over it!" I ran upstairs then and slammed the door. I hadn't done so in a long time and it didn't feel so good this time around. I literally fell, worn out, onto my bed and started crying. I wasn't sure what hurt worse:

that my parents didn't believe me, or that they had no reason not to.

"Katybug?" It was my dad. He knocked on the door and then came inside without being asked.

"Please just go away." I didn't feel like talking.

"I'm sorry that we might have overreacted but we were worried."

"But you didn't have anything to worry about."

"You shouldn't underestimate yourself, Kathryn. You're a beautiful girl and your mother and I have a lot of worries when you're with boys."

"But I'm not with boys. I was with Jason and he's my friend. Please leave me alone, Dad. I have a headache and I just want to go to sleep." He came over and gave me a sorrowful hug and then he strode back out of the room.

I had a hard time going to sleep that night. I kept thinking about Jason and how close we were lying next to each other and I wished we could do that again. I just hated how things had to end like they did. Why are parents so impossible sometimes?

❧ ☙

The next morning, Sunday morning, I didn't get out of bed until almost noon. I just felt so drained that I wasn't sure what was wrong with me. When I finally dragged myself out of bed, I went downstairs to find my parents sitting on the couch, doing a crossword puzzle from the newspaper.

"Well, I guess the princess decided to get up and join us," Dad joked.

"We had pancakes for breakfast, Kathryn. Would you like me to make you some?" Mother asked, not taking her eyes off the puzzle.

"No thanks. I'm not hungry," I replied. Then I saw my mother look at Dad. They kind of talked with their eyes for a minute before I realized what was going on.

"Can't I just not be hungry and it be okay?" I knew I was getting upset over nothing, but lately I'd been getting more and more angry or upset. I hadn't been going to my therapy sessions as often as I used to because since I felt better, it seemed like a waste of time. And since my weight was good, my parents didn't force me.

"I think I'll go to the beach for a while," I told them, looking for an escape and went upstairs to prepare to do just that. I called Jason first though. It rang three times before I heard a raspy, "Hello?" It was Jason, only he sounded sleepy.

"Did I wake you up?"

"Kind of. But it's all good."

"Do you want to go to the beach for a while? I'm headed that way and I thought you might want to go too."

"Kathryn?"

"Duh, who did you think it was?" And then it occurred to me that he thought I was Breeana. My heart sank.

"Sorry, I just woke up," he explained. "Let me take a shower and I'll meet you there in half an hour." I was relieved that he wanted to go, so I tried not to feel too bad about him getting me mixed up with his girlfriend.

We hung up then and I jumped in the shower. It was sunny outside so I put on a purple belly shirt, something I never thought I'd wear but wanted to since I knew Jason liked them. (Breeana wore them all the time). I also put on a pair of denim shorts that were almost too short but looked cool. I had to sneak out of the house though. My parents didn't know about the belly shirt and I didn't think they'd let me out of the house wearing shorts that short. For footwear, I wore my purple thongs that I'd bought at the Shoe Department in the mall. Fully dressed, I looked at myself in the mirror. I didn't look bad, so I ran to the bottom of the stairs. My parents were still in the living room so I didn't go in there.

"Mother, Dad ... I'm going to walk to the beach for a while."

"Okay, don't be gone too long," Mother said. Breathing a sigh of relief that I'd gotten away without my outfit being detected, I went out through the kitchen.

I arrived at the beach before Jason did, so I climbed onto the rock and waited for him. I felt kind of nervous about seeing him because of the night before. While I waited, I watched families playing with their children, some throwing Frisbees and some just running around on the sand. The water was still too cold to go swimming but everyone looked like they were having fun.

"Hey, sorry I'm late," I heard Jason say from behind me. I stood up so he would notice my shirt. He eyed me up and down, but his blank expression hid his thoughts.

"What's with the shirt?"

"What, you don't like it?" My heart fell. I guess my face showed what I was feeling because he quickly said, "Oh, I like it. You look great. It's just not something you'd normally wear."

I shrugged. "Maybe I wanted to try a new look."

"Or maybe you are just trying to look like Breeana," he accused. He knew me too well.

"No, I'm not," I shot back angrily at him. "It's just hot outside." That sounded so lame, even to my own ears.

"Look, just be yourself, Katy. Don't try to imitate anyone." I sat down on the rock and didn't know what to say. By that point, I was wishing I hadn't even called him. He was being so weird that I didn't even know what to talk about. I didn't want to hear about Breeana and I didn't know if I should ask him about his dad. We were quiet for the longest time. A couple of times I tried to talk but he just answered me with a simple yes or no. Finally, he just stood up.

"My head just isn't here, Katy. I have to go." I felt like my heart had just been crushed into a million pieces.

"Why? What's wrong?" My voice was shaking, like I was about to cry, and I didn't want to cry in front of him.

"Don't be upset, Katy. I'll call you tonight. I just need to be alone right now." He didn't hug me; he just climbed off the rock and left. I sat there, all alone, for the longest time. I couldn't figure it out. Something was definitely wrong but I didn't know what it was. He was completely shutting me out and I couldn't stand it. I had felt so close to him the night before and now it was like it all had never happened. I don't know how long I sat out there, but since I didn't want to witness a scene like the one I'd encountered the night before, I started home before my parents freaked about where I was.

As I approached the house, I peeked in the window and saw my parents sitting in the living room. They were occupied with watching TV, so I came back in through the kitchen.

"Is that you, Katybug?" Dad called out when I walked in the door.

"Yes, it's me." Who else would it be? I wanted to ask, but I didn't. I'll be down in a little while. I have a headache." I ran upstairs, took off my Breeana-look belly shirt and shorts, rolled them up in a paper bag and threw them away. I never wanted to look at those clothes again. In fact, I never wanted to be reminded of this day again.

I then got into my Atlanta Braves T-shirt and just got back into bed. Everything went whirling through my mind at once. Was Jason mad at me? Did this mean that he didn't want to come with us on Friday night? If he didn't go, did I really want to go out with just my parents? I couldn't take that humiliation. I decided to just shut everything off ... my mind, especially my thoughts about Jason. I felt my eyelids growing heavy and I just gave into sleep.

I'm not sure how long I slept, but the next thing I knew, my mother was sitting on the edge of my bed, shaking me awake.

"Are you okay, Kathryn?" I felt disoriented. What was going on? What time was it? I looked over at my clock. It was already eight o'clock. I couldn't believe I'd slept the entire afternoon away.

"Do we need to take you back to see Dr. Brandt?" My mother had a different tone in her voice. She sounded so concerned that it confused me. Not that she wasn't always concerned, it's just that usually she was in a panic. This time she just elicited a soft, calm tone. For once, she seemed like a regular Mom.

"What? What are you talking about?" I sat up and crossed my legs in front of me.

"I'm talking about how you're acting just like you were before and I feel it's my fault. You need to start back to therapy regularly."

"Mother, it's not like that."

"You always say it's not like that. So please tell me, Kathryn. What is it like?" I sat up in bed and debated whether I could tell her or not. After a moment of contemplation, I figured why not. So I told her. I told her how something was wrong with Jason and how he was shutting me out. And I told her how I was scared that he was mad at me. I also told her how I had started liking him but that I wasn't pretty like Breeana and that Breeana was his girlfriend. Finally, I told her that I didn't know how to make him like me. It all came rushing out and then something happened that I'd never forget. Mom looked at me and smiled. Then she hugged me and said, "It's a normal teenage problem, Kathryn." When she started laughing, I started laughing too. And before long, we were laughing so hard that I didn't even know what was funny. Dad was passing by my room and stopped at the sound of our giggles.

"Is everything okay in here?" he asked, looking at us in puzzlement. We were still laughing but Mom said, "Yes, William, everything is perfect." And for the first time in a long time, I felt like things were going to be good.

# ಬಿ Chapter Thirty-Nine ೞ

Mrs. Bell arrived on Monday morning as usual but my mind just wasn't on schoolwork. I hadn't heard from Jason and I was caught somewhere between sadness and anger. How could he just blow me off like that? How could he say he'd call then not follow through on that promise? My mind wouldn't shut him out. I kept going over everything, wondering what I'd done. Most of all, I wondered if I'd said something to make him mad at me. I thought about everything but it was useless. My mind was just going around and around in circles but nothing was getting solved. What I couldn't stop thinking about, however, was that night when Jason and I had been lying in his bed, as close as we'd ever been and just two days later, he wasn't even talking to me.

I guess Mrs. Bell could see that I wasn't really concentrating because she finally just gave up and handed me a list of things I needed to have completed by Wednesday. I saw her talking to Mom on the way out, but since Mom didn't come and say anything to me about it, I guess it wasn't anything bad.

The rest of the day passed slowly. I kept watching the clock. I hoped that once school let out, Jason would call me. It was Mom's day to volunteer at the hospital, so she left around noon, instructing me to do my schoolwork in her absence.

"I only have to be there a few hours, Kathryn, so if you need me, just call the cell phone. Also, don't do your schoolwork in front of the TV and please eat some lunch. I left some pizza in the refrigerator. Just reheat it." I assured her I'd be fine and I felt relief wash over me once she was gone.

I took my books into the living room and spread everything out. Then I turned on MTV. They were having a *Punk'd* marathon. But looking at Ashton made me think about Jeremy's hair and I didn't want to think about Jeremy anymore than I wanted to think about Jason. So, I turned the channel over to a game show and tried to concentrate on the work Mrs. Bell had left for me. Algebra was the hardest of my subjects and although I had gotten caught up, I was having trouble again. I really wished that Jason were there to help me. Finally, after giving it a few halfhearted attempts, I just gave up and slammed my books down. I went into the kitchen and ate a few bites of the pizza straight out of the fridge and then I went into my room. I decided to catch up on the reading list Mrs. Bell had assigned for me to complete by the end of the school year. I turned on my radio and curled up on my bed. I started reading *To Kill a Mockingbird*. It was pretty good once you got through the uneducated grammar, but it wasn't as engrossing as I'd hoped. And although I hadn't meant to fall asleep, I guess I did because soon I was dreaming that the fire alarm was going off at school and we all had to get out, only my legs wouldn't go. I felt trapped because the harder I tried to run the slower I went. Finally, I realized that it wasn't the fire alarm after all but was in fact the phone.

"Hello?" My voice sounded faraway and groggy.

"Katy?" My heart started beating too quickly. It was Jason. I tried to be cool about it though.

"Yeah?"

"Did I wake you up?"

"It's okay. I was reading but I guess I just fell asleep."

"Yeah, well, I'm sorry I didn't call you yesterday." I didn't say anything for a minute. I wanted to play it off like I hadn't noticed, but I mean, of course I'd noticed. And if I acted flippant, I knew he'd know. I guess I took too long to answer because he asked, "Are you mad at me?"

"No," I told him truthfully. I wasn't mad at him. I just felt confused.

"I need to talk to you. Can you come over?" he asked.

"I'm here alone. I don't have a way to get there."

"Dad and I will come over and pick you up. We'll even bring you home when you're ready. You can stay for dinner, just please come over." He sounded strange so I told him I'd be ready in twenty minutes. I called Mom on her cell phone to let her know where I'd be and to my surprise she was actually cool about it.

"Just don't be out too late." I promised her I wouldn't then I got up and got ready. I didn't do anything special except brush my hair. I didn't even put on lip-gloss this time. And I wore what I already had on, a white T-shirt and navy shorts. Apparently the last time I had tried to look good, Jason hadn't been impressed. Now he'd just have to see me the way I was.

Jason was knocking on my door just as I was putting on my shoes. Once we got in the car, Mr. Neely told us that he would drop us at the house and then he'd run to the store. He was going to barbeque chicken that evening and he needed some spices. I knew that my parents had gone postal the last time I was there with Jason alone, but this was daytime and Mr. Neely was only going to be a minute away. I didn't care anyway. I just wanted to find out what was going on. Jason sat in the front seat with his dad and all the way to his house we were quiet. Not even the radio was on. I felt uncomfortable and couldn't wait until we were alone so we could talk in private.

# ❧ Chapter Forty ☙

Jason had barely let the car roll to a stop in front of his house before he bounded out and ran up the sidewalk. I thanked Mr. Neely for the ride and for letting me come over then I followed Jason inside. We went straight to his room, not even so much as turning around to look at me. This time, he didn't even turn any music on. I noticed right away that his room was a mess. Clothes were strewn all over the floor, CDs weren't in their cases and his bed was unmade. It was also very dark in his room thanks to the window being closed and the being blinds tightly shut. I had an urge to go open the blinds but I thought about how I hated it when my own mother did that. So, I just stood there. Jason still hadn't said anything to me, but he took his shoes off and sat down in the middle of the bed. His legs crossed in front of him, he told me to sit down. I plopped down across from him, waiting for him to say something. After a few minutes of utter silence, I couldn't take it anymore and broke the spell.

"What is going on, Jason?"

"Dad isn't just going to visit Mom in California, Kathryn. He's moving there." He paused a minute then continued. "*We're* moving there."

My mind was whirling. "But you said that he was just going out there for a visit."

"It's what I thought, but he told me that he was going out there to talk things out with my mom and that after school lets out, we're leaving." His voice sounded so edgy and my mind was spinning. "We're moving back, Katy and there isn't anything I can do about it."

I felt a heaviness weighing down my heart. This sounded way too familiar. After all, it was just last year that I was going through this same thing.

I nodded. "I had the same problem moving here."

He just stared at me.

"But at least you're going to be going back to the same place. You'll know people; you'll have your same friends that you had before."

"I don't want those friends, Katy. I like the ones I have now." He looked so deeply into my eyes when he said it that I had to look away. "You're the best friend I've ever had and I actually like it here. I like school, I like the people at school ... I like Sarasota. I don't want to move to LA."

"That's just the thing, Jason. We're kids and we don't get choices. It's not fair. Parents are so selfish and it's like all they think about is what's best for them. They say it's about us, but it's never about us."

"Yeah, you got that right. Screw them though. I might have to go, but there will be hell to pay for it." The anger in his voice scared me. I didn't want to see him go through a destructive phase in retaliation like I had.

"Please, Jason, it won't be worth it. Getting back at your parents only ends up hurting you. I went through this ... I used food against my parents. Look where it got me ... I've missed an entire year of school, I've spent way too much time in the hospital and this is a year that I'll never get back. And the fact remains, I'm still in Sarasota, so nothing has changed."

He looked at me again, his eyes piercing through me. "But it hasn't been so bad, has it?" It wasn't even a question. I shook my head.

"It's turned out a lot better than I ever thought it would have," I told him quietly and it was the truth, I realized. But of course, the only reason it was good was because of him. He had to know that, and his moving was going to be hard on me too. Then it hit me ... Breeana.

"Have you told Breeana about it yet?" His eyes clouded over at my question. He didn't say anything for a minute.

"What is it, Jason?"

"Yesterday, when you and I were at the beach and I told you that my mind just wasn't there, I knew I had to tell her. I wanted to tell you first but Bree's family knows mine and I knew she'd find out if I didn't tell her first. So, I went over there ..." We heard a car door then, and we knew that Mr. Neely had returned. He waited a minute and then said, "I went over there to talk to her and she broke up with me."

"What? She broke up with you? But why?"

"She said she couldn't deal with anything long distance. I told her that I wasn't leaving until the end of the school year but she said what was the point? She pointed out that we would have to be over soon anyway and she didn't want to be tied down with someone who was moving."

I was shocked. What a colossal monster! "Tied down?" I was really stuck on that part.

"Yeah, I know. It was all her anyway. She bugged me forever to go out with her." He got quiet then. "But the messed up part is that I liked her, Kathryn. I mean, she had her moments, but I really liked her." I tried to be sympathetic, but it upset me to know he was hurting over someone who wasn't worth it. I just didn't know what to say. His eyes looked so sad that I wanted to hug him but I wasn't sure if I should move.

"Are you okay?"

"Yeah, it was just weird today at school. I mean, she totally dissed me during lunch. I sat with Pitman and Jake at the table behind her, but I felt like crap. And she was over there laughing and having the best time of her life, like losing me didn't even matter."

"It was all just an act, Jase. You have to know that."

"No, I don't. She was already talking to that guy Trent from homeroom." I didn't know him but I nodded so he'd go on.

"He'd been flirting with her for a while but I didn't think about it. It just sucks to know that I can be replaced that fast."

Like I didn't know that feeling. After all, Jeremy had replaced me in four seconds. But I didn't mention that; I just let him talk. After he stopped and took a deep breath, he said, "So now you know everything. Dad leaves tomorrow and he won't be back until Saturday night."

"But you're staying here right?"

"Yeah, Dad wanted me to go, but with school and everything, he agreed that I better not. And anyway, I think he wants to be alone with my mom. They have a lot to talk about I guess."

"Will it be weird for you to be here alone?" I was trying to picture my parents leaving town for almost a week. I couldn't picture them ever doing something like that."

"No, it won't be weird. We have lots of friends in the neighborhood and they'll be around. I'm actually looking forward to the time alone." I could understand that.

"But you're still coming Friday night, right?" I guess I sounded worried because he said, "It's all good, Katy. I'll be there."

He smiled at me then and for the first time that afternoon, he looked like he was going to be okay. I had to settle for hoping he would be, because his dad called us to come and help him set the table. We got up and he hugged me tightly. "Thank you for being such a great friend."

I sighed. I hated being just a friend, but at least I was something. We walked into the kitchen and together talked and worked. It actually turned out to be fun. Mr. Neely kept threatening to show me pictures of Jason when he was a baby and he even wanted to drag out the family videos. Jason said if his dad did that, he was going to run away to my house and he wasn't coming back. I laughed, but for a minute, I wished that he could do just that.

ଚଡ     ଔଓ

The rest of the week went by slowly. I was looking forward to my birthday but the days leading up to it passed at a snaillike pace because I didn't talk to Jason as much as I'd wanted. He was too busy brooding over some spoiled rotten brat who wasn't worth it. He was also hanging out with his friends more, so I saw less and less of him that week than I had since meeting him. I missed him terribly.

On Thursday, I got a package from Jane. It turned out to be a birthday present. Of course, the front of the box said, "Don't open until your birthday," but by the time the package arrived, that was only one day away so I just ripped into it. Inside, there was a 'Friends Forever' picture frame with our picture in it. It had been taken last summer at the swimming pool. I was shocked by how much we'd changed in less than a year. The two girls staring back at me weren't the same girls we were now. Jane was so thin in her bright pink two-piece bathing suit, with her hair long and flowing. I was standing there in my black one piece, and I had a towel wrapped around my waist so no one could see my thunder thighs. My hair was stringy from the water, but I was smiling as though I was having the time of my life. And come to think of it, I probably was. It was hard to remember how I had felt back then since I'd gone through so many changes since.

As I riffed through the packaging peanuts I discover that there was something else in the box and I took it out. It was an Usher CD—the same one that had been playing that night so long ago at Woodland Park. I anxiously opened the accompanying card.

*"I was feeling nostalgic so I thought these things would make you feel the same way. Have a wonderful birthday. And since I know you opened it early, go ahead and call me!*

*BFF, Jane*

I laughed out loud at how well she knew me and called Jane right away. We talked for almost an hour. After I got off the phone, I felt nostalgic too, although I had to look that word up in the dictionary before I knew what the heck Jane was talking about. She's always had a bigger vocabulary than I had.

# ๛ Chapter Forty-One ๙

"Happy Birthday to you, happy birthday to you, happy birthday, dear Katybug ... happy birthday to you." My parents were standing over my bed the morning of my birthday, waking me up with their singing, which, if you ever had the misfortune of hearing them together you would know is not pretty. It was a wonderful gesture nonetheless and I smiled as I sat up in bed. My mother was holding a tray of food out in front of me and my dad had come bearing gifts. My mother pushed the tray in front of me, urging me to eat.

"How cute," I told her. She'd made pancakes in the shape of the numbers one and five and she'd put a candle on each number. It was so corny, but I couldn't hurt her feelings.

My dad handed me a small box. "This is from me, Katybug."

My eyes were shining with anticipation. The box was wrapped in beautiful gift paper, but I'm not one of those people who open things up slowly to keep the gift-wrap perfect. Who cares anyway? So, as was my custom, I ripped it off. The package disrobed, I quickly opened the box. Inside, I discovered a flower ring with small diamonds around it. The flower was constructed of white gold in the shape of four petals, and it was so dainty. I couldn't believe how pretty it was. I looked up at my dad, who was smiling at me with so much pride in his eyes that I could tell he had picked it out himself.

"I love it, Dad. Thank you so much!"

I tried the ring on all my fingers, but it fit my middle right one best. I hugged him and then he handed me Mother's gift. I opened it and literally squealed out loud when I saw it. "A cell phone!" It was one of those flip phone kinds with a camera and I felt like I was going to explode ... I just was too excited.

"Oh thank you, thank you, thank you!!" I hopped out of bed and jumped up and down with delight. Then I hugged my mother. "This is so great. I can't wait to use it."

My parents started laughing. "Well, we thought this would cut down on long distance. This way, you can call your friends in Atlanta and it won't be a long distance charge. Also, you need to call Nana more often." I couldn't believe she would say a thing like that, but she was right. Since Thanksgiving, I hadn't talked to my grandmother as often as I should have. I felt bad about that, but now I could call her anytime. Satisfied that their gifts were a big hit, my parents left me to my breakfast and my gifts. I read the instructions for the phone and found out how to use it and take pictures. I was just so thrilled. It was turning out to be a great day already and it was barely seven thirty.

The rest of the day passed slowly though. Mrs. Bell had made me do schoolwork even though I told her it was my birthday and hinted that I should at least have a day off. She didn't see things my way, though and we ended up spending most of the morning working on algebra. I truly hated math.

She didn't even slack up on me when I told her I was exhausted and had to have a break. She seriously was every student's nightmare. Finally, it was time for Mrs. Bell to leave and I went upstairs and tried to take a nap. I knew that I wanted to be completely rested for that night.

I found it hard to nap though. I kept thinking about everything and I was just so excited about hanging out with Jason that I just finally got up. Even though my parents would be there, I kept hoping that we would have some time alone together.

I decided to go ahead and start getting ready so I could take my time and look my best.

I put some almond bath oil in my water and while I soaked, I thought about Jason and how much I liked him. I just wished he didn't like Breeana so much. She SO wasn't worth it.

The warm bath was so relaxing that I was feeling really drowsy when the phone rang. My mother knocked on the bathroom door. "Sweetie, it's for you."

I kept my eyes closed, not wanting to get out of the warm tub. "Who is it?"

"I think it's Leslie."

I knew I needed to get to the phone, but I was just so comfortable. "Will you tell her I'll call her back?"

"Sure, I'll tell her." Twenty minutes later, I finally emerged from my water oasis and put lotion all over my body. It was a new scent that I'd gotten from Nana. Her package of lotion, body wash, and bath beads had arrived that morning. They smelled delicious! She had also sent me a light blue cashmere sweater that I couldn't wait to wear. When I was finished, I wrapped myself in a towel and went out to call Leslie. I let the phone ring four times before hanging up and trying again. The second time it rang seven times, and then the machine came on.

"Hi, Leslie, it's me. I was returning your call. Give me a call back as soon as you can." After I hung up, I started working on my hair. Since it was a special occasion, I decided to use the flat iron on it. My hair is straight anyway, but if I use the flat iron, it makes it shinier and it takes away all the bumps and frizzes. Once I was satisfied with my tresses, I worked on my makeup ... something I rarely used, except for lip-gloss. But again, this was a special occasion and I wanted to look my best.

The end result was good and I actually felt pretty. By the time Jason got there, I was completely ready and actually a little nervous, though I didn't know why. I guess it was because I had been ready fifteen minutes early, giving me plenty of time to make myself nervous. In anticipation of Jason's arrival, I kept pacing my bedroom floor until I thought I would make a hole in the carpet. Mom and Dad must have heard me because they came in to check on me. They looked great. Mom wore a black dress that looked good on her, even though she was old and Dad wore a suit because that's just what dads wore I guess.

Together though, they made an amazing couple. I had just never thought about them being like that until now.

"You look beautiful, Katybug," Dad said before letting me know that he was going to go downstairs and make a drink. "Do you want anything, Abby?"

"No thanks." Then my mother turned to me and we talked about what jewelry I should wear. We were just deciding between two necklaces when the doorbell rang. Except for this past week, I'd seen Jason almost every day over the past few months, but for some reason this felt different and I thought I was going to throw up.

"You're going to be fine, Kathryn. Don't be scared. Jason is your friend. This is going to be fun." I knew she was right, but I just felt so scared. Mom went down first and I clasped my necklace for moral support.

As I descended the stairs, I saw immediately that Jason looked amazing. He was wearing a jacket and tie and I'd never seen him look so grown up or so incredible before. I could tell right away by his expression that he was happy with my choice of dresses. I hugged him when I got to the bottom of the stairs.

"You're beautiful, Kathryn," he whispered in my ear before he released the hug. Just the way he said my name gave me goose bumps.

"You look beautiful yourself." I giggled because I wasn't sure what else to say.

In the grand tradition of mothers everywhere, mine took out her camera and started snapping about a thousand pictures—pictures of Jason and me, pictures of Dad and me. Then, as if that weren't humiliating enough, she asked Jason to take a picture of all three of us. She even took one of me alone and that was even more embarrassing.

"Don't we have a reservation?" I finally asked, wanting to extricate myself from the situation at hand. They took the hint and we left.

ઝ    ૐ

It took almost a half-hour to get to the restaurant, but conversation flowed and the time went by fast. On the way, Dad told funny birthday stories of when I was younger, while Jason and I sat in the backseat and laughed until I thought my sides would split. It was the way my dad told a story that made it so hysterical. If anyone else had been telling it, I'm sure it wouldn't have been as funny, but he was very animated and he kept us thoroughly entertained. Even Mother laughed, although she kept insisting my dad was exaggerating things a bit.

At one point, Jason leaned toward me in the car and I could feel his leg on mine. I felt an electric shock course through my body when he did so, but I didn't think he noticed. For a minute, I thought about what it would be like to be a grown-up and to go on a date with Jason, just Jason and me, without my parents. I got butterflies in my stomach just thinking about it. I glanced at him and found that he was staring straight ahead. He didn't have a sad look on his face though, so that gave me hope that he wasn't brooding about Breeana anymore.

Before I knew it though, we were at the restaurant. As we walked in, Dad gave the hostess our name and we were seated right away.

The restaurant was even more amazing than I had imagined. Because it was a warm, breezy night we decided to eat outside in the courtyard. It overlooked a garden and on one side of us, there was a reflecting pool. Shortly after we were situated, the waiter came out and handed us these huge menus, bigger than any I'd ever seen. And when I opened it, I found out quickly that everything was written in French. Thankfully, my parents could speak a little French; otherwise, I don't know what we would have done. Of course later, Jason reminded me that all we'd have had to do was ask.

Dad asked to see the wine list and I looked at him expectantly. But he answered my unspoken question quickly. "And while we wait, the kids will have a Sprite." Sprite? In a restaurant like this? I was mortified, but Jason didn't seem to notice. When the waiter came back with a wine list, my dad looked it over twice and then decided on one I couldn't even pronounce. Apparently it was a good choice though, because the waiter made an appreciated comment on the selection. Mother raised her eyebrows a little and leaned over to Dad. "Going over the top, aren't you, William?"

"It's a special occasion. Lighten up, Abby," my dad chided, but it was all said in good humor.

Then the waiter asked if we were ready to order. I loved hearing him talk. He had a thick French accent and I actually felt like we were in France, or at least somewhere far, far from home instead of less than an hour away.

"I think we'll start out with Pâté de Foies de Volailles Maison," Dad said.

Jason and I looked at each other and shrugged. I didn't have a clue but soon found out that it meant chicken liver pâté, and that they served it with French bread (which was delicious) and, of all things, tiny pickles called gherkins. I didn't think that went too well, so I didn't eat any. I made up for it in bread, but I didn't touch the liver. That sounded too gross, but everyone else loved it, even Jason, who I wouldn't have guessed would touch the stuff.

"Well, it's not like I get to eat like this every day, Katy." He laughed and kept right on savoring the first course.

Then, for the main course, Dad ordered Filet Mignon for himself, which ended up being just steak. Mother ordered Canard à l'Orange, which was duck. Dad asked Jason what he would like, but he said he didn't know. So, Dad offered to order for him and Jason gladly accepted. After a few seconds of looking over the menu, Dad asked Jason if he ate red meat. I knew that was a stab at me since I was the one who had cut red meat from my diet. But Jason said he loved it, so Dad ordered him Faux Filet Grillé au Bleu, which was New York strip steak with a French blue cheese sauce.

I asked Dad to go ahead and order for me too since I had no idea what to get. I got jumbo shrimp and sea scallops. And he told me not to worry, that I would love it. "They sauté it in a lemon butter sauce," he informed me, like I was supposed to care.

We talked non-stop until the food came. Until that moment, I hadn't realized how talkative Jason could be around parents. I'm never like that around strangers because I always feel shy. But Jason made himself right at home. He and Dad talked about sports and about school and Dad even thanked him for helping me with my algebra.

"I can't wait until Katy can get back to school. This time maybe it'll be better for her since she'll have a friend like you with her." Jason and I exchanged disappointed glances. I hadn't told my parents what was going on and I was scared that bringing it up now would bring Jason's mood down. But he seemed to let it go and then gratefully the food came so nothing else was said about it.

Everyone agreed that the food was delicious. I had never eaten seafood like that and it was just so good. I guess it was just a habit for me to eat very slowly and carefully, cutting my food into smaller bites. I could see my parents exchange worried looks, but I ignored them. I was fine—I just couldn't break all my habits at once.

The conversation continued as we ate. Jason talked about college and told us something even I didn't know. "I've always wanted to go into medicine, Mr. Bailey."

I was surprised by that admission. I'd had no idea. I looked over at my mother and noticed she had an impressed look on her face. My parents were huge fans of goals. They thought everyone should have them, no matter how old or young. I knew they were liking Jason more and more the better they got to know him. It was just too bad he was leaving once school got out. "You know," Dad said to Jason, "I've been trying to talk Mrs. Bailey into going back to school to pursue something in the medical field. She's always at the hospital anyway. She should be getting paid for it, instead of just volunteering her hours."

"Well, dear, after this dinner, I might have to." They laughed but I guess it was just something funny between grown-ups because I didn't think it was funny.

After dinner we ordered dessert, although I wasn't sure I wanted any. My parents insisted, however, since it was my birthday and my mother hadn't baked a cake. I couldn't have cared less about a cake, but I ordered anyway to appease them. "Only if Jason and I share," I compromised.

Jason said that was fine with him, although he had earlier insisted he couldn't eat another bite. We chose strawberry cheesecake because it was my favorite. Jason liked it too and he ended up eating more than I did, which was a relief to me.

Dad ordered turtle cheesecake and my head immediately popped up. "No, Katy, it's not real turtle."

He made me feel foolish for even thinking it, but I was relieved that it wasn't real turtle. He explained that it was just a name and that it had chocolate chips and caramel sauce over it. I didn't know what that had to do with turtle, but I wasn't going to say so.

Mother wanted her own dessert, which surprised me because I honestly didn't know where she put it. She ordered strawberry crepes. My parents drank coffee with theirs, but Jason and I stuck to Sprite.

After dinner, people began dancing. Inside, the restaurant had a dance floor and a band that played music Jason and I didn't recognize. It was more Jazz-type music than the pop stuff we preferred but my parents loved it. Jason asked if I wanted to dance but I wasn't sure. These people weren't dancing like we did at school. They were grown-ups and I didn't want to look stupid.

"Oh, come on, Katy. You know it'll be fun."

Not taking 'no' for an answer, he practically dragged me out to the dance floor and at first I kind of froze up. But after a few minutes of Jason leading me around, I loosened up and found out that it was fun. We just did what everyone else was doing and my dress was perfect for it. I noticed a couple of people glancing at us and I initially thought they might be making fun of us. I tried not to think about it, but as we were walking off the floor, another couple pulled us aside and told us we were absolutely great. "You're both so adorable," they kept saying. They were older, so I'm sure they thought everyone was adorable.

"You two make a great dancing couple," Dad told us when we got back to the table.

"Thanks, Mr. Bailey, it's fun. You and Mrs. Bailey should try it."

Dad shook his head. "I'm not the dancer of the family." He just laughed but Mother looked a little annoyed. I knew she wanted to dance, but Dad was always like that.

"Mrs. Bailey, would you dance with me?" Jason graciously offered.

Mother's face broke into a smile. "Thank you, Jason, but I think I'll sit this one out."

"What is with this family? Are you all against dancing?" As he'd done with me, Jason dragged Mother out to the dance floor and by watching them from the sidelines you could tell they were having a lot of fun. Mother looked so much younger than she had just sitting there next to my dad ten minutes ago.

Dad looked at me. "You'd better watch out, Katybug. Mom might steal your boyfriend." He laughed at his own joke.

"Are you kidding me? You should worry—he's not even my boyfriend, but she's your wife!" We both laughed and then before I knew it, they were back at the table, with Mother breathless.

"Thank you, Jason, that was the most fun I've had in years." She glared at Dad when she said it, but he was oblivious to her verbal stab, as usual.

It was late when we left the restaurant, but I took a chance and asked if Jason and I could hang out at our house for a while. "You'll have to take him home though. His dad isn't home."

"That'll be fine. Just let me know when you're ready," Dad consented.

The ride home was quiet, but at one point, Jason put his hand over mine. And although I didn't know what he meant by it, I did know it made me happy. When we got home, my parents went upstairs to change their clothes. They said they'd let us have the living room and they'd watch TV in their bedroom. Dad just told us to let him know when Jason was ready to leave. I looked at the clock. It was already almost ten o'clock. I didn't know how long Dad would want to wait, but I didn't want Jason to leave yet.

We sat down on the couch and put in a DVD, but neither of us really watched it. I didn't even know what I'd put in; I just grabbed the closest disc to the DVD player.

"I've been waiting all night to give this to you, Katy. It seemed like your parents were always around and I didn't want to give it to you at the restaurant." I smiled and couldn't imagine what it could be. He reached into his pocket and handed me a gift-wrapped box. It was small and inside lay a silver ankle bracelet with little hearts around it. My stomach did a flip-flop. It was beautiful and I immediately put it on. Then I hugged him so hard I thought I was going to break him.

"So, I take it you like?" He laughed after I finally let him go.

"I love it, Jason. You're so great."

"Well, happy birthday, Katy. You deserve to be happy. You've had a hell of a year."

# ℬ Chapter Forty-Two ℭ

Saturday morning I woke up flooded with a happiness that I hadn't felt in a while. Dad and I had taken Jason home right around midnight and I had walked him into the house while Dad waited in the car. I told Dad I would only be a minute. When we got inside, I told Jason that I wanted to borrow a CD, but what I was really doing was stalling for time. I simply never wanted our time together to end. We walked into his bedroom, but he didn't turn the lights on. He just handed me a CD. It was the Alanis Morrisette CD, the one we'd played that night we fell asleep on his bed. I wondered how he knew that was the one I wanted. I guess he'd remembered that night too.

"I'll burn a copy and get this back to you," I'd told him.

"Keep it." He moved closer to me. Then he put his arms around me. We were standing in the middle of his bedroom floor and just gazing into each other's eyes. I couldn't stop staring at him and before I even realized what happened, he had kissed me. It was so unlike any kiss I'd ever had before. His lips were so soft yet his kiss wasn't soft at all. It was an almost urgent probing of his lips and I felt like my body was on fire. I'd never felt that good in my entire life and I never wanted it to end. But unfortunately, it did end and I wasn't even sure who pulled away first. I just knew that once it was over, I felt lightheaded. After that, I barely remembered walking to the car.

Now, I looked at the clock and it was only nine in the morning. I thought I would have slept later than that considering it took me forever to fall asleep. Every time I would start to doze off, I would think about that kiss and I would be wide-awake all over again. I didn't think I would ever get to sleep. But now I was wide-awake and still thinking about Jason. I really needed to find a hobby. I was just about to get out of bed when the phone rang. I hoped it was Jason so I picked it up on the half ring.

"Hello?"

"Is this Kathryn Bailey?" a voice that I didn't recognize asked me.

"Yes, this is Kathryn. Who is this?"

"I'm Sandra Ross and I'm so sorry to have to call you." Her voice sounded funny and my mind was thinking about everyone I knew. But I didn't know a Sandra Ross and anyway, she sounded like an older person. "I'm Leslie's mother," she offered when I didn't say anything.

Then I remembered that Leslie had called me when I was in the bathtub. When I called her back, no one answered so I left a message but never heard back from her. But why would her mother be calling?

"Leslie had to go to the hospital this morning around two with complications," she started telling me, her voice shaking. My heart started beating too quickly and I sat straight up in bed.

"What kind of complications?" I didn't want her to drag this on. I wanted her to tell me what was wrong.

"I'm not sure if you knew it or not, but Leslie really wasn't getting better. She wasn't eating, though she tried to hide it. Last night ..." Her voice broke and I could tell she was crying. To make matters worse, I couldn't understand what she was saying.

"What is it, Mrs. Ross? Just tell me!" By that point, I was almost screaming, but she couldn't talk for crying and then I threw the phone receiver down. I didn't want to hear it. Even though I knew, I couldn't hear it. I let out a shrill scream for my Mom and within seconds, she came rushing into my room.

"What's wrong, Kathryn?" She had a horrorstruck look on her face. I normally didn't scream like that for my mother.

I just pointed to the phone. She picked it up from the floor and said, "Hello? This is Mrs. Bailey."

I couldn't tell what Mrs. Ross was saying, but I saw my mother look at me with very sad eyes. There was something in them so very haunting. I knew that I'd never forget that look. My mother didn't say much at first, just things like 'yes' and 'oh no', and 'I'm so sorry', and 'yes, I'll tell her'. I felt like the room was spinning. Then she took a piece of paper from my nightstand and wrote something down. After a few agonizing moments, she hung up.

"Kathryn, that was Leslie's mother."

I nodded. "I know, but she was crying."

"Leslie wasn't getting better, Kathryn. There were complications. Things with her heart ..." My mother paused and then added, "Leslie went to the hospital, but she didn't make it, Kathryn. They did everything they could for her, but she was just too sick. She died of heart complications brought on by her anorexia."

Even though I knew it already, I wasn't prepared to hear it. I couldn't bear to hear any more. I felt like my heart was beating too fast and I couldn't stop it. I jumped out of bed and threw on a pair of blue sweats. I ran out of the house, sprinting all the way to Jason's house, about a thirty-minute run. I had to see him though. I couldn't stay in my house any longer.

I was still wearing my old Atlanta Braves T-shirt and I was sure that with the gray sweats, I looked frightening. Even my hair was a mess, but I didn't care. I knocked three times before he came to the door. By that point, I was completely out of breath and felt dehydrated from thirst.

He came to the door wearing only boxers and I could tell I'd woken him up. As soon as I saw him, I started crying. "Leslie's dead," I blurted out.

The meaning of my words not registering, he opened the door enough to let me in. He was rubbing his eyes and squinting because the sun was so bright. "Who?"

"Leslie!" I told him. "From the hospital. My friend from the hospital." I gave him all the details in between crying and he hugged me close to him.

"I'm so sorry, Kathryn. I really don't know what to say." We walked into the kitchen and he poured us some juice. I sat down and stared out the window.

"How did you get here?" he asked me.

"I ran," I said, still exhausted from the long distance I'd spanned from his house to mine.

"God, Katy, that's a long way to run. Here." He took away my juice and handed me bottled water. "Drink this first and then drink the juice." I drank the water so fast that he said, "No, slowly. You're going to throw up." I slowed down but I was so thirsty I didn't think I would ever stop drinking.

Finally, after I finished the water and the juice, I said, "I didn't even talk to her that night."

"What do you mean?" Jason was looking at me, his eyes narrowed like he didn't understand.

"She called me, Jason and I didn't even go to the phone." I explained to him that she'd called me while I was in the bathtub but that I hadn't gotten out to go to the phone. "I called her back, but she didn't answer. She needed me and I wasn't there. I could have saved her!" I was almost hysterical thinking about that, but Jason stayed calm.

"There was nothing you could do, Kathryn, nothing!" He walked over to me then and put his hands on my shoulders. "Do you understand? Honestly, you couldn't have helped her even if you'd talked to her all night."

I shook my head. "Maybe there was something and I just didn't do it."

The phone rang then and we both looked at it. Finally, after about a million rings, Jason answered it.

"Hello ... Yes, she's here ... No, she's okay. Okay, I'll tell her ... Okay, 'bye." Then to me he said, "That was your mother. She's worried about you."

"I should go home. I'm sorry I just barged in on you like this, but I didn't know where else to go or what else to do." I realized how much I'd depended on him. But then of course I would. After all, he was really my only friend who lived around here.

"You don't have to go. She just wanted to know if you were here."

"I just don't feel well. I don't know what to do." I felt so confused.

"Well, you can't go home now. You can't make that long walk back. And you certainly can't run. Just stay here for a while and let me take care of you." I loved how he said that. I nodded and he led me to his bedroom. His bed was still unmade. He told me to lie down and he'd bring some toast and some more juice. I crawled into his bed and discovered it was still warm from where he'd been lying. It felt so good to be that close to him. I felt so safe. I could even smell his shampoo on his pillow. The scent was so powerful that I buried my head into the pillow and started crying. After a minute, he came in carrying toast and tea on a tray. Then he set it down on his nightstand and sat on the edge of the bed.

"Katy ... please don't cry." He was rubbing my shoulders but I couldn't stop crying. I just felt so guilty. Why did it have to be Leslie? Why hadn't she tried to get better? What's more, I felt selfish for even thinking about myself at this time. I mean, it could have been me who died. If I hadn't gotten better, I could have died too. And right now, the pain was so intense that I wondered if death could be any worse.

"Do you want some toast?" Jason asked me, almost whispering.

I shook my head.

"Can I get you anything?" he urged. I knew he was trying but I couldn't think of anything I wanted—except to just have this all go away. Finally, after a minute of stunned silence, he crawled onto the bed beside me. He hugged me close to him, running his fingers through my hair and whispering that it would be okay. But how could it be okay? For that moment, in Jason's arms, however, I felt safe and I fell asleep against his chest. For that moment he was right; everything was okay.

ᛤ   ᙅ

I woke up in a panic. I didn't know where I was. Initially I thought I was at home, so I looked over at my clock only it wasn't in the right place. I sat straight up then with a startled scream. It wasn't loud, but it was loud enough for Jason to come running.

"What's wrong? What is it?" I felt foolish. I remembered then. Everything suddenly came rushing back.

"Oh nothing, sorry. I guess I had a bad dream." He hugged me and assured me I was safe. I felt safe but I knew that I'd have to go home soon.

"I'll get you something to drink." He left the room and came back a few minutes later with Sprite. I was so thirsty and the Sprite was so good that I kept drinking without letting up.

"Sip it, Katy," he reminded me. "You need to eat something. I'm going to fix you something and you're going to eat." He was starting to sound parental and I kind of just wanted to laugh. Only I couldn't laugh, so I just nodded.

"What time is it?" I looked around but I couldn't find a clock.

"It's four."

"Oh no! I'm in so much trouble!" I felt panicked and I jumped up, but Jason came over and reassuringly put his hands on my shoulders. "Stop it, Katy. You're not in trouble. I've talked to your mom on and off all day. She knows you're okay. She told me that when you were ready, to just call her and she'd come and get you. Now just lie back down and I'll bring you some food." I got back under the covers and immediately felt drowsy again. Jason's room was dark and the temperature was cool. It was the perfect sleeping atmosphere. I started dozing off again, but then Jason brought in a tray of food. He sat down on the other side of the bed and handed me a ham and cheese sandwich. He also had a big bowl of grapes that he started munching on. He had a sandwich of his own as well, but he only took a small bite.

"I'm really worried about you, Katy," he admitted.

"Don't be. I'll be okay." I took a bite of sandwich. "This is really good, Jason. Thank you."

He ignored that. "I just don't want you getting sick like you were. And every time I think about how you and Leslie were roommates! It could have been you, Kathryn. You could have died." He sounded almost angry.

"But I didn't and I'm okay, Jason. Really, I'm okay." I took another bite of sandwich. "See, I'm eating."

He nodded but didn't seem convinced.

ℰ ℭ

My mother came to get me around six o'clock so I could have dinner with her and Dad. Jason and I sat around and played Halo 2 on his XBOX until I had to leave. Even though I didn't know how to play, I caught on kind of quickly. We were having so much fun that I almost forgot about why I was even there.

When she arrived, Mom came inside to get me and thanked Jason for everything. I felt embarrassed because it almost seemed like he had been babysitting me. I half expected her to pay him for tending to me. On the way out though, he hugged me and told me he'd call me later.

Once we got home, I went straight to my room and stayed there until Mom called me for dinner. I just sat at my window seat and thought about everything that was going on. I felt so guilty and yet, at the same time, I felt so angry. Why hadn't Leslie even tried to feel better? Why was she so determined to kill herself? Then my anger would momentarily go away and I would feel guilty all over again. Maybe she was calling that night to tell me something. Maybe I could have helped her; maybe I could have saved her life. Now I would never know. All I could think about was how we'd planned to get better together, to become friends again and to even go college together. I thought about how she had wanted to become a therapist. Ironically, she had wanted to help people, but she hadn't even been able to help herself. I felt so mixed up that I went from crying to anger and back to crying again.

A half-hour later, Mother knocked on my door and told me that it was time for dinner. I went downstairs looking as worn out as I had that morning. I hadn't even bothered to brush my hair. I sat down at the table and Dad asked me if I was okay. I was really getting tired of that question but to satisfy him I said I was fine.

Mom was putting the last of the food on the table and she and my dad started piling food on their plates. I got a roll and started eating.

"You know, if you want to go to the funeral, we can work something out," Mother said, breaking the silence.

I knew that it would be in Chicago and I told her that.

"But if you want to go ..." she started again, but I interrupted her.

"No, I just want to think about Leslie the way she was when I met her ... I don't want to remember her in a casket with people crying all around her." I was glad that my parents understood: a fact they demonstrated when they said nothing else about me going.

"Well, if you change your mind, Kathryn, just let us know," Dad said.

The rest of the meal was eaten in silence. Dad looked at Mom when he noticed me toying with my food, but she said, "It's okay; she ate a really good lunch at Jason's." I thought it was so amazing how they could communicate like that, without even saying anything to each other. But Dad kind of lowered his voice and probed her further. "Did *she* tell you that or did he?"

"He did, William. And everything is going to be okay."

# ജ Chapter Forty-Three ൽ

I found out the next morning that I had an appointment to see my therapist that day. I think my mother moved it up because although I knew I had one, I didn't think it was that soon. I didn't argue though, because I really needed to talk to someone.

I went in looking like I'd slept in my clothes. My hair was still tangled and I didn't even care. But despite by haggard appearance, my therapist, Dr. Cline, was great. She didn't even comment about how terrible I looked. In fact, she and I talked longer than the usual hour. She listened to me talk about how guilty I felt for not going to the phone that night to talk to Leslie. She also listened while I described how I had bonded with Leslie and how I felt like it could have been me. I explained to her that my guilt stemmed from both of us being sick with the same illness, only I'd gotten better and a part of me was glad that it wasn't me. But of course, that confession made me feel guilty too.

Dr. Cline started out by reassuring me that I couldn't have done anything over the phone to help Leslie and that feeling guilty wasn't going to bring her back. It was only going to make me sick. She also told me that we all have choices—mine was to get better and live. Leslie, on the other hand, had chosen to stay sick. Eventually that choice had killed her. Before wrapping things up, she told me that I shouldn't feel guilty for living. After leaving her office, I have to admit I felt much better. I knew that I would always have sad feelings when I thought about Leslie, but I would also always try to find a way to cope.

When I got home, I called Jane on my cell phone. I realized that I hadn't talked to her in a while and I wondered how things were going back in Atlanta. We talked for almost two hours straight. I told her about Leslie and how hard it was to know someone who had died. After all, we were only kids and kids weren't supposed to die.

I told her about how I was having all these weird feelings for Jason and how he was moving. I even told her about how Bree had broken up with him and how he seemed to not have taken it so well.

She told me about how school was going great and how she couldn't wait until it was out for summer. She also told me how she and Kevin were going to the spring dance together. And then she hesitated, before adding, "And well, Kammy and Jeremy are going out now." When I heard that, I almost chocked on the Sprite I was drinking. For a minute, I felt so jealous that I wanted to scream, but I didn't say anything.

"It's just because he's now as tall as Brent and she's grown even more, so she's like the tallest girl in our class," she assured me. I laughed, but it still made me feel awful to know that Kammy was with Jeremy—Jeremy with his Ashton hair and a smile that made my knees weak. For a minute, I hated Kammy, but I knew that I couldn't hate her forever ... she was still my friend and I was far away. I couldn't be with Jeremy, even if Kammy wasn't. I had to let it go.

That night, Jason called me to see how I was feeling. When I told him I was fine, he sounded relieved. He said that he was worried because he was afraid I was going to relapse. I admitted that in a way, I was kind of scared of the same thing.

"But Jason, I'm not going to relapse because I don't want to end up like Leslie. And I'm worried about you because when you talk about moving, you get an anger inside of you that I completely relate to. Please don't get that angry over something you can't control." We talked for over an hour during which he said that he couldn't help the way he was feeling, but that he wouldn't do anything self-destructive either. He also told me how his dad had told him that things had gone so well with his mom that he couldn't wait to get out to California to be with her.

"I can kind of understand where he's at with it, Katy, but it still sucks that I have to leave." I admitted him it sucked just as much for me.

"You're the only friend I feel like I have," I told him quietly. Before we hung up, he made a final confession that nearly broke my heart. "You know, Katy, no matter how many friends I have, I'm going to miss you more than anyone else."

# ഇ Chapter Forty-Four ദ

Things went smoothly for the next couple of months. Very typical days ... school with Mrs. Bell, talking on the phone with Jane (the cell phone had been a great idea) and hanging out with Jason. I kept going to therapy and Dr. Cline told me I was much better. On my last visit, my weight was one hundred fifteen pounds and I was up to five feet three inches. That meant I was at a perfect weight for my height. I knew that I'd always have food issues, but I didn't dwell on that fact. I just accepted it.

Jason and I spent so much time together that all his friends thought we were a couple, although he never acted like it. To him, we were just friends ... good friends ... but still, only friends. I had to accept that too. It was like the kiss we'd had on my birthday hadn't happened at all. He never kissed me like that again and we never talked about it afterwards.

Sometimes, Jason and I went to movies together; other times we went to the beach. And since it was getting warmer, we even swam in the ocean. Of course, we spent a lot of our time in the pool in my backyard. Since this was the first summer in the house, Dad had hired a pool guy and we started swimming almost everyday. We had a built-in pool with a diving board at the deepest end, which went to nine feet. We also had a slide that spiraled in at the five-foot level. I'd never thought I'd even get in the pool when I had first moved to Sarasota, but now I loved it. I had a great tan and the funny thing was, while I had been so worried about not looking good in a bathing suit, I now practically lived in one. A couple of times we even invited his friends, Jake and Kelly, over to swim with us. We had a lot of fun as a group and I really liked Kelly. In confidence, she admitted to me that she wasn't really hanging out with Breeana anymore. She agreed that Bree was just a self-centered brat and it bothered her that she could just blow off Jason like that. The more Kelly and I talked, the more I liked her and before long, we were talking on the phone regularly. In fact, we even went shopping together a couple of times. Mom was thrilled that I had found another friend.

ভ   ভ

One Monday, during the first week of May, Jason came over after school. We were sitting in my room, listening to CDs. While we were trying to do homework, we kept talking and neither of us was getting much done. Mom was at the hospital working, so we were home alone. Mom and Dad didn't say much about things like that anymore. I guess they trusted Jason and realized it really didn't matter.

Jason kept looking at me but not saying anything. Finally, I couldn't take his silence any longer and just yelled out, "What's with you?"

"Nothing," He narrowed his eyes. "I was going to ask you something but now forget it."

"Why forget it?"

"'Cause it's lame and you'll say no anyway." By that point, I was curious and getting mad at him for not just telling me.

"What are you talking about?"

"Well, it's just that Seth McCormick is giving a party in a couple of weeks. It's like an end-of-school party and I thought you might want to go."

I was silent for a minute as I assessed his roundabout date asking. He took my silence as an indication that I didn't want to go.

"See, I told you it was lame."

"No, it's not lame, Jason. It's just that I don't know anyone. I'm kind of nervous about meeting new people." I wanted him to believe me and I wanted him to know that I really wanted to go, but I was just nervous about it.

"You know Jake and Kelly. They're going to be there."

"Will Breeana be there?" I asked.

He shrugged. "I don't know. But who cares anyway? Just come, Katy. You need to meet new people. I don't want to bring this up, but when school starts you won't have me here and I want you to be okay. You have to have other friends besides me." I knew he was right but it hurt me to think about it.

"Okay, I'll go," I told him quietly. I still wasn't sure about it but he was right about one thing: I did have to make new friends.

"By the way, when do you and your dad have to be in LA?" I really didn't want to ask but I needed to know. We never talked about it and most of the time, I just pretended it wasn't happening.

"We're leaving on June fifth. He wants to leave right after school lets out at the end of this month." The reality of it hanging in the air, we got quiet then. I didn't want to think about it anymore.

"So, what do I wear to this party, Jase?" I asked, changing the subject.

"It's a pool party, so you can wear anything. Just bring your bathing suit." At that prospect, I felt nervous all over again, but then I remembered that I wasn't the beach ball on legs I once was. So, I tried not to be scared. "When is the party?" He had said a couple of weeks but that wasn't specific enough.

"It's in two weeks, on Saturday night. I'll pick you up around seven."

I told him I'd have to ask my parents first, but I was sure they would say yes. And they did ... with an excitement and enthusiasm I hadn't heard from them in a really long time.

# ❧ Chapter Forty-Five ❧

The day of the party I was really nervous. Mom let me buy a new bathing suit and it was a cute one piece. It was just a plain pink bathing suit with tiny straps on the shoulders. I liked it, but I just hoped that Jason didn't think I looked like a huge bottle of Pepto Bismol. I didn't know if people would be wearing their suits over there or just under their clothes. I decided to bring a swim bag so I could carry everything I needed. Since it was casual, I just wore my pink Old Navy tee so when I did change into my bathing suit, I would match. I also decided on white Levi shorts. They were cute and they showed off my tan. For finishing touches, I wore my sandals that matched my pink T-shirt and Mom French braided my hair. My hair was much longer now that it was growing back, so the braid looked nice. I didn't put on much makeup ... just lip-gloss ... and then I was ready to go.

Jason was at my house at seven ten. I was so nervous by the time he got there that I almost backed out. He came to the door and told my parents that his dad would pick us up once the party was over and that we'd be home right after.

"Just have fun," Mom said. "I know Kathryn is fine when she's with you."

We climbed into Mr. Neely's car and we chatted all the way to Seth's house. Seth doesn't live in a neighborhood. He lives in a really huge house on the edge of town that is surrounded by a privacy fence and you have to drive up a really long driveway to get there. It's the biggest house I've ever seen.

"And you said my house was big," I told Jason as Mr. Neely dropped us off.

"Well yeah, but I'd never been to Seth's. I should have known though. His dad is a cardiologist."

We walked up to the door and knocked. Someone in a uniform greeted us. I think she was like the maid or something. Anyway, she told us where the party was, like we couldn't hear the music blaring and led us downstairs to the biggest basement I'd ever seen. Seth had a killer stereo system around which there were dozens of kids dancing. The room was so big that there was plenty of room to dance and still be able to move around freely. They also had a bar set up that was littered with food and drinks. They even had a pool table where some of the kids were hanging out. There were so many kids and yet I didn't recognize any of them. I held on to Jason's hand protectively because I was scared I would get separated from him. He squeezed it to let me know that I was okay.

"Hey, Neely! Glad you could make it. You can hang out here or change into your swim clothes and head out to the pool," Seth greeted us. We then made our way outside to see what was going on. I'd never seen so many kids in my life. The kids in the pool were splashing around and playing water volleyball. The pool had lights around it so everyone could see well and the kids who weren't in the pool were lounging around on the chairs just chatting and laughing and goofing off.

Lots of people called out to Jason and I felt proud to be with him. I immediately saw that I was dressed appropriately so I didn't feel out of place at all. We were walking over to the chairs to sit by the pool when two kids I didn't know came up to us. "Hey, Jason!" the boy with the blonde hair yelled out. "Is this Katy?" I was surprised he knew my name but I was glad to know that Jason had been talking about me.

"Yeah, Katy, this is Mike and his girlfriend Hannah." We said hello and they asked us to come over and sit with them. They were sitting at an outdoor table with an umbrella overhead and several chairs surrounding it. Before long, Jake and Kelly came up to us and sat down as well and the next thing I know, we're all laughing and talking like old friends. I didn't feel like I was on the outside at all. They were actually including me. They asked me about Vanguard and we laughed about how snobby all the kids there were. Everyone was just so nice.

We all decided to go swimming. Kelly, Hannah and I went into the pool house to change then came back out in our swimsuits and jumped right into the water. It felt great. The boys joined us and we started splashing and playing. This was what I'd missed. I'd missed having friends around ... I'd missed having fun without worrying about what everyone was thinking. And for that moment, I was a typical teenager again, having typical fun. It was great.

After a while, our skin starting to wrinkle and our energy drained, we emerged from the pool and dried off. Hungry from our exertion, we went inside and got some food then went back out to the table to sit, eat, and talk. The boys were goofing off while Kelly, Hannah, and I watched them make fools of themselves. In their character play, they were making fun of one of the teachers, Mrs. Garner, and apparently they were doing a great job of imitating her because everyone started laughing. I didn't know her but even I thought it was funny. Then suddenly everyone stopped laughing. It grew deathly quiet when we noticed someone standing over us.

"Jason, I need to talk to you." It was Breeana and even I have to admit she looked amazing. Her hair was even longer and even more blonde than the last time I'd seen her. Further adding to my humiliation, she was wearing a purple bikini that showed off her rock-hard abs. You could tell she worked out by her muscle tone. She was also tanned to a golden bronze and if I didn't know better, I'd have sworn she was a model. I just sat there looking stupid, staring at her but not knowing what to say.

"What do you want, Bree?" Jason asked her agitatedly.

"To talk to you in private." She glared at me. I looked away and Jason looked around uncomfortably. Then he looked right at me. I begged him with my eyes not to leave me, but I guess he didn't pick up on it, or simply didn't care, because he got up and walked away with her.

"What does she want with him?" Kelly asked to no one in particular.

"Who knows?" Hannah asked. "And who even cares? He's too stupid just for talking to her." Then Hannah looked at me apologetically. "Sorry, Katy. I know how you like him, but that was just rude for him to walk away from you like that."

I shrugged. "We're not dating," I had to admit. "He can do what he wants." I tried to act like it wasn't bothering me, but the performance was excruciating.

"You're not?" the two girls said at the same time. The guys, Jake and Mike, had long lost interest and had gone to get more food. So, it was just the three of us left sitting there.

"No, we're just friends."

They glanced at each other before Kelly blurted out, "But he talks about you all the time. I was just sure that you two were completely together." My stomach fluttered a little when she said that.

I longingly watched Jason talk to Bree. He has his arms crossed and his eyes were narrowed, but I couldn't see what they were saying. Then she reached out and touched the ends of his hair. Anger swelled up inside me when I witnessed that affectionate gesture but I did nothing. He did nothing either. He just let her touch his hair. He even uncrossed his arms and moved them to his side, opening up his body language to encourage her caress. She said something to him then and he smiled. Then she giggled. I glanced over at Kelly, who was watching me.

"It's okay. I'm sure they're just talking." I nodded but I felt hurt. Finally, after what seemed like forever, Jason came back over to us.

"Where did Jake and Mike go?" he asked, not even acknowledging I was there.

"Food," Kelly said and Jason sat down to wait for them.

"What did the queen bee want Jason?" Hannah asked.

He shrugged. "Nothing really." Then he seemed to remember I was there. He took my hand and squeezed it

reassuringly. The gesture made me feel good but I still
wondered what they had said.

After I put the Bree incident out of my mind, the rest of the
party proved fun. Bree left not long after she and Jason talked
and we all got back in the water and played water volleyball.
Completely spent, we then went inside the pool house and
changed back into our regular clothes. My hair was still damp
but we went inside anyway and listened to music while we
watched other people dance. Then that song, "Over and Over
Again," came on. "So, Katy, you know you like this song," Jason
teased, jabbing me lightly with his elbow.

"It's redundant." I laughed at my own joke since it was a new
vocabulary word I'd learned that week. Since Jason didn't laugh,
I guess he didn't get it. Or maybe he did and just didn't think it
was funny. "But yeah, I like it." I smiled.

"So, let's dance." He pulled me up and drew me so close
that I felt my heart beating in my ears. "You look great tonight
Katy," he whispered in my ear.

"So do you." And he did too. He had on a green polo that
made his eyes look almost hypnotic.

I wanted to ask him what Breeana had said to him earlier,
but I didn't want to ruin the moment. He pulled me closer and I
moved my head up to his. Then, in a magical moment I'd been
waiting for forever it seemed, we kissed. I didn't even care if we
were in a room full of people I didn't know. For that moment,
we were the only two people who existed anyway. When the
song ended, we walked back outside, seeking solace away from
everyone else. On the way, Jason grabbed two bottled waters and
we shared a lounge chair.

"You know, Bree asked me to hang out with her tonight," he
said nonchalantly once he'd taken a drink of water.

"What do you mean?" I was playing with the water bottle
top so he couldn't see the disappointment rising to my face.

"She and some of her friends were ditching the party, and
she wanted me to go along."

"What did you say?"

"I told her that I didn't want to go."

"And what did she say to that?"

"She said it was only because I'd brought you along. Then I told her to get over herself, that even if you weren't here, I wouldn't have gone anywhere with her." I smiled at that. Then, after about a minute of silence, he added quietly, "I also told her we were going out." He looked at me sideways, waiting for a reaction.

"Are we going out, Jason?" My heart felt like it had stopped for a minute.

"If I weren't moving, would you want to?"

I nodded. "Yeah." It was all I could say. We were sitting so close and he wrapped his fingers around mine.

"You know I like you. It's just that with moving, I don't know. Maybe I'm being a jerk like Jeremy."

"No, you're not. It's just a fact that we're too young to make a long distance thing work. God, we'll be on opposite ends of the coast." The thought was depressing.

"But we'll stay in touch and we'll always be friends, right?" I nodded my reassurance. "Katy, you're the best friend I've ever had."

Jason's face was really close to mine when he confessed that and we kissed for a minute before I joked, "Well, you're the only friend I've ever had that I've kissed." He laughed and I wished for the millionth time that he didn't have to move.

# ❧ Chapter Forty-Six ☙

The next few weeks sped by like a blur. Kelly and I were talking on the phone a lot more and we hung out at the mall more frequently as well. Sometimes she and Hannah would spend the night at my house and when they did, it was almost like hanging out with Jane and my old friends. I talked to Jane more often because of the cell phone and I felt like I was more in touch with what was going on back in Georgia. I even asked about Kammy and Jeremy. It didn't bother me as much, but sometimes I still felt a stab of jealousy. I decided to put those feelings aside, however and focus on the here and now instead.

I confided in Kelly about my feelings for Jason. She said the same thing I did—it sucked that he was moving. All four of us, Jake, Kelly, Jason and I, spent time together and once, while we were at the mall, we all jammed ourselves into one of those photo booths and got our pictures taken. All you could make out was our heads, but I knew I'd keep those photos forever.

When school let out, Jason and I spent the last week we had together at the beach. Despite his looming departure, we were more like a couple than we'd ever been. We kissed a lot more and we talked about things we'd never talked about before. I felt so close to him in those moments. I didn't want him to move and I knew I'd miss him more than I'd ever missed anyone else. But despite my sentimentality over the situation, I knew I'd survive it. I'd have to. But I would be so lost without him. Kelly said that I shouldn't worry about school starting ... that I'd made lots of new friends and she was right. Seth's party had proved to be a good thing for me. In the days that followed, one of Seth's friends had asked Seth about me. He wanted me to go out with him but Seth told him I was dating Jason. For the first time in my life, I felt like I was a regular teenager and I loved it.

ॐ ❧

Jason called me the day before he and his dad were leaving. It was around three o'clock in the afternoon and I was watching silly game shows when the phone rang. I was supposed to go over to Jason's after dinner so we could hang out one last time before he left. But when he called, he yelled, "Come over here, quick!" I told him I'd be over there as soon as my Mom got home.

"What time will that be?"

"In about an hour."

"It can't wait that long. I'll have my dad drive me to you."

I started laughing over his urgency. "Okay," I told him then went upstairs to brush my teeth and hair. I hadn't expected to see anyone, so I wasn't even dressed properly for company. I changed into shorts and a T-shirt, which was becoming my uniform for life in Sarasota. Jason was at my door within minutes.

"What's going on?" I asked him when I let him in then led him into the kitchen. "Do you want anything?" I asked him.

His eyes were gleaming. "No, I don't want anything. I have everything I want."

"What are you talking about?" He seemed way too happy for someone who was about to leave and his enthusiasm was starting to make me angry.

"We aren't moving, Katy!" His words, the words I'd hoped to hear since he had first told me he was moving, didn't sink in right away."

"What do you mean?" I asked him. "What do you mean, you're *not* moving?"

"You won't believe it." He was really dragging the agony out.

"Then tell me, Jason. What won't I believe?"

"Remember when my Dad went out to LA to work things out with Mom?" I nodded. Of course I remembered. "Well, apparently they worked things out quite well, because I'm going to have a brother or a sister in few months and since she's going to have a baby, she can't do the sitcom after all. They've decided to live here, Katy! Mom has decided to move to Sarasota because Dad likes his job here, I like school here and I can be here with you and all my friends." He was talking so fast that I could barely catch everything he was saying.

"You mean you're staying because your mother is having a baby?" He nodded and I squealed out loud with delight. I was glad no one was home to hear me. I started jumping up and down. "Oh, Jason! We can start school together in the fall."

"Let's not even think about school, Katy! Let's have an awesome summer together and let's spend it doing whatever we want, whenever we want." I was smiling so hard that my face was hurting.

"Does that mean we're like going out now?" I was shocked that I'd asked but I wanted to know. I'd wanted this moment forever and I was going to just grab it while I could.

"It's exactly what it means." He laughed then. I couldn't wait until I could call Jane and tell her.

"Does anyone else know about you not moving?" I asked.

"Nope, you're the first. Dad dropped me off, so let's walk over to Jake's and tell him. You call Kelly and let's all go out tonight." I was so excited I just started dialing. When she heard the news, Kelly squealed out loud too ... she said she couldn't wait until that night. When I got off the phone, a deflating thought occurred to me. "What about Bree?"

"What about her Katy?" Jason looked at me puzzled, obviously a bit taken back that I'd brought up her name and spoiled the mood. .

"Well, she only broke up with you 'cause you were moving. What if she wants you back now that you're not?"

"Well, I'll just have to tell her that I'm busy ... with my girlfriend." He winked at me and I laughed. We walked over to Jake's house hand in hand and I just started thinking about how quickly life could change. A year ago I couldn't have imagined ever being happy in Florida, but now I couldn't imagine not loving it here. I thought about all the things I had had to get through to find this kind of happiness, but now that I had found it, I was hanging on to it. Because the only thing you could count on in life was that it is always changing. Everything I'd gone through had made me the person I was today ... the person Jason liked. I knew that I'd grown up a lot in the past year. I was lucky though ... I hadn't ended up like Leslie and I when I thought about her I felt sadness over the fact that she couldn't be helped. I knew I couldn't have saved her even if I'd talked to her that night. But for once, I didn't dwell on any of the bad stuff ... I felt good and all the way to Jake's house, as I held tightly to Jason's hand, I felt lucky and happy to be alive.

# Watch for Zoey's next novel . . .
# Brockway High

Being part of *Brockway High*'s "in" crowd isn't all it's cracked up to be for sophomore Alyssa Drake. Feeling invincible in her popularity role, she trades in her hunky, sought-after boyfriend for the school's resident geek, William Jordan. That rash decision proves an unwise one for Alyssa, however, when she soon finds herself ex-communicated from her former clique, the Brockway Beta Girls' sorority.

Spearheaded by the cruel Jill Landon, Alyssa's former friends begin making her life at *Brockway High* a living hell. Forced to accept that it's the popular way or the highway at *Brockway High*, Alyssa must reevaluate her priorities. With no one else to blame for her newfound estrangement, Alyssa turns her resentment on William and backs out of the relationship.

Drowning in his own sea of personal problems, Alyssa's alienation sends William over the edge. Feeling trapped and without options, William decides to take matters into his own hands and deal with the situation the only way he knows how. Will it take a *Brockway High* tragedy for Alyssa to realize what really matters in life?

Visit us at: www.EudonPublishing.com for more information about Zoey's upcoming novels.